THE BEST OF YOUTH

ALSO BY MICHAEL DAHLIE

A Gentleman's Guide to Graceful Living: A Novel

THE BEST OF YOUTH

a novel

MICHAEL DAHLIE

W. W. NORTON & COMPANY   NEW YORK • LONDON

For information about permission to reproduce selections from this book,
write to Permissions, W. W. Norton & Company, Inc.,
500 Fifth Avenue, New York, NY 10110

For information about special discounts for bulk purchases, please contact
W. W. Norton Special Sales at specialsales@wwnorton.com or 800-233-4830

Manufacturing by Courier Westford
Book design by Brooke Koven
Production manager: Louise Mattarelliano

Library of Congress Cataloging-in-Publication Data

Dahlie, Michael.
The best of youth : a novel / Michael Dahlie. — 1st ed.
p. cm.
ISBN 978-0-393-08185-5 (hardcover)
1. Benefactors—Fiction. 2. Ghostwriters—Fiction. 3. Publishers and
publishing—Fiction. 4. Brooklyn (New York, N.Y.)—Fiction. [1. Courtesy—
Fiction.] I. Title.
PS3604.A344B47 2013
813'.6—dc23

2012029249

W. W. Norton & Company, Inc.
500 Fifth Avenue, New York, N.Y. 10110
www.wwnorton.com

W. W. Norton & Company Ltd.
Castle House, 75/76 Wells Street, London W1T 3QT

1 2 3 4 5 6 7 8 9 0

for Allison and for Evan

ACKNOWLEDGMENTS

For help with this novel, the author would like to thank Doug Stewart and Jill Bialosky, Madeleine Clark, Steve Colca, Dave Cole, Seth Fishman, Rebecca Leicht, Alison Liss, George Nicholson, Vivian Reinert, and Rebecca Schultz. Butler University, the Ernest Hemingway Foundation, PEN New England, the Mrs. Giles Whiting Foundation, the Ucross Foundation, the Universty of Idaho, the Spruce Knot–Upper St. Regis Writing Residency, 5Chapters, and Broad Ripple Tavern. Dan Barden, Hilene Flanzbaum, Andrew Levy, Susan Neville, Brynnar Swenson, and everyone involved in the MFA Program and the English Department at Butler. Chris Bannon, Dave Daley, Kathrin Kollman, Frederick Mendelsohn, Christopher Miller, Gillian Munson, Esther Padilla, Lynne Sharon Schwartz, Ado Shmnovic, and Alexander Williams. Elizabeth Dahlie, Anne Dahlie, Susan Dahlie, David Wimberly, Trevor McProud, Gary Goldberger, Susan Lynn, Mort Lynn, Heath Albert, Cassie Albert, Gordon Goldberger, and Tatum Goldberger. And, Allison Lynn and Evan Dahlie.

PART I

1

IT WAS TRUE THAT Henry didn't entirely understand what, exactly, their magazine was really trying to achieve, although he enjoyed the fervor of his friends and the sort of conviction that everyone else seemed to feel over the importance of the project. And the fact was that he was happy to be included in it all, and the money he contributed was hardly substantial, at least as far as he was concerned. Thirty thousand dollars for what his comrades were billing as a magazine that would finally "challenge all this shit that gets published these days" seemed entirely reasonable, even if he himself did not feel the sort of anger everyone else seemed to feel about what publishers were putting out. Henry had even once had a job of sorts in publishing, although it had ended badly. He wasn't particularly good at what a human resources person called "interpersonal relations," on a professional basis at least, and after a two-month internship at a major magazine ("with a literary slant") he left without so much as the promise of a good recommendation, to say nothing of a full-time job.

But it had been a difficult time. That was true. So maybe he wasn't to blame for it all. Both his parents had recently died in a boating accident in Katama Bay, off Martha's Vineyard, leaving him without much stamina for the various demands of a magazine job. The tragedy had also left him with quite a bit of money, which, if he were being completely honest with himself (and, in fact, he often tried to be), probably wasn't very good for the more competitive aspects of his character, for as much as these dimensions of his character existed in the first place. Fifteen million dollars was hardly the sort of thing that lit a fire under him, as the saying goes. In fact, it was exactly the sort of sum that allowed Henry to imagine that he could take his time to figure out what exactly he wanted to do with his life, although even this seemed not to be such a pressing question. Mostly he wanted to meet a girl he liked and make some friends (real friends) around Brooklyn, and these things, surely, in their truest sense, in the sense that Henry believed in, were not dependent on money.

2

AND THERE WAS, in fact, a girl he was interested in. She happened to be his fourth cousin, which (according to his research) was a relation that was not only legal to date but posed absolutely none of the genetic problems that might be associated with so-called inbreeding. They only shared some kind of colonial ancestor, after all. It did, however, present a sort of psychological barrier, at least as far as this girl (named Abby) was concerned.

"I don't want to go there, Henry," she said one evening when, after eating a fairly heavy meal of sausages and noodles at an Austrian restaurant in Williamsburg, he confessed that he was having confusing feelings toward her.

"I mean, of course," Henry said in response. "Of course, I don't want to go there either. I suppose that's why I'm bringing it up. I suppose I wanted to talk about it."

"Yeah," Abby replied, "but I don't even want to talk about it. I mean, when I say I don't want to go there, I mean I don't even want to talk about the possibility of going there."

"Well, that's what I mean too," Henry said.

"Yeah, but you brought it up," Abby said.

"But only so we didn't have to talk about it."

Abby stared at Henry for several seconds before saying, "Well, I suppose I should have expected this kind of thing.

You're a strange guy, Henry. Really. But that's good. I mean it. I really like you. In fact, I think that maybe you're the nicest, best guy I've ever met. But I like you as a friend. As a cousin. Yikes! And I think we need to leave it at that. We really need to leave it at that."

"Okay. All right. Let's leave it at that," Henry replied. "This is exactly why I brought it up."

Of course, Henry understood that it was probably very unlikely that he would have the ability to "leave it at that." He even found himself suddenly thinking he ought to try to kiss Abby—perhaps that was the sort of bold act that would really tilt things to his advantage. And perhaps Abby didn't know about the research he had done into the legal and biological aspects of this sort of thing. That was important, after all. But just as he was having these thoughts, Abby said, "But really, Henry, let's drop it. Let's promise to drop it. And it's not just that we're cousins. We're not a good match. So don't try to talk me into it."

"Of course not," Henry said. "Of course not. We'll leave it alone. I won't bring it up again."

And this time, as he said this, he decided that maybe he wouldn't bring it up again. But the fact was that he really did want to kiss her, and he wondered if this particular desire really would ever go away. And he also wondered if maybe he had more of a shot with her than she was letting on. It was always so difficult to know with this sort of thing and perhaps, with time, her feelings would change.

3

IT SHOULD BE pointed out that despite the various failings in Henry's life (whether he was bumbling as a magazine intern or awkwardly trying to seduce a relative), he was, in fact, quite capable in many other ways. He'd been, for instance, an excellent student, and not just in the colder and less humane disciplines. He'd done very well in his college creative writing classes, for example—both poetry and fiction. And this was at Harvard, of all places, so surely no one could accuse him of not having some kind of subtle and imaginative mind. One of his professors even said he ought to continue to work at his writing because he had "a real talent for this." What exactly "real talent" meant, Henry didn't know. But for this particular professor he'd written a lengthy, three-part short story about a ninety-one-year-old man who was caring for his younger sister, who was suffering from kidney cancer.

"It was very moving," the instructor had said, "and I don't say that about most of what I get in this class. Generally speaking, Ivy Leaguers don't always make the best fiction writers."

Henry was quite happy with this praise—it had come at a good time, since he had, only the night before, been rejected by a young woman (not a relative) who said she adored him as a friend but that the "romantic spark" just wasn't there. It was very disappointing—and something he seemed to hear at least once a semester—but the next day he really was buoyed up by his professor's comments.

It was a question, though, why Henry's story had captivated his teacher, and Henry spent quite a bit of time over the next several days rereading his story and thinking about how to recapture whatever it was that had made this one turn out so well. He did at times suspect that maybe it was a one-off sort of thing, a kind of transitory inspiration, but he also determined that he was, in fact, particularly good at writing about diseases. He had done extensive and creative research concerning nephrology and cancer statistics in the United States, and, as he considered this, he thought that perhaps he might one day become one of the great advocates for people who suffered from cancer of the kidney.

There was also the possibility that he had a certain kind of affinity for old people, although Henry was much less excited about this prospect. That being said, it seemed to him more and more (as he thought about writing other stories and about who, in fact, he got along with in the world) that this might be the most accurate conclusion. He had always gotten on well with old people, and the fact of the matter was that he spent a lot of time thinking about what it would be like being old—an old person with a terrible illness, an old person who couldn't afford to take care of himself, an old person who had never been in love (real love, that is, love that was returned). Maybe that would be his stake in the world of modern literature. Certainly he hadn't read many novels about people in their nineties. It was an appealing idea, and it stayed with him over the years following his graduation from Harvard and into his postgrad years in Williamsburg, when he eventually put up the $30,000 to launch the magazine.

4

WHY EXACTLY THE magazine was to be called *Suckerhead* was at first a mystery to Henry, although it was explained to him by the editor-in-chief that "it's just so fucking funny it's got to be the name." It was true that Henry also found the name funny, but the fact that it was a funny name hardly justified it being the title of their literary venture.

All the same, Henry didn't complain. "Perhaps we could call you sucker-in-chief and I could be sucker-at-large," Henry said—after making his financial contributions, he had been named an editor-at-large. To Henry's surprise, though, this suggestion did not go over very well. In fact, the editor-in-chief, a twenty-five-year-old named Tully—a graduate of Wesleyan—seemed quite offended. After a rushed bite of his pumpkin ravioli, Henry quickly added, "I mean, it might be pretty funny to have something like that on the masthead."

"I want people to take us seriously," Tully replied quickly. "We're really trying to do something here. They're the suckers, not us."

Henry thought about this for a moment. "I guess that's right," he said at last, feeling a bit like he was somehow losing the thread of this particular conversation. "I guess that's right."

Losing the thread of a conversation, or the thread of his entire social world, was not uncommon for Henry, especially since he had moved to Brooklyn. But it was also the case that Henry loved Brooklyn, loved Williamsburg especially—the bars, the parties, and the people—and despite his difficulties navigating the intricacies of Brooklyn society, he embraced it all without any sort of resentment or cynicism. True, he did always feel as though things were happening just a bit beyond his reach. He was present for many of the great events—he frequented the popular music venues, ate at the newest restaurants, and was even invited to what he imagined were the most exciting parties. But he never really felt quite like he was at the heart of it all—or like he even particularly belonged to the periphery. He often suspected this was because, while there were lots of people he was friendly with and would hang around with, there was no one in Brooklyn who counted as a close friend, no one who really seemed to like him with any sort of enthusiasm, with the single (and confusing) exception of Abby.

It was not what Henry had hoped life would be like when he moved to Brooklyn (following a strange semester as a graduate student in the English literature department at the University of Michigan). He had moved to Williamsburg because of a woman—one of the few who didn't reject him outright after he made his customary long confession (again, over starchy Northern European food) about how he was having feelings that were "just a little beyond friendship."

This woman seemed unfazed by the confession, didn't say she "really just wanted to be friends," and even seemed not displeased when, after a month of dating, as she was leaving Ann Arbor for Brooklyn, Henry said that he'd like to move to Brooklyn too.

It was only four weeks after he arrived in Williamsburg (and had even bought a fairly impressive loft in one of the newer buildings on McCarren Park) that this particular woman, named Helena, left him. Or she didn't really leave him so much as tell Henry that maybe they shouldn't be romantically involved anymore, especially because she had started dating someone else who had indicated that he'd like to "be exclusive" with her.

It had been devastating to Henry. He was entirely shocked that she was dating someone else, that their own relationship wasn't, itself, "exclusive," and that she was throwing him over for this other person. To this woman, their relationship seemed to be nothing more than an odd and minor adventure. She even said as much: "I just can't believe you're crying like this. This is nothing. I like you. I do. But we're only twenty-three. Why are you crying like this?"

Over the next several weeks Henry transformed a short story about an eighty-five-year-old man who had never been in love into a story about an eighty-five-year-old who had never been properly loved by another person, and he found it so moving that he sent it to about a dozen literary magazines with an unusually assertive cover letter. The typed form rejection letters came swiftly, although he did get several small handwritten notes at the bottom of the letters that said things like "Not bad!" and "This was interesting!" It was always good to get a note. Henry knew this. But the fact was that they seemed to make him feel even worse about his romantic and literary failures because somehow his feelings and artistic expression ended up meriting only a kind of booby prize. That is, his pain and his art weren't laughed at as cliché and ridiculous—his pain and his art were appreciated. But they were appreciated only enough to justify a few mild words of encouragement. And mild words of encouragement are hardly what a man wants to hear when he's digging deeply into his emotions and his artistic imagination.

All the same, Henry didn't give up on the story, and later

he even passed it along to the fiction editor at *Suckerhead*, although with the clear understanding that there was, of course, no obligation to publish it.

"Only if you like it," Henry said.

"Sure," the fiction editor replied. "I'll give it a read and let you know what I think."

5

DESPITE HENRY'S difficulties in Brooklyn, however, he was sure that he had a friend in Abby. She was a real friend—someone with whom he had meaningful conversations, and who seemed to like him a great deal, and all this continued even after his embarrassing confession. And because Henry needed Abby's friendship, and because he secretly believed they might, in fact, one day "get together," as the saying goes, he didn't flee the friendship after the rejection, as he might have done in the past, but instead put forth a brave face and accepted his lot.

And just a month or so after they'd had the conversation about Henry's confusing feelings, Abby even invited him away for a weekend to visit a farm in Vermont. The farm was owned by her aunt (an aunt who was no relation to Henry) and the trip away was "just as friends," as Abby made clear, adding with a bit of a smile, "So don't try any of that incest shit with me, all right?"

"But it's not incest!" Henry replied, and was about to point out that in most places in the world a fourth cousin wasn't even really considered a relative. But Abby evidentially saw how distressed he was and quickly said, "I'm kidding. I'm kidding. It's not incest. I know. I know. We're not even really related. Dude, you've got to lighten up. But seriously, though, don't try to kiss me. I'm only inviting you along because I know we'll have fun together."

Henry paused, then said, "Yes, well, I was kidding too. And don't worry. I don't want to kiss you. I just wanted, that night, to talk about kissing you, because it seemed to be an issue."

"Well, it's not," Abby replied, again flashing Henry a smile, although now with just a bit of effort. "It's really not. But let's not even ever again talk about kissing being an issue."

Henry nodded and agreed. He thought that perhaps he might take the opportunity to say that it was Abby who had, in fact, brought it up this time, but he decided it might be best to just leave things alone at this point.

At any rate, on the following Friday, midday, they found their way to Henry's parking space in Greenpoint, got into his car (it was a silver Volvo station wagon that he had inherited), and headed north. The farm was in southern Vermont, not far from Manchester, and this was, in fact, Abby's second trip there that month. Abby kept herself alive in Brooklyn by doing various odd jobs—dog-walking, freelance Web design, etc. She even played viola in a so-called alternative musical band made up of women who all played obscure instruments, and they occasionally made very small amounts of money at bars. And when she could, Abby slipped away for two- or three-day stretches to work on her aunt's farm, making a little money there as well and enjoying a break from the city. The truth was that she was also very interested in farming, as she insisted over and over in the car.

"It's just really strange how alienated we are from what we eat," she said. "I mean, it's incredible the kind of care and labor that goes into it all. And the economics of it. And the weirdo luck. You can have a great harvest one year and then a terrible season the next, and usually that's because of something like a drought in the Ukraine or overproduction of turnips in Arkansas."

"Yes, I've heard that's true," Henry said, and, although it was not something he had thought much about, he began looking forward to learning more about all this, and to getting an insider's view of American farming.

It was a fact, however, that this particular farm, although clearly "working" by any definition, was hardly the sort of thing that would qualify as an example of the American farm. Rather, as Abby explained, it was a very expensively run organic farm that had been financed by Abby's uncle, who managed a hedge fund in Greenwich. His wife had bought the farm (called Highgate Meadows) several years earlier after his fund had had a particularly astonishing year, purchasing it from an older couple who were retiring and moving to Florida. This husband and wife were real farmers. They made their living that way. But they were fairly well off, as these things go, and the land they owned was spectacular—nice enough to finance an extremely comfortable retirement in sunnier climates.

Abby's aunt (named Hannah) put another $4 million into the property, building a greenhouse, buying harvesting machinery and equipment to make cheese, and, apparently, tending a flock of Libyan heirloom goats that were entirely unique in North America.

"And she's a little affected," Abby said. "She can't quite understand why everyone can't pay twenty bucks for a pound of hamburger meat. I mean, by worldwide standards I've got some cash, and I definitely can't pay that much. But she doesn't really get that. But I like her. There are things I like about her. And I like going to the farm. It might be a bit utopian. Rich-person utopian. But I like it there. And I do think it's important. Maybe it's the farm that I like."

6

HENRY WAS ABLE to piece together more of the story when they finally arrived. They drove up the long gravel drive, parked at a surprisingly impressive stone farmhouse that looked to be at least two hundred years old, and then walked around back to find Abby's aunt standing in a patch of sunflowers that she was cutting with a large pair of gardening sheers.

"These things will grow right into the first snowfall," she said with a strange kind of mania when Henry and Abby approached her. "But it's best to cut them back now. That's what they say, at least."

She clipped two more sunflowers and then walked over to embrace Abby and shake Henry's hand.

For the next few moments they exchanged customary greetings, which included remarks about the now-diminishing autumn leaves and Abby's extraordinary slimness. The two young people were then offered something "hot to drink" and before long they were in the modern and expansive kitchen of Highgate Meadows, chatting about the farm.

"I'm worried that I'm a little too obsessed with all this," Hannah said, pulling a large copper kettle off one of twelve Viking burners. "I used to scream at my husband about being such a workaholic, but now I feel like I'm the neglectful one in the relationship. But it's all so fascinating. And what I'm doing is very, very important."

"Abby told me a lot about it on the way up," Henry said, putting his hands on an antique butcher block that had an alarming amount of cleaver scars. "It does actually seem very important to me as well."

"Well, I'll show you around just as soon as the tea is ready."

After they each had a cup of tea in their hands, they commenced the tour, which took them through assorted venues, including the new greenhouse (with a large crop of a strange kind of hydroponically grown yellow tomato), a large aging barn filled with various tools and farming equipment, an empty field where, as Hannah explained, a crop of organic acorn squash had been harvested a month earlier, and then to what Hannah described as the pride and joy of Highgate Meadows—the goats and the cheese facility.

"I built all this from scratch," Hannah said as they approached a single-story shingled building with a low-pitched roof.

Henry did remark to himself—and this really was the only cynical reflection he had on the entire tour—that Hannah didn't look like she'd ever really built anything at all physical on her own. Despite her ragged clothes and a few dirt smudges on her hands and forearms, she still looked like she was some kind of grand Connecticut lady—tall, athletic, fully exfoliated and moisturized. But the farm was beautiful and obviously a success, so who was he to say what an authentic farmer or builder should look like? And certainly he too was a complete failure when it came to physical labor and building things, so he really was in no position at all to judge anyone.

And the fact was that it truly was impressive. They stepped into what Hannah was now calling the cheese house, and it all seemed to be from the set of some sort of futuristic movie. Everything was either white, stainless steel, or transparent plastic, and it felt like a kind of high-end science lab without so much as a hint of germs or dust. It was also entirely empty—not unlike utopian (or dystopian) movies.

"Not much action now," Hannah said. "We've shut down for a little bit. We just made a huge batch of cheese and we're not putting up anything else till February. There's no room to store it. Anyway, there's no rush, and it's always best to do things right."

All the same, without the so-called action, it was very striking—the mixers, the beakers, the refrigeration units, the stacks of cheese wheels in the large storage room. It wasn't, however, as interesting as their next stop. They left the cheese house, walked across a small quadrangle, and came to another shingled building that was attached to a large fenced pen.

"This is the goat barn," Hannah said as they stepped inside. They walked into a little anteroom, then opened another door and entered a dark, low-ceilinged chamber, filled with what Henry determined were at least eighty surprisingly tall and confused-looking goats. The room was smaller than Henry would have expected, but, as Hannah explained, "They get skittish when they have too much space."

Hannah also gave a fairly detailed description of the goats and their value. Apparently she had purchased them from a farmer in Delaware who had started with only seven goats in the 1950s and, since then, jealously managed the flock. They were one-of-a-kind in North America, since none of the flock's generations had ever been sold off. Perhaps more relevant, they had originally come from Libya—where they were also fairly rare—and importation of Libyan goods, to say nothing of goats, hadn't been permitted for quite a long while.

"And even today," Hannah said, "with Gaddafi supposedly joining the 'world community,' it would be next to impossible." (It was then about time that George W. Bush was applauding Mr. Gaddafi's generous and courageous abandonment of

WMDs). "And there are all sorts of strange diseases to worry about and endless FDA reviews," Hannah said. "It would take decades. And they're hard to take care of because they're very temperamental. And they need to be kept warm. That's something that's hard to do in Vermont. They hate temperature shifts, especially when temperatures fall, and it shows in the quality of the milk. But they're worth it. They're worth the trouble."

One of the reasons the goats were worth so much trouble was that their milk was unusually sweet, which allowed for various opportunities in cheese-making that other goats couldn't match. There was also the general wealthy person's interest in exotic provenances and one-of-a-kind culinary experiences. Cheese made from these goats commanded excessive prices at high-end restaurants around the Northeast, where proprietors wanted to say that they bought locally, as it were, but still offer products that had the cachet and obscurity of the deserts of North Africa. Hannah used about a quarter of the milk herself and was able to sell the rest to artisanal cheese makers around New England for "top dollar," as she insisted. The goat milk was, in fact, the only part of the farm that produced any real revenue.

"But as for profits, not revenue, but profits," Hannah said, "that's going to take a while. This was a huge capital investment."

"How much does a goat like this cost?" Henry asked.

"They're expensive," Hannah said, "because you can sell their milk at such a high price. And they're one-of-a-kind. So each goat, and I have about a hundred, cost around ten thousand dollars."

For just a second the number ten thousand registered in Henry's mind as the value of the flock, so the first impression he had—again, just for that second—was that $10,000 seemed like a very reasonable price for such a valuable commodity.

But then he reconsidered Hannah's statement, and then did just a little math, and realized that this particular flock of goats that was now before him was worth a million dollars.

"Oh, my god," Henry said, although he regretted his reaction just a bit. After all, it's hardly polite to gasp at the price of another person's possessions, even if it is a million-dollar flock of goats. "Of course, it's obviously a very wise investment," Henry quickly added, "seeing that they bring in good revenue."

"Yes, well," Hannah said, a little more quietly, "I know it's a large sum. But the point of this farm is bigger than making money, even though I want it to be profitable." Hannah paused for a moment. "I was actually fine with it at first. I mean, I still am. But there's just a bit of resentment in Vermont over people buying up farms and launching this kind of project. I mean, it's always been this way. This farm was built by a Quaker family that had a lot of money, and they did very well. Farming and landowning, after all, used to be one of the ways rich people got rich. And there's always been poorer farmers—or farmhands, mostly—who weren't crazy about that. I mean, I guess they might have some reason. And we really try to pay everyone well. And health insurance. Those we can." Hannah paused again, laughed in a bit of an exaggerated way, then said, "I guess this is on my mind because there've been a lot of pretty hostile articles about my kind of farm in Vermont newspapers—Burlington, Manchester, a lot of our newspapers. I've been mentioned once or twice. Particularly by a columnist in Manchester who writes about farming in the state. He likes to talk about know-nothing city people and rich New Yorkers ruining Vermont's way of life. And I suppose I know how it sounds in the abstract, out of context—a million dollars for a hundred goats—and somehow he found out what I paid and has talked about it in his column. But I'm really trying to do something important here. What's important is the mission, not the price. I mean, how can you put a value on doing what's best for the world and the environment?"

Hannah paused, although she looked like she had more to say. She was certainly a little flustered at this exact moment. But after another second she announced that she had to work on some rabbit hutches she was building and that perhaps this would be a good time to conclude the tour. "The rabbits are arriving in a few days and I've got to be ready! I don't think this is a work weekend for you, Abby, so do whatever you like. Maybe tomorrow I can get you to help mend a fence that's fallen, but for now, why don't you two just enjoy yourselves, and there's plenty of beer and wine, if you just want to sit by the fire."

Henry and Abby spent the rest of the day in various ways. They walked the perimeter of the harvested squash field and then along several other fields that grew, at different times, alfalfa, yams, pumpkins, and numerous other crops that could survive in Vermont. They wandered through the machine shed, and Henry examined the tractor attachments and a portable generator, and also looked over the long workbench. Every kind of tool imaginable hung above the bench, and the long wooden work area was flanked by two space heaters, a paint-covered portable radio, and a small fridge that, Henry saw when he opened it, was filled with Miller Lite.

Henry and Abby also passed a little time watching three very strange Wiltonshire pigs, each of which had an unusual meaty growth on its forehead. Apparently there was quite a market in the city for this kind of pig. Fashionable restaurants were now naming their pork and beef by breed, and the *New York Times* dining section had profiled this particular variety of pig (as Abby informed Henry) and said that its meat was the best a person could get.

"Can you eat that thing that hangs off the top of their

heads?" Henry asked. As he asked this, he did think that perhaps this was something of a gruesome question. But he was
honestly curious.

Abby didn't know. "And, frankly, that's kind of disgusting,"
she said.

"But it might be good," Henry replied, trying to affect a
sort of worldly ease with the grim realities of farm life. "I once
heard that on farms nothing is wasted."

"I'll ask my aunt if she'll cook you one tonight," Abby said,
punching Henry softly in the shoulder. "Wiltonshire forehead
flap with applesauce."

"That sounds good to me," Henry said.

Dinner was, in fact, duck, roasted whole with shallots and
butter, parsnips (from the farm), and bread baked by a bak-
ery down the road that had also been started by the wife of a
hedge fund manager.

Hannah hesitated a bit as she added this last bit of information—the three of them were in the dining room, all
pleasantly lit by two silver candelabras, and eating with great
enthusiasm—and she now looked just a bit remorseful for
bringing this up.

"I suppose sometimes it's embarrassing," she continued.
"For all the reasons that I told you, I'm a little embarrassed
by the goats. But what are you going to do? Money has to
come from somewhere. And I could be spending it in Miami
or Gstaad, so it seems like my husband's professional wind-
fall is being put to good use. But 'wife of a hedge fund manager' has such an ugly ring to it. And, like I've said, I haven't
quite been accepted as part of the farming community here.
I understand the criticism. Or where it comes from, at least.
The important thing is to keep my head down and keep my
mouth shut—even though I could spend the rest of my life
talking about sustainable agriculture. If I stick it out, they'll
accept me. I hope so, at any rate."

It was an interesting moment of introspection—interesting and just a bit moving, to Henry, at least—and the wine they were drinking certainly made everything more appealing. It was a type from California that Henry knew nothing about, although he knew absolutely nothing about any kind of wine at all, so this wasn't surprising. As Henry took a bite of his duck, he thought he might actually like to spend more time learning about wine, and then, leaning back in his chair and surveying the austere but beautiful farmhouse dining room, he thought that maybe he might one day even like to own a farm like this. He couldn't quite imagine actually managing a farm, but country living held quite a bit of appeal to him. This farm did, at any rate. It really was a wonderful place.

And this struck him again, later that night, and the next day, when he and Abby were invited for another visit. "You can come as much as you like, Henry," Hannah said as he and Abby packed up for their return to Brooklyn. "It's hard on me being mostly alone up here. My husband can't make it up as much as I'd like. And as I said, I'm hardly in a position to accuse him of being obsessed with work, since it seems to be my problem as well." They were standing by Henry's silver Volvo as she said this, and Henry once more had the vague idea that perhaps one day he'd like to have a place like this. He looked to his right, across an empty patch of gravel, and at the goats, which were now outside, wandering around their pen. Maybe if he got his own farm he'd even get his own flock of goats to take care of—a flock of Libyans, perhaps, although he concluded that this was probably unlikely.

"I'd love to visit again," he said. "It really is nice up here."

7

IT DIDN'T TAKE more than a few weeks for plans along these lines to unfold. About a week or so into November, Abby proposed another visit for the two of them over Christmas.

Holidays were, needless to say, a troubling matter for Henry because he had lost his parents. It was true that he was on good terms with plenty of relatives from assorted branches of the family and he managed to see them every so often. Some lived in the city, others in Connecticut, and still others in places like California and Washington, D.C., although he saw these particular people with much less frequency. Festive events, of course, provided the main occasion for visits, but ever since Henry's parents had died, he shied from these sorts of things because, rather than making him feel safe and secure in the bosom of family, he found that he mostly felt very lonely and missed his parents terribly.

For this reason, Henry found that he liked to spend holidays alone. The first time around it was a bit hard, but this was mostly because he felt as if he were missing out on something, not because he was staring into the abyss of death and misery. And staring into the abyss of death and misery was obviously much worse than missing a happy event. Henry did, the previous year, try having Thanksgiving dim sum with some foreign friends, but these people, who had no reason at all to celebrate Thanksgiving, seemed just a bit too interested in why he wasn't with family over the holiday, and he didn't particularly like having to explain himself on this matter. Mostly, what he liked to do on holidays was walk around and drink coffee and read and think (in a pleasant way) about what he had loved most about his mother and father. The fact was that this was generally what he liked to do anyway, and perhaps it was the routine and the ordinariness that gave Henry some relief from contemplating the unhappiness of it all.

That particular Christmas, however, Henry decided to agree to the plan proposed by Abby. "I know you're a strict loner at Christmas," she had said. (They were drinking wine and eating a small dish of roasted Brussels sprouts at some sort of Czech restaurant.) "And that's totally cool. But my aunt and uncle are going to be in the Caribbean, in St. Croix, for the week of Christmas, and their caretaker has plans as well, and they've asked me to head up to Vermont to keep an eye on the place. I'll go up on Christmas Day—after presents and breakfast at home—and you could meet me then. Or you could even go up on Christmas Eve and have the place to yourself. No one else will be there. The caretaker is leaving that day for Cleveland or somewhere for a few days, so you can still do your I-want-to-be-alone thing."

"Well, it's very nice of you to invite me," Henry said. "And maybe I'll take you up on it. Let me think. I probably shouldn't say yes right away."

But it did seem to Henry as he first considered the offer that he probably would, in fact, take Abby up on it. Henry really had liked the farm. And he especially liked the goats. And if he was alone at least until the afternoon of Christmas Day, that seemed like it would be all right. As far as he was concerned, it was Christmas Eve that had always counted most, and the holiday had always felt over by noon of Christmas Day anyway. And the fact was that Henry thought it would be fun to spend time with Abby, even if he was still concerned that he hadn't quite left his crush behind. At any rate, it didn't take more than a day for Henry to consider it all. He called Abby at the place where she was house-sitting in Park Slope to tell her that he'd love to come.

"I like the idea of at least spending an afternoon over Christmas with someone I know," he said.

"I like that idea too," Abby replied.

8

AND HENRY REALLY was looking forward to the trip, but he did have several other issues that were also occupying his thoughts.

First, there was the matter of *Suckerhead,* which had an organizational meeting one evening at a place called Tamerlane, a bar that offered beers of the Pabst Blue Ribbon sort, a wide array of grilled sandwiches, and, for reasons Henry couldn't quite understand, an extraordinarily expensive wine list, which included several bottles that went for over $300.

Henry did like Tamerlane quite a bit, though. It had old leaded windows and pressed-tin ceilings and antler chandeliers (which were clearly not original but gave the bar a sort of old-time feel). And the music was always good. Henry didn't really know that much about music, other than the things that all people in Brooklyn knew, but he found that the bartender's iPod always seemed to have interesting material on it.

The organizational meeting consisted of twenty-three people—the various editors, editors-at-large, a publicity person who had a day job at Simon & Schuster, and even an astonishingly handsome young man of British origins who had the unlikely name of Whitney. It was all just a little unnerving to Henry, for several reasons, but most on his mind was the fact that the fiction editor was still reviewing the story he had submitted. On this front, Henry mostly felt embarrassed. After all, he was using an unfair advantage to publish his work, and how would it look for him to appear in the magazine, given that he was himself an editor-at-large (and the principal financier)? But he assured himself that this sort of thing happened all the time. "This is how publishing gets done," he even once said to himself out loud, parroting something he had once heard at the magazine where he had interned. Still, the fiction editor seemed oblivious to Henry's anxiety and didn't say a word about his story even though they greeted each other warmly before the meeting started. The fiction editor, named Max, had even introduced Henry to his new girlfriend as "a fellow writer and important patron of the magazine." This made Henry feel a little uneasy—the word "patron" evoked memories of charitable widows in Lexington, Mass, who doled out money to gardening clubs.

But Henry was quickly released from his discomfort because he suddenly found himself entirely taken with the fact that this woman he'd been introduced to—Sasha was her name— had more tattoos than anyone he'd ever met, even ones that crept up her neck to her face. Henry was not a prude about this kind of self-expression. He admired such things, or so he told himself as he said hello to Sasha. But just as he said, "Nice to meet you," she was distracted by another friend who'd just arrived and only managed to give Henry a quick smile before turning away, leading Henry to believe suddenly that he ought to take a more dismissive position toward people with tattoos. After all, Henry was now convinced, this was precisely the kind of woman who tended to dislike him, generally using words like "dull" and "tiresome" if the subject of his character or personality came up.

At any rate, the meeting soon began, and Henry sat quietly in a corner listening to reports on things like advertising, typefaces, the possibilities of color art, and whether or not they should solicit work from poets with whom the poetry editor had studied. The main topic, though, was where they should have their printing done. One of the associate editors, a woman named Karen, whom Henry had always found very attractive, had been researching the possibility of sending the work to a printer in a developing country. This was, in fact, not such a far-fetched idea, and certainly many publishers had books and magazines printed in countries other than the United States. Karen had concluded, though, that the best place to have *Suckerhead* produced was at a company in Ontario, Canada, "because they're totally green, they pay their employees well, and, frankly, there's not going to be any hassle. These guys are pros."

There was quite a bit of debate following this, including the obvious point, raised by several people, that Canada was not, technically speaking, a developing country. But Karen made fairly complex arguments about uncertain labor practices, questionable workmanship, and environmental issues in the other locations she looked into. Henry, at least, was impressed, although he made an effort to evaluate the matter carefully, from all perspectives and divorced from the fact that he really did find Karen attractive.

And after the meeting was over, Henry was surprised to find himself delivering a fairly well reasoned explanation of his views to Karen over beers at the bar, where he said things like, "It really seems you've done a very thorough job with all this," and "I really think you're onto something with this Canada idea."

Perhaps more surprising, Karen seemed to be interested in everything he was saying, including his views on modern literature, the viability of print literary journals in the electronic age, and even his opinions on visual art, something Henry knew very little about. Karen, in fact, responded to most of what he was saying by replying, "Yeah, I think that's right," and "I never really thought of it that way, but that's pretty interesting."

And after all this, after what Henry decided was truly an exciting conversation, Karen finally suggested that they grab something to eat. "Let's go to '404.' Texas barbecue. Just opened. It's supposed to be great."

"That sounds good to me," Henry replied, and, after visiting the men's room, he soon found himself walking under the BQE on his way to dinner.

In the spirit of authenticity (which, of course, New York was famous for), 404 sold its food by the pound from one of various "stations," and if it was meat it was wrapped in beige waxed butcher's paper. (Sides such as baked beans and coleslaw were served in white Styrofoam containers with opaque plastic lids with straw holes.) Henry and Karen decided to buy a pound of brisket and a pound of pork ribs, two orders of beans, and one order of coleslaw. It was far too much. That was obvious. But they had been drinking, and they were having fun together, so it seemed reasonable to make a celebration of the evening. In this spirit they also each got a beer and a shot of Maker's Mark, and before long they were seated at a long table surrounded by other diners and with clusters of condiments and rolls of paper towels laid out before them at regular three-foot intervals.

"I'm really excited to be here," Karen said as she unwrapped the pork ribs.

"Yeah, it's a really cool place," Henry replied. "I'm glad we came." He looked down at the ribs and started to wonder if there was a dignified way to pull the fat off one before eating it. He wanted to do what was appropriate. But Karen quickly grabbed a rib from the pile and shoved the end in her mouth without any of the trimming Henry was planning, and thus Henry did the same, eating the fat with feigned abandon.

In any event, the food was magnificent (as was the bourbon) and the conversation flowed well, and as the piles of paper-wrapped meat diminished, Henry started to wonder if he ought to start planning out his next moves. After all, this was precisely the sort of occasion where young men in Brooklyn ended up having sex—as far as he could tell—and if sex was a possibility, he should certainly have a plan.

It turned out, though, that no plan was needed. Near the end of dinner, Karen took a large bite of coleslaw, nibbled on the end of a rib, and then said, "Why don't you come over to my place after we're done here? My housemate's out of town. We could have another drink. And then maybe we could sleep together."

Needless to say, this particular proposal was stunning for an almost endless number of reasons. Mostly, though, it seemed to be very clear evidence of something that Henry had long suspected—that sex for everyone else was an entirely natural and easy arrangement, and (and this was the important corollary to this suspicion) Henry was somehow, due to a kind of cosmic injustice, excluded from this easy sexual exchange— excluded for reasons that Henry could never quite decipher but which he imagined had to do with his outrageous self-consciousness, unreasonable fears of perfectly normal things, and the general confusion that he seemed to feel when he was around women.

It was a very interesting matter. But Karen's was not a complex proposal, and Henry had to answer with some ease and speed if he was to keep up this spirit of casual intimacy. "That sounds cool to me," Henry finally said.

Henry ate the rest of his brisket with alarming speed, and soon he was back at Karen's apartment in Greenpoint, sipping another glass of bourbon and wondering (again) just how to make the first move. But Karen once more took the lead, kissing Henry and slowly unbuttoning his jeans, and before long Henry found himself in precisely the sort of heroic and, to Henry's surprise, just a bit raw situation he had always wanted to be in with Karen.

9

AND (to Henry's happy astonishment) they saw each other again. Six times, in fact, by Henry's exact count, and each time was the same: an indulgent dinner of fatty meat and distilled alcohol followed by interesting bedroom acts that kept Henry in a state of delight and self-congratulation well into the next day.

Still, it was hard to say what all this meant. They were both in their mid-twenties, after all, and in this day and age exclusivity had to be affirmed and not assumed, as Henry sadly found out when he first arrived in Brooklyn. And Henry could never quite escape the suspicion that Karen was just a bit too good for him—just a little too attractive and a little too savvy. But by the sixth date (now the first week in December) he felt some small amount of confidence. Henry decided that perhaps this so-called relationship might have some kind of future. However (and this, sadly, surprised Henry not one bit), the whole thing ended very badly.

It had been decided, after some discussion, that people friendly with other people Henry knew were gathering to watch the New England Patriots play the New York Jets at a bar on Metropolitan Avenue, a bar which was known for having several popular video games. The idea for this particular gathering had started with Karen, who had proposed it to a friend in an email (as such things were done then), an email which had been (quite thoughtlessly, as it turned out) forwarded to subsequent people and, finally, after perhaps thirty people had received it, to Henry. The thing was that the first email, the email that had proposed the plan, included (obviously due to a careless and also catastrophic mistake) information about Henry, and Karen's feelings toward him. In response to a mercifully deleted question, it said the following:

Yeah. Henry. Strange guy. Or not strange as much as a bore. Milquetoast, as my mom says. But all that money he's got is pretty appealing. Ha, but even that's not enough for me to stick around. Only taking one for the team! All for the good of Suckerhead's *finances! Oh, and one thing I've got to say, because I've got to tell somebody, is that he makes the freakiest facial expressions during sex. Crazy shit.*

Henry was so completely startled as he finished reading this (again, it was far at the beginning of a long string of emails) that he found he had an absolutely shocking and adrenaline-fueled sense of awareness of every single aspect of just how terrible this was. The fact that he was called milquetoast and a bore was, needless to say, entirely demoralizing. Worse was that somehow the sex had been turned into a type of painful barter for the $30,000 he'd put up for the magazine, and the future money they'd probably need. More worse, and his hair really did feel like it was standing on end when he contemplated this, was that he made strange (and clearly disturbing) faces when he had sex. And the worst of all (by far the worst): people around Brooklyn now knew about these particular faces he made. Karen was telling people. And even if she wasn't telling *a lot of people*, it was now on an email circulating throughout Williamsburg. How long would it be before some other person read back to the beginning of the exchange and then posted his discovery on one of the then-new and popular social networking sites?

It was all more than Henry could bear. And after just two or three seconds of the adrenaline-fueled awareness, his thoughts began to dissolve, and, without any ability to stop himself, he burst into tears.

He was at home and he was alone. At least he had that. Henry had, on more than one occasion, burst into tears in public, so he was happy, at least, that he wasn't using some café's Wi-Fi and weeping into his coffee.

The crying lasted for nearly five minutes, but then quickly subsided, although the agony did not, and soon he was walking alone through Williamsburg with his collar pulled tight around his neck and wondering how he was going to get through all this. He began thinking about those relatives he had in California and how he had always had a vague desire to live close to a proper, sun-drenched beach. But after that fantasy ceased and he concluded that he would actually not be that happy spending more than a month or so living on the beach, as it were, he decided that what he really needed to do was take some sort of action. If not an angry phone call or a hostile email, then, at the very least, the announcement that he was not interested in going out with Karen again. Surprisingly, however, by the time he got home, now just a few hours after his horrifying discovery, Henry found that he had an email from Karen, canceling their next date and adding, almost as an afterthought, that she had decided that they probably shouldn't be romantically involved anymore. Of course, in this era, especially in Williamsburg, it had long been entirely appropriate to break up with someone on email, and this wasn't even a breakup, given the fact that they had only gone out on a handful of dates. Still, Henry wondered if she hadn't suddenly realized that she had disseminated her offensive thoughts about him and decided to bail out before he did. Henry even formulated a long email response that accused her of this, discussing the importance of privacy, the lack of care and kindness in our troubling world, and how it was nobody's business—not even that of her closest friends—what he looked like while having sex.

It felt good to write this hostile email. In the end, though, Henry decided not to send it, thinking it would only make him look worse, and probably be more fodder for Karen to make fun of him to her friends.

And so he abandoned his email, and began to cope with his feelings of humiliation by starting work (and it actually went very, very well in those next hours) on a story he had long wanted to write about a ninety-year-old man who had to struggle with the sorrow of having to commit his hundred-and-six-year-old mother to a nursing home. This project took him well into the night, and, mercifully, through the next week and a half. And, with some amount of thanks for the distraction, Henry even sent it out to several literary journals as soon as he had finished, although, given the odds and his recent luck, it seemed likely that he would not be particularly successful with this project either.

10

GIVEN THESE RECENT events, by the time Christmas came Henry was relieved that a return trip north to Highgate Meadows would take him far from the city and, better yet, allow him to spend time alone with Abby. She'd been doing quite a bit of freelancing at some sort of textile arts website and had been unable to meet Henry at all following his most recent humiliations, although Henry did his best to pretend that nothing bad had happened to him. He was, however, not very good at this.

"What's with all the moaning?" Abby asked on the phone one evening. "You'll see me soon enough. We're spending Christmas together."

"I suppose," Henry replied. "And I'm not moaning. I guess I'm just looking for something to do."

"Well, find a hobby," Abby said. "I'm making great money and getting a billion hours and things with my band are going really well, so I'm not seeing anyone till I split for upstate." (Abby's family lived in Saratoga Springs.)

It did occur to Henry that perhaps Abby herself had seen the email that Karen had sent out, although Abby's address didn't appear on any of the forwarded emails—he had checked three times. And, given the fact that Abby had always been skeptical of the *Suckerhead* crowd, if she did get the email, she might have dismissed the whole thing entirely.

So it was all a puzzle, but by the time Henry loaded his bags into the back of his Volvo early on Christmas Eve, his mind had relaxed somewhat. He'd spend time in the country doing things like inspecting picked-over squash fields, walking along old stone walls, and feeding the prized heirloom goats, who wouldn't care one bit how Henry looked in bed.

The plan for the trip involved Henry staying at Highgate Meadows alone on Christmas Eve. The caretaker would be gone by noon, as would the other employees, and Abby would not be up until the afternoon of Christmas Day. She had a few small duties to take care of, but Henry was encouraged to "have fun and make yourself at home!" as Hannah was kind enough to say in an email she sent just before departing for St. Croix. Abby gave Henry more specific instructions— which room he was staying in, where he could find towels, etc. "There are things I've got to do when I get there," Abby also said. "But it's all minor. Everything is on autopilot, basically, so there's nothing really to think about. We'll just be there to make sure no catastrophes occur." Abby also gave Henry various other bits of information—assorted things involving Henry's comfort, including where the woodshed was and where the liquor was kept.

The promise of liquor was, in fact, on Henry's mind as he drove north. He had somehow arrived at a vision of himself in front of the fireplace with some kind of brandy as the final symbol of him relaxing and putting Williamsburg behind him, if only for a day or so. He even had a fairly methodical plan for how to build a fire and pour himself a drink in as little time as possible—he would wait to unpack his car, wait to use the bathroom, and wait to make himself something to eat before the fire was built and the brandy was poured.

And there was another thing that was making him long for the warmth of a fire and a drink. On the trip north, it started to snow. Heavily. It was really quite beautiful. Henry's Volvo had a number of so-called cross-country upgrades, and was very well equipped to handle difficult weather, so he wasn't worried about road conditions, and he even allowed himself to enjoy the scenery and think (with some irrational optimism) about the various possibilities that might unfold on a snow-covered Vermont farm alone with Abby. The snow certainly was heavy, and as he drove up through Massachusetts and then approached the Vermont border, it occurred to him that this was one of the heaviest snowfalls he had ever seen. He turned on the radio to get the weather report (he had been listening to music thus far) and his suspicions were confirmed as several newscasters discussed what they were predicting would be—and maybe this was a bit surprising—the worst storm to hit the region in thirty years. Henry had heard that snow was coming when he was still in Brooklyn. Or, he had read about it online. But there'd been none of the drama and seriousness that he was now hearing in the voices on the radio. And by the time he pulled onto the road where Highgate Meadows lay, he was hearing specific reports of record temperature drops and the possibility of as much as forty-two inches of snow—it was supposed to last all the way through Christmas and into the following day.

Henry could, of course, see for himself what was being discussed by the weather forecasters. The festive and Christmassy snow had turned into a freezing blizzard, and Henry had trouble even making out the silhouettes of the buildings as he passed up the drive. But he had arrived. So there was really little for him to worry about at this point. At least he wouldn't freeze to death on the side of the road, and that, after all, was something to be thankful for.

11

AND SO, ONCE he arrived, Henry executed his well-made plans, although he did have to make one small adjustment and use the bathroom before he built the fire. Within fifteen minutes of his arrival, however, he was sipping a glass of some kind of expensive-looking Armagnac and watching a large oak log catch fire atop a pile of pine kindling.

It was very peaceful and took him far away from his life in Williamsburg, and after a few moments of taking it all in—the leather-bound books, the antique sideboard, the soft yellow couch with two quilts draped along the back—Henry wondered again, as he had the last time he'd been to Highgate Meadows, if this wasn't, in fact, exactly the life for him. And the corollary thought—this was new, however—was that maybe what he really needed was a woman like Hannah, although, of course, a much younger version of her. Maybe he needed someone who enjoyed the country more, someone who liked sitting by the fire, arranging quilts in appealing ways, and cooking elaborate meals. Unfortunately, at the same time he also had the uncomfortable realization that Hannah reminded him a bit of his mother. His mother was sweeter, if that was a thing a person could really be, and quite a bit less ambitious than Hannah. But his mother was an emotionally astute woman and an excellent storyteller, having somehow memorized the entirety of the details of every maternal relative Henry had ever met, or known to exist. It was, in truth, nearly the only thing his mother liked to talk about, although the stories were never repetitive or dull, and they always left Henry with a very strong urge to write something about it all himself.

It was when he was in his last year of college (the semester before he started his so-called internship at the magazine) that she died, along with his father, in the boating accident near their house on Martha's Vineyard. Again, it had been entirely unexpected, as boating accidents always are, and so shocking that Henry was sure he still hadn't recovered. In fact, what he generally felt at the times when he thought about it all was that he hadn't yet even really experienced the event in its full form and was instead moving helplessly away from that first horrible phone call in a state of increasing confusion. It was odd, never quite feeling that you had really grasped the depths of a terrible event, to say nothing of having recovered from it. And the fact was that Henry had been very close to his parents, as different as they were from him.

Henry had grown up in Lexington, Massachusetts, in an enormous house on nine acres of land, with an old barn, a pond, and a reasonable commute for his father into Boston. His father managed a sort of investment fund, which consisted partly of the family's money and partly of money from other investors—generally other wealthy families that didn't have someone as smart as Henry's father to manage their estates.

Henry's father had had a more formal job once, before taking the reins of the fund he ran. He was an equities analyst for a large brokerage in Boston. He bowed out without too much trouble, though, following a disagreeable change in management. But Henry's father was never possessed with the kind of financial mania that most successful money runners are, and he slipped easily into his new and calmer life without too much trouble. He was an excellent sailor and he loved to play tennis and to hunt, and the truth was that he was devoted to his family. In fact, Henry came home at least five or six weekends a semester when he was at Deerfield (a fairly unusual thing among his peers) and his father always loved to spend time with him.

It was the case, though (and this had been completely clear to Henry for all his life), that Henry and his father were very different people. Even when he was in grade school he could tell that he was frailer and more sensitive (in the bad way) than his father, and these first suspicions bore themselves out as he grew older, and as he grew even more sensitive and into even less of an athlete. But the thing was, and this was something Henry understood deeply and with great emotional precision, his father loved him with a heroic sense of gratitude and acceptance. Never once—really, not once—did his father ever make a single disparaging remark about things like Henry's irrational fear of water, his lack of physical stamina, his crippling shyness around girls, or anything else that marked him as functioning far on the other side of his father's robust and masculine vigor.

"You and I are different guys," his father once said, just after they discussed Henry's decision to abandon his tenuous alternate's position on Deerfield's junior varsity cross-country team. "We're different. But Henry, you're the best man I know. You really are. I couldn't be happier that you're my son. I learn something from you every day. And you know why? Because you're the most emotionally generous person I've ever met. I don't think I've ever heard one mean or petty thing come out of your mouth. Ever. Not even when you were little. And that's pretty unusual. About as unusual a thing as I've ever seen."

This conclusion had always puzzled Henry. Certainly he had held thoughts and opinions that were far from generous and very well might land squarely under the heading of petty.

But it was true that Henry had few enemies and had never really mistreated a friend.

One thing was clear, however—clear at least on the couch at Highgate Meadows that Christmas Eve: Henry's father had loved him. And Henry knew it. And while there are, of course, any number of perfectly obvious reasons why losing your father is entirely devastating, in Henry's case the most important loss had to do with the fact that he felt as though he would never find anyone who thought as well of him, who liked him quite as much, who really seemed so happy to be around him.

All the same, it was still a pleasant thought, despite the tragedy that lay behind it. Or comforting that there at least had once been someone like that in his life. And it was part of a constellation of ideas and memories that Henry decided he might nurse for the entire evening, now that the fire was built and he had secured something good to drink.

But just as he began to consider that he might try another variety of Hannah's Armagnacs in order to contemplate his past more deeply, his cell phone rang. At first Henry thought he might ignore it, not recognizing the number on the telephone. But he eventually answered, thinking it might be some elderly relative calling to wish him a merry Christmas. Instead, it was Abby, and although she did at first say she was calling from Saratoga Springs to wish him a merry Christmas, she also said she had more specific matters to discuss.

"So I guess the storm is pretty bad up there," she said.

Henry looked out the window. He'd almost forgotten about the storm, now that he was in front of the fire. The storm was still raging—almost worse now. "It is pretty bad," Henry finally agreed.

"We're getting killed here," Abby said. "But it seems like you're even worse off. I guess a lot of roads are closed for the night."

"That doesn't surprise me. The roads were terrible getting here."

"Anyway, Hannah wanted me to make sure you're not dead and that the farm's all right. She also wants you to check on the goats. Make sure they're all right. But that's it. I'm going to try to leave early tomorrow. Hopefully the roads will be passable by then. I should make it there one way or another, though. I'm taking my dad's car. But you'll be on your own tonight and a lot of tomorrow."

"That sounds fine to me," Henry said. He thought for a moment that perhaps he'd buy some Armagnac when he got home. He wondered, specifically, how much this particular bottle cost and he even considered that maybe he'd like to open a small shop in Williamsburg that sold nothing but Armagnac. "Everything is great here, though," he finally added.

"Do you have a fire?"

"I have a fire. And I found the liquor cabinet. We'll have lots of fun tomorrow. We can play gin rummy in front of the fireplace."

Henry expected Abby to say something like, *I can't wait* or even, *Don't drink everything before I get up there.* But there was no response, and Henry had the vague idea that Abby was about to scold him for some inadvertent offense. But there was nothing. At last, Henry said, "Hello? Hello?" several times.

There was still no response. Henry pulled the phone away from his ear and looked at it. The screen read, "No Reception."

He stared at his phone for another second, then stood up and walked to a cordless phone at the far side of the room. He'd call her back that way. But the cordless phone was dead as well. And then, in the next instant, the one small lamp that Henry had on in the living room flickered, and then it flickered again, and then it went out.

Henry walked through the back hall to the kitchen and tried the lights there. They were also off. It was still light outside, so he could see fairly well in the house. But after trying several other light switches, he determined that the electricity was now clearly out. This was probably not a very good development, Henry thought, although also probably nothing to worry about. He'd just have to keep an eye on things.

And perhaps this ought to begin with the goats, seeing as they were the one thing that really concerned Abby and Hannah.

12

HENRY COULD HARDLY help but think that these so-
called Libyan goats were—even to the layman—magnificent-
looking animals. They had intense glaring eyes, and black
shining horns, and, although their coats were technically
gray, in the now-dimming light of the Vermont winter, with
the sun filtered through a terrible snowstorm and the large
Plexiglas windows of the small barn, the goats looked blue.
And not just gray with a bluish tint. Their coats were a sort
of pure dark blue, unmistakable and with almost no gray in
it at all.

They were certainly puzzling animals, and Henry thought
that he'd definitely like to spend more time with them in the
next day or so. But before he could think too deeply about
the mysteries of animal life, he noticed something else. It
was just a little colder than it should have been in the barn.
The heat was electric—Henry could see that quickly enough
from the ceiling installations—so it would now be out just like
everything else electrical on the farm. And there was another
problem. One of the windows had blown open, and freezing,
snowy air was tumbling in—probably had been for some time.

Henry quickly walked to the window to shut it. He didn't
know the exact temperature inside, but it certainly was cold,
and Henry remembered that Hannah had made the point on

her tour that the goats needed to be warm—that their milk suffered from cold temperatures, and perhaps (Henry could only imagine) their bodies in general might have trouble with temperature drops.

Of course, how exactly to warm up a goat was just a little beyond Henry's expertise. And, after all, they did have long woolly coats, and they were huddling together, and surely a barn was better than the wilderness, although Henry wasn't sure if this species of goat had ever actually lived in the wilderness.

But the matter of the barn's temperature was a question, and Henry decided he should think the matter over a bit, although he really wasn't sure what his options were. He went back inside, put another log on the fire, poured another glass of Armagnac, and decided tentatively that it was probably foolish to worry about animals and cold weather because surely their natural instincts would somehow lead them through the trouble.

About ten minutes later, however, Henry was up and pacing again, and he eventually determined that he really ought to do something. He looked at the thermometer outside the kitchen window and noticed the temperature had dropped about four degrees in the past half hour—astonishingly, it was now close to zero—and it was also quickly getting darker. He found several flashlights in a kitchen cupboard, although he didn't quite need them yet, then put on his coat and hat and headed back to the barn.

The wind was now much more powerful, and the snow was moving in a nearly horizontal direction. In fact, because of the tremendous wind gusts, the snow was also exploding in big clouds blowing up from the ground. And it really was much, much colder—Henry didn't need the kitchen thermometer to see that. He wasn't sure what sort of weather systems caused this kind of thing, but this really did feel like what a blizzard was supposed to be, both by formal definition and by direct experience.

It was unclear, however, whether or not the goats under-stood that things were getting worse for them. When Henry arrived in the barn, he saw that the window had stayed shut, but it was already much, much colder. The goats were still huddled together, more tightly now, though, and when Henry approached them, he thought he saw one or two of them shiver, although the physical movements of goats were, of course, something that Henry had no familiarity with at all. Still, it seemed like he should do something. It seemed that he needed to deal with the fact that their barn was without heat and that the temperatures would soon drop below zero and stay that way for the night and probably the next day. The goats were only going to get colder, and they were, after all, the most important (the most irreplaceable) asset on the farm. The question was, what to do.

For just a moment, Henry did arrive at a somewhat inter-esting idea stemming from a book he'd read in college about the history of "rural dwellings" in early modern Europe. It pointed out that livestock often slept right in the house with the owner to protect it from inclimate weather and bandits and whatever else might harm it. And it did (just for a brief moment) seem to Henry that it might be possible to bring the goats into the house and keep them warm by the various fire-places. It was not a very serious consideration, though, mostly because it was quickly transplanted by another, better, and much more sensible idea. He remembered on his first tour with Hannah at Highgate Meadows that there was a large gas-powered generator—large but reasonably portable because it was on wheels—located in the machine shed. He also remembered seeing the two space heaters in the shed, near the long workbench where various repairs were carried out. If he wheeled the generator over and hooked it up to the space heaters, he'd be able to heat up the goat barn quickly—again, because of the goats' skittishness regarding open spaces, the barn was enclosed, relatively small, and easily sealed off, now that the window was secured. It wouldn't take more than twenty minutes for the barn to warm up.

Without thinking much more about it, Henry left the goats with the promise, "I'll be right back!" and then headed out to the large snowy lot and then across to the machine shed.

13

HENRY ACTUALLY FELT quite happy as he opened the door to the machine shed and turned on one of his flashlights. There was still dim light coming through the windows, but using a flashlight seemed exciting to Henry, since he was doing something that might fall under the category of farm work. Moreover, it was, in fact, innovative and resourceful farmwork, farmwork to protect the farm's most unique feature, which he decided was mainly why he was now feeling something of a thrill. And when he spotted the generator near the door, and then the two space heaters, he decided he was very much looking forward to telling Abby what he had come up with when she arrived the following day.

Moving the heaters and the generator would take two trips, and he decided to carry over the space heaters first. They were small, although heavy under each of his arms. He managed well enough, though, and by the time he was back and pushing the generator out of one of the large vehicle-sized shed doors, he was happy with how simple all this was, and even happier with the prospect that he'd soon be back in front of the fire with his glass of Armagnac and the knowledge that the goats were secure.

Because of the generator's wheels, which were inflatable and good-quality, it was fairly easy to push, although Henry could tell how heavy it was because of how hard it was to steer. It had quite a bit of momentum after it got going, and there were several moments when the generator seemed to strike out on its own course. But Henry eventually arrived at the goat barn and parked the generator beneath a large over-hanging roof. He had found extension cords in the machine shed as well, which were long enough to make it into the barn, although as he pulled the cords over a railing and in through the barn's front door, he had another idea. Henry had begun to think that maybe the two space heaters ought to be supple-mented somehow, and, not having seen any other heaters in the machine shed, and deciding that the goats ought to be warmed up as quickly as possible, he arrived at a new method of adding to the goats' heating system. He ran back outside and started pushing the generator to a small gate in the out-door corral, and then toward the so-called barn door, which opened between the corral and the actual goat barn. The engine itself would also generate heat, Henry concluded, and why not use that heat as well to warm the barn?

He passed through the corral's gate, flipped the latch of the barn door, and was soon pushing the generator into the barn. The goats were still huddled at the far corner and now, Henry decided, looking just a little more concerned about the threatening weather. Henry quickly looked around and estimated their enclosure was about fifteen hundred square feet—not that large—and he figured with confidence that with the added heat of the hot engine, the goats might start to feel a bit better in only ten minutes or so.

There were two cement sections of the floor—they sur-rounded drains that Henry assumed were used for quick cleanings with a hose. He positioned the generator over one of these, thinking that he didn't want to risk any sort of fire starting. Next, he checked the enormous, emergency-sized gas tank—it was full—and then he turned a small black key that was already in the ignition. The engine turned over immediately, and after popping a few times, it smoothed out and began to hum like the engine of a car, the exhaust hitting Henry in the legs and heating up his shins. Everything was in working order, although the goats suddenly seemed to be a little more nervous with all the noise. Still, it couldn't be helped. Surely it was better for them to be nervous than to freeze to death.

Henry then plugged in the space heaters to the generator's panel of outlets and turned them up to high. Their coils took less than twenty seconds to start glowing, and with the space heaters' fans behind the coils, warm air was soon blowing into the freezing barn. It was really all very satisfying for Henry, and, what's more, within five minutes the barn started feeling a tiny bit warmer. Henry remained with the goats for another ten minutes, monitoring the progress of his plan, and soon the goats seemed to be huddling just a bit less tightly. One even drifted away from the pack. It seemed perhaps that it was even possible that Henry could now return to the fire and his Armagnac, knowing he'd really done something very useful. He'd check on things in another hour, but for now everything seemed to be going smoothly.

And Henry did return in about an hour—now definitely a little drunk—and the flock of heirloom Libyan goats seemed to be in very high spirits. They weren't huddled together anymore and several were at their feeding trough, happily munching on their strange granular feed in their now-warmer barn. Again, Henry felt a very deep kind of satisfaction, looking over all this—aided, of course, by his intoxication—and he couldn't help but anticipate, once again, the pleasure he'd feel the following day when he showed all this to Abby. With that, he turned and headed back to the house, thinking that it was finally time to eat his dinner.

14

HENRY'S DINNER WAS simple—a cold plate of cheese and cured meats, and the end of a whole-grain bâtard that had been wrapped in paper above the refrigerator. And pickles of various sorts—Hannah was clearly an enthusiastic vegetable pickler, and Henry could hardly help but conclude that she was very, very good at this particular craft. The pickled turnips and pickled green beans were exceptional, and they went perfectly with the local, organically made beer Henry had also decided to open.

Henry ate an enormous amount, quickly working through the bread, smearing it with mustard and fresh Vermont butter and layering it with cheese and meat, and soon he began to feel very sleepy. It was always this way with him, especially after drinking hard liquor, and before long, without cleaning his dishes or even finishing his beer, Henry wandered upstairs to his bedroom—the one that had been assigned to him and was waiting with fresh sheets and towels. It was now getting very cold in the house as well, and Henry was happy to crawl beneath a thick down comforter, and also happy that an early night would mean he'd be up early in the morning, ready to manage the farm and the goats and prepare for Abby's arrival.

Henry slept very well, waking at seven o'clock, feeling fresh and ready for the day. He was just a bit hung-over, in that his mind seemed a little hazy. But it was somewhat pleasant, especially since he was alone on a beautiful farm, the snow was deep (and still falling rapidly), and he really had little to do besides sit by the fire, read, eat, and experiment with expensive alcohol.

He wandered into the kitchen (it was now entirely freezing, so Henry was fully dressed) and turned on the gas stove to heat a kettle. Henry then put on his boots and hat, preparing to head out to check on the goats. He'd take a quick peek at them and then return to build a fire and make some kind of breakfast.

Now, with a cup of tea, on the walk across the open quadrangle, Henry could hardly help but remark once again about how cold it was. But the unbelievable and almost unnatural temperatures only made Henry even happier when he walked into the barn and felt how warm it was. The generator was purring and the space heaters were glowing red, and the burst of hot air that met him at the door was very pleasant.

The scene inside, however, was initially somewhat puzzling. The goats seemed fine at first—certainly they must be warm enough—but they were all sleeping in a state of bewildering silence. Henry had no idea what a sleeping goat was supposed to look like, but these goats looked as though they had halcyon in their feed. And they seemed to be sleeping in unexpected positions—not curled around themselves like dogs, but lying rigidly, on their sides, and one or two seemed to have legs sticking up into the air.

Henry looked over everything for a moment, and then approached the goat that was closest to him and noticed that all four of its legs were perfectly straight and raised just slightly above the ground, unsupported by anything. He bent down to stroke it, but recoiled when he realized that the goat was astonishingly hard. He touched the goat next to it, and it was just as stiff, just as immobile. And when he shook it, trying to rouse it from its sleep, he found that it shifted as though it were a single, solid piece. It moved like a sack of concrete, not a living thing filled with fluids and organs. As Henry stood up and looked over the rest of the goats before him—not one of which was awake, moving, making noise, or doing anything else that might indicate it was alive—he realized that something was terribly wrong. And it didn't take long for Henry to figure out what it was. He suddenly recalled a friend in prep school who had a brother who had died while working on his sports car one winter because he ran the engine in an enclosed garage, and he immediately turned and sprinted for the door. He glanced to his right at the generator, gently humming and powering the space heaters, and thought he ought to turn it off. But he had to get out before he was poisoned by the carbon monoxide fumes that he now understood filled the barn. And he did manage to make it through the door, although as he stepped through the outer room and then outside, he felt very far from fortunate to still be alive. Quickly, he ran outside, around to the windows, and forced them open, breaking two in the process. He waited for another few minutes, then took a deep breath and reentered the barn, dashing to the generator and turning the key. Henry could feel the wind blowing through the open windows now, so he assumed he was mostly safe. Nevertheless, he left the barn for another fifteen minutes to make sure, spending the whole time pacing in circles in the shockingly deep snow, thinking about what to do next and the fact that a million dollars' worth of goats (irreplaceable Libyan goats) were now lying stiff and immobile before him. Henry did look several times into the open windows to see if there was any sign of life. There was none, although Henry told himself several times, in instants of wild hope, that maybe the goats could somehow be revived, that maybe they all weren't as stiff as those few he had inspected. But after ten minutes had passed, and Henry felt it was safe to return, he did a careful inspection and concluded that it was completely unlikely that any of the goats would ever be up and walking around again.

15

ALL THE SAME, despite the entirely obvious scene before him, Henry still felt he had to try to do something, and after once again inspecting the warm stiff goats, he ran into the house to look for a copy of the yellow pages. He spent some time searching the obvious places, but with no luck, and, given modern technology, there was a good chance Hannah didn't even keep a copy around. The Internet was not an option since the power was out, but finally Henry noticed a bulletin board next to the kitchen phone that had the listing he was looking for. A card read "Strafford Valley Farming and Veterinarian Services" and, more promising, said below in bold type, "7 DAYS A WEEK / 24 HOURS A DAY / ALL MAJOR HOLIDAYS."

Phoning was still impossible, so Henry found a map and plotted a course to the Strafford Valley Vet's, and soon he was outside running to his car. It would be a rough trip with the snow, but Henry had good tires and all wheel drive and by this point he was thinking that it might be more dignified for him to crash into a tree or freeze to death in a ditch than to sit around the farm in the presence of an astonishingly expensive and rare flock of dead heirloom Libyan goats.

Of course, what a vet could do was a mystery to Henry, but since it was clearly such a catastrophe it seemed that he had to make some kind of attempt to save the flock, that he had to turn to some sort of expert or institution or authority. Henry was already trying to figure out what he was going to say to Hannah, and at the very least he wanted to be able to tell her something like, *I naturally charged off to the veterinarian's immediately, despite the terrible and dangerous snowstorm.* It seemed better than the alternative—saying that he wandered around the farm weeping, doing nothing at all to change the situation.

Although the roads were terrible, the larger of them seemed to have been plowed within the last two or three hours, and when Henry arrived at the vet's, he was happy to see that Christmas and the storm had not prevented Strafford Valley Veterinary Services from keeping the promises made on their business card. He dashed in, consciously trying to look as hysterical as possible to impress on everyone that a disaster had occurred, and after a brief explanation to a youngish woman about possibly having killed a hundred extremely rare ten-thousand-dollar-apiece goats, he was once again back on the snowy roads, but now followed in a pickup truck by the vet—the woman to whom he had so hastily explained himself.

It took about twenty minutes to make it back to the farm, although during this leg of the journey Henry seemed to not have any coherent thoughts. What was going on in his brain seemed to be purely physical, his mind producing a sort of buzzing and rattling that somehow extended down his neck. And this sensation didn't leave Henry as he and the vet left their vehicles, ran across the quadrangle, then entered the goat barn, where he was able to see, once again, just exactly what he had done.

The vet stopped as soon as she viewed the scene, not so much out of horror but out of what Henry determined was utter hopelessness. She had told Henry that she ought to take a look at the goats before he panicked too much—maybe he was mistaken—but it was now perfectly clear by the way she walked among the goats, and the almost perfunctory way she inspected several of them, that she knew that the damage was done and there was no possibility of reversing it.

"I'm so, so sorry," she said at last as she stood up from a goat. "They've been dead for a while. You shouldn't blame yourself. It was an honest mistake. But I'm truly sorry."

Henry couldn't quite figure out if he appreciated this sympathy or if her compassion was making him feel worse, although by the time she had said she was sorry the third time, Henry was in tears, now realizing (by way of the vet's pity) that he really had done something very horrible and that the consequences were almost too great to calculate. And this was just the beginning. Standing there, crying and shamefaced in front of the vet, surely wasn't as bad as it would be when Abby arrived and when Hannah found out.

"Was your phone working at your offices?" Henry finally asked, thinking that maybe he ought to make a phone call to Abby.

"No. It's still down," the vet replied, adding, "I'm assuming I'm the only one you've told so far?"

"Yes," Henry said. "But I have a friend. Or a fourth cousin, really, although that's not really a relative, and she'll be here later today. So I'll be telling her soon enough."

"I'm so, so sorry," the vet said again.

16

ABBY FINALLY ARRIVED at the farm several hours after the vet had left—left after also telling Henry that veterinarians didn't really deal with dead animals and that they'd probably have to be incinerated on the property. Henry spent the next several hours rehearsing his story, wondering over and over if there was any reasonable way to explain how he had killed a singular and hugely expensive flock of goats. And when Abby at last arrived at Highgate Meadows, and he finally told her what had happened (slowly, in the kitchen, over a carefully prepared pot of tea that Henry insisted on making for her), she just sat there, stunned and wide-eyed and staring into the space just to the right of Henry's head. And then they walked to the barn, and together they looked over the terrible carnage that Henry had caused, and eventually, in the now, once again, freezing cold barn, she said, "Oh, Henry, what have you done?"

But it was said sweetly. A little sweetly, Henry hoped. Henry thought he could detect just a bit of kindness. But there was also apprehension (or anger, perhaps) because Henry was her friend and, as blameless as she was, she was also somehow going to have to answer for this. And this fact Henry found almost unbearable. Of all the things Henry didn't want to happen, he certainly didn't want Abby to take any of the blame.

And, in fact, Henry didn't have to face Hannah at all. Not right away, at least. As they stood there in the goat barn, after thinking silently for a few moments, Abby told Henry that he should go back to Brooklyn. She'd get in touch with Hannah, she said. And she'd let the caretaker know when he got back the next day. She'd handle it.

"Just go back to Brooklyn," she said.

"But this is all my fault," he replied with more desperation than he would have liked.

"Yeah, but I can deal better with what's next," she said.

"I should be the one to tell Hannah."

"Henry, I think that would be a bad, bad, bad idea. You just need to go home. I know you didn't mean for this to happen. I know it was an accident. I know you were just trying to help. But I think it's better if I explain this to Hannah, not you. She's going to lose it. I can't imagine what it's going to be like. And if you're on the phone it's going to be a million times worse. For me too. I don't think I could bear that. Anyway, I'll still have to talk to her, even if you break the news. So do this for me? Head back to Brooklyn?"

Abby now looked close to tears herself as she said these last few sentences, so how could Henry reply? And the fact was that he did vaguely believe that she might be right. Hannah would be more furious than he could really reasonably imagine, and Henry was hardly the best foil for such emotions to be properly expressed. Henry did not, however, feel any relief over the fact that he wouldn't be the one to break the news. Abby's face appeared entirely drained of blood. Even her lips seemed white. And her mouth couldn't quite close. And she kept scratching her neck in a sort of distracted and upset way that made her seem to be a very different person, a person very far from the tough and intrepid young woman that Henry normally knew.

"All right," Henry said after a moment.

Abby stared at him for a second, almost as if she had forgotten what Henry was agreeing to. But then she said, "Go pack. I'm going to stay here. I need to think about this."

17

NEEDLESS TO SAY, the drive back to Brooklyn was excruciating for Henry—all that time alone with his thoughts. It was exactly what he didn't want at that point, and he began conflating everything he was thinking into a single saturated emotion based on his general and recent failures with women, his shameful facial expressions during sex (probably being discussed at that moment throughout Williamsburg), and now the fact that he had killed a million-dollar herd of goats, which, because of their unique origin, no amount of money, Henry's or an insurance company's, could replace.

Henry wasn't even able to resort to his customary emotional trick of thinking about writing a short story (and thereby winning literary glory) to give himself a bit of relief. After all, on the level of great literature, he was feeling like a complete failure as well.

And, ironically, this particular failure was confirmed once again when he arrived home. There was mail—clearly it was the last delivery made on Christmas Eve—which contained a rejection letter from the fiction editor at *Suckerhead*. It was for the somewhat sentimental story he had written about the elderly man who had never been properly loved by another person, and, quite shockingly, it was a form rejection letter that politely told him his work wasn't "needed at this time," with a tepid note of encouragement at the bottom: "A good but uneven effort. Keep trying!—Max."

It was almost too horrible to bear, although there was one surprising addition to the rejection slip. On the back was a note in different script that said, "Disagree. I loved it—Sasha."

So that was good. For just an instant, Henry felt good about that. The tattooed woman liked it. Still, it wasn't enough to diminish the humiliation of Max's completely patronizing response and Henry was soon taking off his clothes and getting into bed, hoping he'd sleep through the entire next day, and maybe even beyond that.

18

ɑ**ND THE NEXT DɑYS** were, in fact, terrible, although
Henry didn't hear anything about the terrible catastrophe
in Vermont. He called Abby about it—repeatedly—but much
to his dismay she didn't return any of his calls. Henry also
made several offers to help alleviate the situation, suggesting
via Abby's voice mail that he could even compensate Hannah
for the loss—it seemed a not-impossible thing to do given
his bank account, although it was a staggering million dollars. Henry did suspect, though, that she was at least partially
insured, so if he was taken up on this, he'd hopefully be in for
substantially less than the entire price of the flock.

All the same, despite his numerous calls and messages,
Abby didn't reply, and although Henry also formulated many
heartfelt apologies he wanted to deliver to Hannah, he didn't
dare call her directly until he heard from Abby. A week after
he returned from Vermont, however, he did finally get an
opportunity to offer these apologies when Hannah (not Abby,
quite shockingly) finally called him. The fact was, though,
and much to his horror, Hannah was calling about another
development in the catastrophe and was not at all open to a
sort of clearing of the air, as it were.

"Why the fuck did you go to the vet?" Hannah screamed,
just after Henry answered the phone.

Henry was extremely surprised by this question. It was not exactly what he had expected to hear. "What?" he finally said, still not able to grasp what was being asked of him.

"Why the fuck did you go to the vet, you stupid fucking dickhead?" Hannah yelled.

Henry was fairly astonished that a fiftysomething woman from Greenwich, of all places, was using this kind of language. But he didn't dwell on this matter.

"I thought there might be something she could do," he replied.

"The goats were dead, Henry. Goats are like humans that way. You can't bring them back to life by calling a doctor, you stupid fucking dickhead."

Henry was still entirely confused, especially that this of all things would be what Hannah was angry about.

"I had to do something," he said. "It seemed best to get the vet. But what does it matter? I can pay, Hannah. I can pay for everything. The goats. The vet bills. Whatever insurance doesn't cover. Even if it doesn't cover anything, I can pay. I have fifteen million dollars."

"Let me tell you why it matters, Henry, you fucking dick." (Hannah said *Henry* and *fucking dick* with a kind of contempt he had never quite heard before from anyone.) "The vet has, at this point, told everyone in the entire state the story of you killing the fucking goats and now I'm on the fucking front page of every Vermont newspaper as the stupid fucking wife of the hedge fund manager who thought she knew better than local farmers and couldn't keep control of her own fucking farm and whose gross mismanagement killed off a million dollars' worth of fucking goats. A million dollars' worth of fucking goats!"

"What?" Henry said.

"On the front page of every fucking newspaper in Vermont, you stupid fucking dick. And all of New England soon enough. I'm a fucking laughingstock, *Henry*. All because of you."

Henry was now speechless. He rapidly thought about how to reply and then finally said, in a voice that he would later recognize as being completely and ridiculously pathetic, "They were just so cold, Hannah, and I wanted to keep them warm, which seemed to be the best thing to do because, really, they seemed very, very unhappy."

"Fuck you, you stupid fucking idiot," Hannah screamed, and before Henry processed these words (and her yet again surprisingly new threshold of anger) she hung up, leaving Henry holding his phone's receiver and thinking that now, certainly, there would be no way to ever make amends.

19

HENRY SPENT THAT day and the next wandering around Brooklyn, and while he ate little, he did stop from time to time for coffee and even drank beer at various bars, hoping that alcohol might give him some relief—it always did for everyone else. And it was true that more than once a few beers did make him feel a little better. But the feelings were temporary and were always followed with an even deeper sense of despair.

Two days after the call from Hannah, he also managed to go online to read the articles that had been written about the killing of the goats, and she certainly wasn't exaggerating when she said she was the laughingstock of the Vermont press. He did notice, however, in the later stories, when Hannah was asked to comment, that she made it very clear that it was all entirely the fault of "a brainless idiot twenty-four-year-old from Brooklyn" and that she was probably going to take legal action against him and maybe even encourage local police to press charges against Henry for "gross cruelty to animals." It was quite chilling, although two separate newspapers pointed out that legal retaliation had little possibility of success, especially because no jury or judge was likely to sympathize with the hedge fund farmer who left her homestead for a week to vacation in the Caribbean: it was hardly the sort of Yankee ethic that most Vermonters could relate to. It did hurt Henry, however, that he was now being discussed like this in the press—surely Vermont farmers were just as unsympathetic toward stupid twenty-four-year-olds from Brooklyn as they were to rich women from Connecticut.

But the pain eased somewhat about a week after Hannah phoned him, because Abby finally called (or finally returned Henry's calls) and suggested they meet for dinner. They went to the Austrian restaurant where Henry had first brought up the matter of a romantic liaison between the two. It seemed the best place to go because Henry was having trouble eating anything at all, and thick wet noodles and sausages were about the only things he thought he could choke down. When the food finally arrived, though, he found it impossible to do anything more than poke at his dinner with his fork.

"You've really got to eat, Henry," Abby said at last when she saw that Henry wasn't at all interested in his food. (They had thus far talked entirely about Abby's somewhat mystifying musical projects with her viola.)

"I'm afraid I already ate an hour or so ago," Henry finally replied, "and I'm not really very hungry."

"You already ate?" Abby said sarcastically. "Sorry, Henry, not buying it. You've got to eat something. You really do. You've lost like ten pounds. Come on, time for you to stop acting like an idiot all the time." Abby forced a smile as she said this, and then leaned forward and poked Henry in the shoulder, although, despite the playful gesture, she now looked fairly angry.

Henry dutifully cut into a sausage. "Well, I don't want to be a skinny idiot," he said quietly.

Abby hesitated, then said at last, "Look, Henry. I know Hannah called you. And I've seen the articles. And I know what she's saying. And I know how bad you feel. I feel bad. I feel completely terrible, in fact. But the truth is, and I guess I think I need to say this, the truth is that I guess I'm also a little pissed off at you too. Maybe at everything. Maybe mostly at you. I don't know. I mean, why do you do such stupid shit? And why do you even hang out with those asshole *Suckerhead* people? And, I don't know, I look at you moping around Williamsburg with fifteen million bucks in your bank account and I don't even know why we're friends, especially when you do things like kill a hundred completely innocent goats who, because they're goats (Henry!) don't have much control when some jackass from New York poisons them with the exhaust of an emergency generator."

Henry was more than a little surprised by this outburst, and while the content of what Abby was saying was of course very damning, he didn't entirely follow it because he was so lost in her tone. This was real anger, and Henry was now doing everything he could not to start crying, although he was sure there was something of a tremor beginning to appear in his mouth.

"I mean, fuck you, Henry," Abby yelled. "I mean, get it together. You've got to fucking sort your shit out. I mean, what are you doing with yourself? That's what I want to know. What are you fucking doing with yourself?" Abby paused, then took a deep breath. "That's what I what to know," she continued. "That's what I think. That's one of the things I think." She paused again, but continued before Henry could gather himself enough to respond—or start weeping. "But I guess, Henry, I think other things too," she said. "I mean, you're an idiot. You really are. But it's all bullshit. Fuck Hannah for saying all that crap to the newspapers and all the crap she said to you. Hannah might have done exactly the same thing. Anyone might have. Not me. Because me, I'm not a fucking idiot. But maybe someone else. So fuck Hannah for being so hard on you. I mean, let's face it, she is exactly that, she is the wife of a fucking hedge fund manager. Who ever heard of a ten-thousand-dollar goat? I mean, really. A ten-thousand-dollar fucking goat? A million-dollar goat herd? You've got to be some kind of freak to spend that on goats. And if you've got a million-dollar flock of goats, you certainly don't jet off to St. Croix for a week. You put your bed in the barn and watch them every minute."

Henry stared very intently at the bite of sausage on his fork. He wasn't sure what he ought to be doing at this particular moment.

"But you are an idiot, Henry," Abby said. "I'm not saying you're not. I mean, you're a total fucking goober. But, and I guess this is what I really want to say, Henry: I'm your friend. One of your best friends. You're one of my best friends. In the world. Ever. And I'm more your friend than I am my aunt's niece. And when the chips are down, I'm with you, although I can't believe I'm saying it. I'm with you, against whatever other problems you're facing, even if you deserve everything that's coming to you. I'm definitely against those *Suckerhead* idiots. I know you feel terrible about the goats. I'd kill myself. I mean it. So you're probably doing better than I would be. But you and me are friends, Henry. We're close. Really close. And that's not going to change. You really are a complete dope. But you're one of my best friends in the world. And I really, really think you're a great person, despite your completely stupid fucking behavior. You're certainly my favorite relative, although, I know, I know, like you've already pointed out"— Abby now cracked a smile—"we're only very loosely related."

It crossed Henry's mind for just an instant to reaffirm this last comment, but only out of some kind of habitual reaction, because, surprisingly, at that exact moment, he wasn't really thinking, as he usually did, about his romantic prospects with Abby. Instead—and it really was surprising—he was thinking of how much she suddenly reminded him of his father. Henry thought again about the time when he had confessed that his prospects of being a Deerfield letterman (or any kind of athlete ever, for that matter) were extremely slim, and how his father replied by saying that he was the "very best man he knew," and in that exact split-second at dinner with Abby, as Henry thought about how much his father saying that had meant to him, he almost, finally, really started crying, although now for entirely new reasons. For a moment, in fact, he felt extremely happy—despite all that had happened to him—although the feeling passed soon enough because Henry could hardly forget that he was still in quite a bit of trouble. Nevertheless, he suddenly managed to eat the piece of sausage he had on his fork, and then he ate another piece after that, and he found that it actually tasted all right to him, which was promising for any number of reasons, including that it was probably very true that he had lost nearly ten pounds in the past week or so. Henry thought for a moment about what he could only describe as a kind of general contempt he'd felt from so many people in recent months: dismissive people at *Suckerhead*, exploitative girls who insulted him online, angry wives of hedge fund managers—the list was long. But it seemed to Henry, just briefly, just at that moment—and he hoped the feeling would continue for longer—that maybe if you at least had a fourth cousin who liked you and was on your side, and you at least had the memory of a father who said you were the best person he ever knew, then maybe things weren't so bad. Or, if they were bad, you could at least somehow find a way to survive. And that was what was important in the end: finding enough of a reason to keep going. This was New York City, after all, and no place for the weak of heart (Henry now thought with some romantic reflection), especially not for a young man trying to find his way in the world, even if he did have $15 million to fall back on. He could tough it out. And the fact was, if you really thought about it, everything that had happened to him had only brought him and Abby closer, which was really just the sort of thing, Henry concluded tentatively, that might lead to deeper feelings between the two.

Henry quickly decided, however, that this was not a good way to think, especially not now. After all, maybe he really should start trying to work at being less of a so-called idiot, and imagining romantic liaisons with women who don't like you in that way was probably a good example of his many problems, and one he ought, perhaps, to correct as soon as possible. He was, all things considered, very lucky to have Abby, and he shouldn't do anything to jeopardize that. That, of all things, was very important.

20

DESPITE ABBY'S FINAL affirmation of friendship and solidarity, however, Henry knew he was still facing quite a few serious problems. But the next day something very fortunate happened that made him feel that perhaps things might really, eventually, turn around for him—at least in some venues in his life.

He had been pacing through his apartment thinking not about Abby or the goats he had killed but (still) about how outrageous it was that *Suckerhead* had sent him a form rejection letter (despite the tepid note of encouragement and the apparent approval of the fiction editor's shockingly tattooed girlfriend). He was also thinking about how it was even more outrageous that Karen referred to sleeping with him as "taking one for the team," and he was then wondering, as he walked between the kitchen, the bedroom, and the terrace, if maybe he should resign his position as editor-at-large, not in protest but because, when it really came down to it, he definitely needed to start cutting people like that out of his life. His $30,000 was irretrievable, but Henry was willing to chalk that up to a lesson learned, and, the truth was, he could afford it. It actually gave Henry a rare and sudden sort of pleasure that he was so rich, because, when you thought about it, people love money, and he had plenty of it, although just a second or so after this thought he felt quite guilty.

It was another development, however—one very surprising—that made Henry feel like the future might be a tiny bit better than he had imagined. He checked his email at about eleven in the morning and discovered that an editor at a magazine called the *Wellfleet Review* had contacted him. The *Wellfleet Review* was a little like *Suckerhead* in that it was new (although already respected) and had recently (two years ago) been founded in New York by people in their twenties. But one of the *Wellfleet Review*'s founding editors had just published a novel to fairly favorable reviews, and the magazine was getting just a little press, and it was a journal where Henry very much wanted to place a story. And, in fact, that's exactly what the email was offering. It came from the fiction editor (the editor who had published the novel) and it said that he and his colleagues all absolutely adored Henry's story—it was the one about the 90-year-old man who struggles with the pain of committing his 106-year-old mother to a nursing home—and that they'd love to publish it. Certainly it was far from a book deal with a top-notch press, or even publication in one of the more famous literary magazines, but Henry could not have been happier about the news. In fact, Henry regarded it as so extraordinary that he once again found himself pacing his apartment, although now with an outlook entirely different from the one that had just been burdening him.

Henry was somewhat nervous at that particular moment, however, thinking about how to respond to the email—whether he ought to write back right away or wait a few hours so that the editors didn't think that he was too needy. At last, though, after about ten minutes, he sat down at his computer and wrote that he would be honored to appear in the *Wellfleet Review*. He actually erased and rewrote the word "honored" several times before finally thinking that it was, in fact, a good word to use, because, after all, it was the truth. And after finishing the email with a friendly, "Let me know what the next steps are!" he stood up from his computer, put on his jacket, and headed out for another walk, although this time with quite a bit more to think about than his recent failures and disgraces. The fact was that the *Suckerhead* people would be truly impressed with this. Certainly most of the people at *Suckerhead* would be extremely glad to place a story with the *Wellfleet Review* (Henry could only assume), so perhaps now spending time with him wouldn't be so easily described as "taking one for the team." Perhaps he wouldn't feel quite so nervous around them all.

This did, however, make Henry think again about what, in fact, he should do about his position at *Suckerhead*, and the depression about the magazine made a brief reappearance. But as Henry thought the matter over (walking through McCarren Park, passing under the BQE, and stopping in three different cafés for cups of coffee), he eventually decided that perhaps he'd just stay in his role as editor-at-large because, after all, he now had a legitimate credential, as they say, and could speak with authority (informally and at meetings) as a *Wellfleet Review* writer.

And along these lines, Henry even decided that he might have a better shot with Abby, although he again quickly forced this prospect from his mind, and with an honest attempt to remove it forever. This was no time to start scheming about how to get Abby to think of him as a romantic suitor because the fact of the matter was that he really needed her, he really needed Abby as a friend. He still wasn't yet out of the woods with the fact that he had killed an entire flock of extremely rare Libyan goats, and there were numerous other things that still might come back to haunt him—perhaps he would soon be known around New York as the young author who kills goats and makes comical faces during sex.

But it was more than that, it was more than somehow preserving Abby as a means of support when things got tough again. Rather, it was the idea that Henry might be better off not worrying so much, not trying to push things so much. Maybe that was his whole problem all along. He was always trying to force things. Maybe in the future, in the next stretch of time, he'd experiment with being a little more relaxed about his life. After all, he now had a story accepted at a good literary journal, so maybe he didn't have to worry so much about whether or not he was doing the right thing with his life. In the end, a man in his mid-twenties with a story published in a literary magazine and $15 million to play around with didn't have such a bad lot in life. Henry knew that he would find plenty of things to be depressed about soon enough. Still, he had Abby to keep him on the straight-and-narrow. And maybe he'd actually learned something in the past few weeks. It wasn't impossible. So maybe now, at last, things really might finally get just a little bit better.

PART
II

1

HENRY WELL UNDERSTOOD that getting an agent was
something of an accomplishment, although it had come
about in such an inadvertent way, and led to such a strange
literary project, that he wondered if he might have done better to have waited and not jumped at the first thing that came
along. Of course, this was often the thinking he used in amo-
rous situations with women (the few that he had) when he
found himself with someone who wasn't quite right for him.
In the end, Henry mostly just stayed with the things that came
his way, and certainly he avoided throwing anyone over. He'd
never broken up with a single girl in his life—the alternative,
loneliness, was simply too grim. And Henry had been feeling
very low recently, before he and his new agent struck a deal, as
they say. It was now September, nearly ten months since he'd
slaughtered the irreplaceable Libyan goats and brought disgrace upon Hannah and her farm. Unfortunately, he was not
able to use these ten months to move on, as it were, since Hannah followed through with her threats of lawsuits and Henry
spent quite a bit of time with his newly hired lawyer, a man
named Lawrence Barnett, who, because of his conviction that
Hannah had no case at all against him, laughed with enthusiasm every time Henry called him in a state of panic because
of some kind of new threat or legal letter he received.

"Look, Henry," he finally said. "She just fucking hates you. This woman absolutely fucking hates you. People sue for anything they can think of when they hate someone. But she doesn't have a case. Not for her reputation, not for any of these things."

It was true that the financial damages were entirely covered by an insurance company. Hannah's hedge fund manager husband was an obsessive insurer of things, apparently. She got exactly what the goats had been valued at—actually something quite a bit more than a million dollars—and the insurance company itself knew enough not to come after Henry, since any case of proper malfeasance against him would be very thin.

"But she seems to think she's owed more from us because they're heirloom goats!" Lawrence said on the phone one day (laughing wildly). "*Heirloom fucking goats!* Well, she may be right that they're irreplaceable, but from a quantifiable and monetary standpoint, she's got well over a million bucks to buy whatever other damned goats she wants. As far as the courts are concerned, she's been made whole, the crazy fucking bitch."

It was a relief to have Lawrence on his side, but as time dragged on over the next many months following that awful Christmas Day, even the most mundane legal issues made Henry sick with worry, including parking tickets, a jury summons, and a drunken night when he'd relieved himself against a fence only to discover that a surveillance camera was pointed at him and that the lot beyond belonged to the city's Department of Corrections. He was not arrested for this, but, given what he often saw on TV, he couldn't rule out the possibility of a vengeful authority doing some kind of high-tech facial scan to locate and arrest the obnoxious Brooklyn kid who didn't properly respect public institutions. It was irrational, of course, but reason was never at the root of Henry's worries, although this particular fear was far-fetched enough that it went away in a few days.

At any rate, the fact was that signing a formal (legal) agreement with an agent had been just a bit unnerving. Still, Henry was well aware that getting an agent really was something to feel good about. Henry had published two more stories that summer and had one coming out in the fall, but a short story writer is a terrible prospect for proper representation, although the truth is that Henry's particular relationship with his new agent was fairly unusual and, in fact, based on a project that took him some distance away from his short stories and his so-called literary work.

2

HENRY HAD MET Merrill at a benefit for an "up-and-coming cancer charity, " which he mostly attended because an aunt of his who sat on the board had asked him to. At that time he had very few romantic prospects and thus invited Abby to be his date, acknowledging to himself (with some equanimity) that she was not a romantic prospect herself. It was now the end of September and, since the past Christmas, Henry had worked with diligence to eradicate any sort of aspirations he had for their relationship, and Abby agreed to Henry's invitation (he'd not announced any sort of confusing feelings for some time), saying that she'd be thrilled to hang out with all the well-heeled people who were sure to be there.

"And there's a great party we can go to later that night," she said as she and Henry walked below the BQE one evening on their way to dinner. "And I've got the perfect thing to wear!"

"Yes, to the party afterwards," Henry replied, "but, so you know, the benefit is black-tie."

"Yeah. I figured," Abby said. "And I've got just the thing to wear."

"I can't wait to see it," Henry said.

Of course, when Henry met Abby at the bar at the Carlyle (the benefit was a block away, at the Mark) it occurred to him that she was wearing what was, if he were ever forced to use such a tedious word, entirely inappropriate. It was, in fact, a wedding dress (a wedding dress that could not be mistaken for anything else), and although it had been retailored and had no train or cumbersome hem to prevent a woman from enjoying herself at a party, the elaborate white lace and somewhat bizarre beading on the elevated shoulder pads made it clear that this dress was meant for things other than attending charity fund-raisers for people dying of cancer—it seemed, rather, the sort of thing a wealthy young woman from 1950s Westport might get married in.

"I told you this was black-tie," Henry whispered as he approached Abby, astonished but not quite allowing himself to be angry.

"I know," Abby replied, "that's why I'm wearing this." Then, seeing that Henry was flustered, she added, "trust me, Henry, this dress goes over well at this kind of thing. I wore it this summer to an event in San Francisco, and those people are the worst with this shit."

"But it's not a formal dress," Henry said, still at a whisper, "it's ceremonial." (It was an interesting distinction—just the sort of insight that might have earned him praise in his literature classes at Harvard—but as Henry said this he also couldn't help but notice how beautiful Abby was and how good she looked in the dress.) And Abby was absolutely right in her predictions about how her appearance would be received. When they arrived at the Mark, Henry quickly saw that the dress didn't look as out of place as he'd imagined it would—Henry, after all, was hardly an authority on current styles and fashions—and Abby simply had a kind of ready and easy charm about her, as Henry also couldn't help but acknowledge. Additionally, since the average age of the guests of the benefit was surely close to sixty, Abby's youth and mysterious Williamsburg élan were quite appealing to nearly everyone, as was clear by how many people (both men and women) turned to smile at them as they first walked through the main ballroom.

The schedule that night was the customary schedule at such events, starting with cocktails, an opportunity to look over the silent auction items, and warm but efficient mingling on the part of the board members and other distinguished volunteers.

Henry was certain he wouldn't know many people, but as he looked over the room when they first arrived, he discovered that his aunt had apparently invited half of his extended family (not Abby's side) and soon Henry was standing with assorted cousins and uncles chatting about family topics and exchanging news of each other's lives. This was, in fact, the first time Henry had seen some of these people since before his parents had died—those who hadn't made it to the funeral—and in these instances, Henry found the discussions to be somewhat awkward. Such discussions always were, though, and there weren't many ways around it, and Henry certainly never felt any sort of anger over some elderly aunt struggling to say something reassuring.

Henry did, however, feel bad for Abby having to be part of all this conversation. This was not her side of the family, after all, and after about ten minutes, Henry began to wonder how he might do a better job of entertaining his guest. But just as he was ready to announce that he'd "really like to get a look at those silent auction items!" (hoping this might allow them to escape), Abby said, "Hey, there's an old boss of mine. I put up a website for her." And before Henry could say, *I'd love to meet her*, she said, "I'll catch up with you," and walked off, leaving Henry with another elderly uncle who was telling Henry with wistfulness about the astonishing and crushing unpredictability of life and death.

It took Henry some time to rejoin Abby—he went to look for her when it was announced that it was time to sit for dinner, and Henry wasn't sure if Abby knew where their table was. When he found her, though, she was not with her former boss but instead standing with a man who looked to be about fifty, and she was laughing quite uncontrollably as he told her some sort of story. Again, Henry's feelings for his fourth cousin were well controlled at this point, but this man in particular made him swallow a bit harder than usual. He was tall and handsome (as far as common notions of such things go) and he was wearing the sort of high-end and modernized tuxedo that Henry himself would have liked to have worn. And on top of that, he was apparently very funny, as Henry again concluded as he approached, because Abby said several times within his earshot, "You are so, so, so funny!"

As Henry arrived, he smiled too, wanting to join in on whatever fun was being had, and Abby seemed delighted to see him. "Henry," she said, "I'm glad you found me! This is Merrill. I've been telling him all about your writing. He's a literary agent."

Merrill smiled, put out his hand, took Henry's, shook it, and said, "It's great to meet you. Abby here made me write down your name. I'll keep an eye out for your stuff. I hear you've had a few stories published this year and, according to Abby, you're absolutely brilliant."

Henry wasn't quite sure how to reply to this. He was happy to hear that Abby had been talking about him, but the situation was still troubling, and, after quickly denying (with appropriate modesty) that "brilliant" was at all correct, he said to Abby, "My aunt wants us to be seated. There are going to be a few remarks before we eat, so we should really sit down."

"I should sit too," Merrill said, smiling. "It was a pleasure to meet you both. Truly."

After a few more smiles and nods, they all turned and went to their respective tables and, to Henry's great relief, did not run into each other again that night. In fact, Henry soon forgot Merrill as he focused on his dinner (a strange kind of mushroom lasagna) and then the small amount of dancing he did with Abby to the fairly pleasing band before she insisted they head back to Brooklyn for the other party that would soon be under way.

"Music people will be there," she said. "I've got to go."

"Yes," Henry said, thinking suddenly about his own career, although just at that moment he couldn't also help but notice once again how appealing she looked in her beaded white dress.

3

AND SO IT WAS a fun night, and Henry didn't have to watch Abby leave with some fifty-year-old handsome literary agent, although he also concluded once again that he was definitely over his feelings for her. But it was subsequently also just a little jarring nearly two weeks later when Henry came home one afternoon to a ringing phone, answered it, and found Merrill on the other end.

It took Henry some time to figure out who was on the line, but at last he understood that it was the man from the benefit, and then assumed (concluded with deep conviction) that he was trying to track down Abby's phone number. After a few customary remarks, however, Merrill said something that truly surprised Henry.

"I read your stories," Merrill said. "Three so far? That's how many you've published?"

"Yes," Henry replied, just a little hopeful now.

"Well, look, Henry, what I'd say is that you've got a long road ahead of you if you're looking to put out a collection. Pretty impossible. And even a novel in your particular vein would be tricky, given what the market is today. But the fact is that your stories, I absolutely adored them. Again, there's not much I can do for you right now. But later on I think I can help. If you wrote a novel. I might be able to sell a novel of yours. Others might not be able to, but I bet I could."

Henry didn't know how to respond, but he did (despite his happiness) wonder what was appropriate concerning his cousin's telephone number. Should he just give it out to this man? Was flattery and the lure of representation enough to justify such a thing?

"The reason that I'm calling," Merrill quickly continued, "has to do with something else. Something related. But I really am sincere with my praise. Your stories were very, very moving, very funny, and extremely heartbreaking. And so, because of that, the purpose of this phone call is that I'm looking to set up one of my clients—not really a long-form writer but a longtime friend—with a ghostwriter."

Here Merrill paused, but just as Henry felt obliged to say something, he continued. "We need the project to have a literary feel," he said, "so we're trying to steer clear of the normal hacks, but it's hard to hire quality writers because, obviously, if you're the real thing, established, you're probably not interested in writing your good stuff for other people. And it's risky to take a chance with less accomplished writers because they haven't done enough to prove themselves yet. But you, believe me, Henry, have done more than prove yourself, to me, at least. And I'm pretty sure my client will agree."

"Well, that's really nice of you to say," Henry said. He thought he ought to add more, but Merrill continued.

"Yeah, and I mean every word. There is one complication, though, or one requirement, and that's that we'll need absolute discretion on your part. And when I say absolute, I mean legal and contractual. You'll have to sign a nondisclosure form before I even tell you who he is. He's a big deal. But he's branching out, or he's expanding on certain things he's already established, and he wants a novel. He has an idea for it. It's actually a young person's novel, for the young adult market. I don't have all the details of his idea, but it has to do with an old guy and a young guy and, well, it seems you're absolutely perfect for this, given your literary inclinations."

"Okay," Henry said. "This sounds interesting to me." Here Henry paused, and for long enough that Merrill apparently felt like he should jump in again.

"By the way," he said. "Your cousin, I already have her number. So this isn't some trick I'm playing. I'm not opposed to sneaky ways of getting phone numbers, and I'll admit that it's why I first looked you up and read your stories, but I wouldn't mess around with my work like this, and I certainly wouldn't fuck my client." Here, Merrill paused. "Henry," he continued at last, "you are a truly gifted writer. The stories blew me away. The pathos—it's something. That's the only reason we're having this telephone call right now. And anyway, Abby and I already went out and it seems like there's nothing there, despite what an obviously wonderful person she is. I'm too old, she's too young, but it wasn't an awkward realization—just so obvious that there was no reason to take things further. So, there's no bad blood. We're going to a Yankees game together. Next week. With a bunch of people. I'm even bringing a date. You can come if you want. I've got extra tickets. I have a whole box, actually, from a client. But all right, aside from that, what do you think about the ghostwriting thing?"

Henry paused for a moment and then said, "Well, again, all this sounds very interesting to me. I suppose I'll have to think about it. And hear more of the details."

"Yes, details," Merrill replied. "You'll be paid well for this kind of thing—I can promise you that—but a lot of what we talk about can only come after you sign the confidentiality agreement. It's a total pain in the ass, but that's how these things work. You'll know the guy immediately, he's a pretty prominent actor, and he's leveraging himself into new things and thinks this might be a good line for him. And I agree. For a lot of reasons. Anyway, since it sounds appealing to you, let's have lunch. We can talk money and I'll let you know what the deal will look like."

"Okay," Henry said.

"I'm going to put you through to my assistant and she'll get us a time. And Henry, I know I've said this, but I'll say it again, the only reason we're having this call is because I loved your stories. Believe me, when we met at the benefit, I never imagined we'd be on the phone right now. This isn't a favor I'm doing for you. I'm simply in need of your talent."

"Thanks. That's really nice to hear," Henry said.

"Okay. Sit tight. I'm transferring you to Joanne."

With that, the phone made several barely audible clicks and Henry was soon talking to Merrill's assistant.

4

NEEDLESS TO SAY, it was quite an unexpected offer, and
for the next few days—Henry and Merrill were meeting two
weeks later because of a trip Merrill was about to leave on—
Henry thought about the proposal. It all seemed so strange,
though, and the truth was that there were other matters in
Henry's life that also took some effort to consider. Among
these was an unexpected development regarding a matter
having to do with his parents. Henry had gotten word, via a
cryptic email and then a formal letter, that the family collec-
tive that managed shares in an ancestral summer home in
upstate New York (called Pembry Cottage) was making some
decisions about the future of the estate. Henry's stake in
the home, following his parents' death, was now one–thirty-
second, the house having been built long ago by a great-great-
grandfather (a close associate of Teddy Roosevelt's, it was said,
although Henry never quite understood all the details). Pembry Cottage was managed by a trust, and Henry had rights
to use it a certain amount of time every year. He occasionally
took advantage of this, but he had spent such happy times
with his parents there that he hadn't been up much recently,
since he found returning to be extremely depressing. It was
quite a beautiful property, though—a sprawling shingled
house on Lake Placid that had even hosted Roosevelt on sev-

eral occasions, as the stories went. The house was also linked to a family trust fund that paid for its upkeep and whatever taxes were levied on a home of this kind—the taxes, Henry had heard over the years, were shocking.

Unfortunately (or fortunately, depending on whom you asked), the money and the estate also came with a bewildering set of legal documents and binding rules, preventing the house from ever being sold and making all decisions about the house a matter of democratic vote by a system that Henry found completely unintelligible. Certainly he had never been asked to vote on anything having to do with the property, although his father had attended family meetings in Boston more than once to assent to one resolution or another (to remount the awning on the boathouse or to resurface the tennis court, for instance). Henry, however, only received a list of already-passed resolutions every six months or so (he was owed at least this because of his one–thirty-second stake), but as for being a full-fledged voting member, he didn't seem to have yet made the cut.

At any rate, it was this strange and tentative association, with its complex parliamentary procedure, that led to the puzzling email and then a fairly surprising letter (written by the trust's executor, Lilly Holloway) telling Henry that the family board had decided to convert a storage room on the ground floor into a studio for "the many family members with serious interests in the arts" and that Henry would have to come up to collect possessions of his parents that had been "illegally left" in the storage room in question. "You may pick up the items anytime over the next six weeks. After six weeks we will donate them to Goodwill."

It struck Henry as a strangely aggressive and mean-spirited letter. Henry did acknowledge that he was not the only person the letter was addressed to—there were two others—so he couldn't take it too personally. But at the bottom of the let-

ter was a handwritten note from Aunt Lilly's father, an elderly
uncle wishing Henry well and apologizing for the inconve-
nience of the request and assuring Henry it was only a car-
load of his family things that he had to retrieve. And then,
in smaller script and squeezed between parentheses—as
though the note were meant to be read in a darkened room
and in a whisper:

*I'm afraid you'll have to do this! You're aunt Lilly is quite cross
with you! Apparently you caused some kind of disaster at a farm
belonging to a friend of hers from Choate! You killed a flock
of priceless goats! My goodness! But I'm on your side, Henry!
Always have been! Sadly, even I can't stand in the way of the
bylaws of the august Pembry Cottage estate! So you shouldn't
ignore this! I know you've rescued your more sentiment-laden
artifacts from the house, but there are a few things here that
have some value, in particular a mahogany lap secretary that
was made, I know from poking around, by Price and Jacobsen
in Philadelphia! All right! More anon! But we should meet for
dinner in the city soon!*

Uncle Louis

Henry remembered the mahogany secretary his uncle
mentioned and he concurred that it must be worth quite a
bit, but more on his mind was his aunt Lilly's anger. Uncle
Louis could do no wrong in Henry's mind, but Lilly was precisely the sort of bitter Protestant matron who gave his people
such a bad name, and it was more than alarming that she
was talking about the goats Henry had killed. Was there some
kind of annual meeting in Narragansett or Litchfield where
well-healed fiftysomething heiresses exchanged the names of
people who had crossed them?

"Are my failures in Vermont going to follow me forever?"
Henry asked Abby not long after receiving the letter. They

were eating at a Vietnamese restaurant in Fort Greene that Henry particularly liked.

"Kill a lot of goats and it follows you for life," Abby said. "And WASPs tend to intermarry, so that's another problem for you. But anyway, enough about the goats, because, frankly I don't ever want to hear about them again. Is Merrill going to rep you or what?"

With this sudden shift in topic, Henry quickly became nervous (from a legal standpoint, because of the confidentiality that was in question with the agreement and his continuing general worry about being sued). He abruptly stood and said he needed to get a beer and then walked to the front counter to place his order. By the time he returned he'd once more rehearsed the story that he'd planned to present, namely that he and Merrill were going to work together, but that he was still a long way off from having a book. Thus, as far as his publishing career went, there really wasn't much to say.

"But he's going to read my stories before I send them out," Henry said. "And if it makes sense, he might even put in a call for me to a few places where he knows people, although agents don't really sell short stories these days. Not to the places where I'd be a good candidate, at least. It sounds like I'll need to write a novel before anything much happens, and that's a long way off. But we're going to stay in close touch. I'm probably going to see him a lot."

"So that's great news, right?" Abby said.

"Yes," Henry replied, "I suppose it is great news."

"It is great news!" Abby repeated, and it looked as if she were about to give Henry a lecture on staying positive when three women Abby knew suddenly appeared, and soon the conversation turned to the matter of a party later that night that they wanted Abby to come to. They invited Henry as well, and although it did sound fun, he was just a little tired and not really in the mood to wander around some stranger's apartment, so he said he needed to get home. And soon they all parted on the street outside the restaurant. As Henry watched them walk away, he did feel just a bit of regret over not joining in. He could put off sleep for a while longer, after all. But he also thought about something else at that moment. As he watched Abby walk away, he wondered again if he was over the crush he'd had on her. He instantly concluded that he was. That moment of his life was well over. And anyway, the fact was that he needed her now too much as a friend to indulge that kind of idea.

At last Henry turned and headed home. His romantic future lay elsewhere, he decided. And probably his social life, its platonic aspects, might lay elsewhere as well. And in this regard, things had been changing somewhat for Henry in Brooklyn recently. For the better. In particular Henry had recently made something of a new and good friend, a friend who was not Abby. And this new friend was a person who had a deep grasp of the social world of Williamsburg and, perhaps most important, he was a person who had absolutely nothing to gain from the friendship other than honest camaraderie— he was not, for instance, trying to secure funding for *Suckerhead*, although it was true that Henry had first met this person at a *Suckerhead* meeting.

The friend's name was Whitney (his mother was British, as he said when his name came up, although Henry had already heard this explanation). He'd been at Harvard when Henry was there, although he was two years older. He'd even studied with the same professors that Henry had, "although I can't say they liked my fiction much," he confessed when they had their first real conversation one evening at a party. "Apparently I have no talent at all, and I didn't have the guts to argue. Of course," he continued, "one day I'll show them, when I publish some magnificent piece of writing. But until then, I'm afraid it's amusing myself in New York for me."

Astonishingly, though, Whitney was not really like Henry at all. He was very handsome and quite a heartbreaker, for instance, although he was also a man who truly regretted each time (was astonished, in fact) when he hurt the feelings of the various women he dated. Whitney was also extremely charming and socially adroit in other venues—also part of the origin of his success with women. He could dominate a conversation with the most aggressive equities analysts and then quickly move into other circles commenting on obscure details about the lives of poets or the more comical mannerisms of composers and painters.

It was writing, though, that led Henry and Whitney to become friends. Henry had met him one night at a party and discovered that Whitney was the so-called literary editor of a free Brooklyn magazine called *Merit*, a sideline as he pursued a graduate degree in romance languages at Columbia. They talked some when they were first introduced about various books Whitney had reviewed and how Henry felt about them, and soon they were in a fairly deep conversation about nearly everything they'd ever read. They left that party at three to go to Whitney's then-girlfriend's house, where she was having people over for some kind of late-night eating event, and the two of them sat together for another few hours eating endless crepes—the girlfriend had just bought a large cast-iron crepe-cooking pan—and talking even more about their lives, books, and then Henry's short stories.

Henry left after they exchanged numbers and he was quite pleased to discover a voice mail on his phone just three days later from Whitney inviting him to dinner (again at his girlfriend's house) "to keep going with our conversation." Whitney also added that he'd read two of Henry's stories online and loved them, although he had "some advice for them to be even better" and that he'd be happy to share it as they ate their dinner. Henry wasn't sure he wanted to hear Whitney's advice, but it might be interesting and perhaps Whitney's insight would give him new perspective on his work.

It turned out that Whitney's feelings about Henry's stories were not very helpful, although Henry found that he still liked Whitney a great deal as he presented his ideas. Whitney seemed to think that it was important for a young writer to write about what he was experiencing. "And all these fucking old people, old people having sex, even, what's it all about? These people have been written about. And here, here, you've got a whole world here, right here, that you could write about. And, Henry, Henry"—they had now eaten their dessert and were drinking coffee mugs filled with what had been described to Henry as grape brandy—"I say this because I loved the stories. I fucking loved them. I mean, I'm so impressed. But what's it all for? Why all the fucking old people? I mean, why all the fucking old people?"

Henry was now quite drunk, and the sugar high he'd just been experiencing (dessert had been crepes with Nutella and ice cream) was now bringing him to a more confused and sleepy state. Still, he managed to follow everything Whitney was saying and then replied, after pausing again to think, "I guess I don't know."

At this point, Whitney leaned very close to Henry. He paused, then said, "You dating anyone?"

Henry blushed at this. He could feel it, the blood in his face. All he could say, though, was—there was no way to be poetic about this—"No. Not now. I came here with a woman from Michigan. But she wanted to see other people. Or she wanted to see another guy and make that exclusive. And I have this cousin, but that's over. So, no, I'm not dating anyone."

Whitney nodded as though he understood exactly what had been said to him and then replied, "Well, I'll do what I can, but god help you. And I say that with the best possible feelings." He then stood up and walked to the kitchen, where his girlfriend was still making crepes.

At any rate, this was how he'd met his new friend, and Henry couldn't have been happier or more surprised that he'd been embraced by this quite popular Brooklyn man.

5

IT SHOULD BE NOTED at this point that just as Henry's career was showing promise—it was an accomplishment, after all, to publish a handful of short stories in respected literary journals—Abby's future in music had also brightened. Abby's band was gaining a foothold in the Brooklyn music scene. It wasn't a contract with Atlantic Records (although that wasn't entirely crucial in the age of the Internet), but her band was being booked at bigger venues, their songs were being downloaded at a swift pace, and Henry had even seen a person walking along Bedford Avenue with a T-shirt that had the band's (new) name on it: Odd Girl Out.

Abby too had been developing quite a bit as a musician, and although there were, of course, limitations for a person who played viola in a group designed to appeal to a broad (if sophisticated) audience, she had an impressive stage presence, as these things go, and Henry couldn't help but notice that she'd slowly moved to the front of the ensemble in the ever-changing seating arrangement. She was also singing more, when she managed to put the viola down, and she got better and better, to Henry's surprise. He'd certainly never grasped that this was a talent she was working on. But she began to be the lead on more and more songs and she'd managed to develop a sort of waiflike inflection to her voice that seemed to be increasingly popular with people around New York.

Henry, of course, did his best to make it to all her events, and the truth was that he'd only missed two over the past many months, both because of stomach viruses, although had he only been feverish and not also throwing up, he would have attended (despite the fact that he was definitely over his feelings for her).

It was about this time—about the time that he had first been given the proposal by Merrill—that a somewhat important show was scheduled at a sort of rentable warehouse in Bushwick. Henry went with Whitney and arrived at eleven to a packed house.

Abby was not onstage (or at the performance end of the warehouse) when they arrived. People were milling about and drinking quite a bit and looking very excited. It was true that Henry had still hardly made a name for himself in the social world of Williamsburg—he did not have a lot of friends, and the people he knew (often attached to *Suckerhead*) now filled him with suspicion and some resentment—but Henry truly, truly loved parties like this. He loved big social gatherings where people were talking and laughing and drinking cocktails and snacking on whatever was being served. (Tonight, because of the higher-than-normal cover charge and the expensive drinks, there were endless tables of artisanal Japanese dumplings, made by some kind of highbrow local Japanese dumpling maker.) And the one person he saw who was from the *Suckerhead* crowd was, in fact, the tattooed girl, and since she had apparently liked his story, it was hard for him to feel any kind of resentment when he saw her. He wanted to say hello, in fact, but she drifted off before he could approach her, and she never rematerialized.

At any rate, Henry found himself to be very drunk and quite

happy by the time Odd Girl Out came on, and he continued to drink with great enthusiasm, standing with Whitney, greeting Whitney's friends as they arrived to say hello, and watching Abby with quite a bit of psychological introspection.

Abby was a truly beautiful woman and it seemed that she was growing aware of this herself. As he watched her sing some kind of old popular song that Henry knew from parties but which he didn't remember the name of, he came to a conclusion that had somehow been in the back of his mind but which was now completely evident: Abby was simply far out of his league. Such things usually never occurred to Henry at all. He believed with conviction that love and friendship (in their truest form) were not about gamesmanship or status evaluation. But watching Abby onstage—she was wearing a white tank top and overalls that no man (Henry was sure) could resist—he grasped that he was simply no match for the many other potential suitors. Or, and this was a more charitable assessment, if she hadn't already decided that Henry was what she was looking for, she probably wasn't going to change her mind now. Of course, a man could never be entirely sure, but the fact was that there really was quite a bit of opportunity for someone like Abby in the world. It was not as though they were living in some kind of tent village in Finland, after all, where a sensitive and artistic man like Henry might stand out a bit more. Maybe more than that, Henry grasped that Abby had somehow become aware of all this, of what kind of world was open to her now.

Henry was thinking very deeply about all this when Whitney approached him—he'd just been talking to some woman he claimed to have a "minor interest in"—and he put his arm around Henry's shoulder in a very gentle way.

"I don't think that's what you should be thinking about," he said to Henry, with kindness and also smiling.

"What?" Henry said. Whitney knew most of the story of Henry and Abby, although Henry had told Whitney that those feelings were long behind him.

"Henry, you're one of the best guys I know," Whitney said. "Abby's appealing, no question, but there are lots of other women here as well, and you're young and this is no time to get hung up on one person, because even if it does go your way, it will probably fall apart eventually. Do you see yourself getting married in the next ten years?"

Henry hesitated for a moment and thought deeply about the question before finally and abruptly saying (and to his own surprise), "You're not interested in Abby, are you?"

Henry expected one of two responses to this question (which he tried, at the last minute, to deliver in the mode of a joke, although it had more of a tone of desperation to it). The first anticipated response was laughter—who would ask such a question in such a way? The second was a heartfelt apology followed by an assertion that, yes, he'd fallen in love with Abby. To his amazement, though, Whitney looked at Henry with great seriousness and said, "Henry, I'll never, ever go after Abby. I promise you that. No matter what. I'll never do that. I know you've moved on. Still, I know how these things can linger. Or, how they can be brought to the fore again when something happens. But I'll never do that. I promise."

Henry paused for a second and then said, "Well, I didn't mean it like that. I mean, I don't want to interfere with what you think you want to do. And really, there would be no hard feelings about it. I'm totally over it."

"No, Henry," Whitney said. "I'd never do that. Never."

Henry didn't quite know what to say. It was such a gallant assertion and he was extremely touched. But just as he was about to make yet another gentlemanly statement about the murky nature of love and his understanding of the ways of the world, two women approached Whitney (quite excited) and asked him what he was doing after the show. It struck Henry as just a bit strange that anyone would assume there was an "after"—it was already far past three a.m. and the event was scheduled to keep going until five. Henry resolved that he needed to make a general point of going to bed later, but once more he turned toward Abby—she was now singing a fairly slow ballad about a romance that began on the G train—and thought about how his life really was drifting into unknown territory.

6

HENRY, THOUGH, HAD other matters in his life that helped distract him from romantic longings, the most important of which was what to do about the prospect of becoming a ghostwriter. He hadn't thought very carefully about the matter over the past several days, but this mostly had to do with the fact that he'd quickly decided, unconsciously at least, that he'd take the job and there wasn't much to consider. Henry didn't really need the money, although the prospect of living the rest of his life only on his inheritance did make him feel somewhat uncomfortable. He felt as though he really ought to be part of the working world, that he ought to contribute some kind of useful labor to the larger society. Merrill was also right that it would be an excellent experience.

And Merrill had sent him some of the financial details via email and the deal seemed very good, although, given the Hollywood origins of the plan, perhaps this was not much money. The fee for the writing would be $60,000. ("Excellent for this kind of thing," Merrill said in the email.) The money, however, would be spread out over time and in parts, each part to be paid upon approval of the mysterious actor. On top of the advance, Henry would receive 10 percent of the royalty that the named author would be making, which was not good on its own, since it would be 10 percent of the actor's

15 percent royalty. But it was good in context because much of the sales, Merrill asserted in his email, would be based on name recognition. "He's sold nearly a million children's picture books," Merrill wrote, "so this guy will be bringing in an enormous amount of money just because of his name."

At any rate, Henry agreed to meet for lunch and, according to the plan, if the discussion went well, they'd head back to Merrill's office to sign the appropriate contracts.

They met at a midtown restaurant that was near Merrill's office. It was not an impressive place from the outside but the food more than measured up to the quite extraordinary prices. And the conversation went very well also. At first Henry and Merrill talked mostly about books and movies they liked, and things they liked to do in New York. They also had a fairly deep discussion about losing loved ones at an early age. Merrill had lost his father when he was ten—a thing Henry couldn't imagine and which he decided might have been even more unbearable than what he himself went through. At last, though, they got to business, which Henry found fairly interesting, seeing as he'd never had such close contact with a man who was clearly involved (as Henry soon learned) with so many high-end editors and publishers. And so it was mostly Merrill who talked, although Henry did interrupt just once because he felt suddenly moved to remark on how delicious his Dungeness crab club sandwich was.

"I think this is one of the best sandwiches I've ever had," he told Merrill. "It's so delicious. Do you want a bite?"

"No, I'm okay," Merrill said. "But thanks. The food's definitely good here. This is what they call a power lunch, Henry. I'm trying to impress you. So now that I know that you like your food, maybe I can be a bit more explicit."

Henry knew most of the broad aspects of what was at stake from the email he'd received, although Merrill wanted to make sure Henry understood that this deal was much better than Henry would have gotten on his own as a first-time novelist for kids. He did also want Henry to understand that there would be stages of approval and his client reserved the right to abandon the project if he didn't feel as though it were going well.

"If you write it and he absolutely hates it," Merrill said, "you'll still get twenty grand. That's good money for this kind of work. And if all goes well you'll make something in royalties, as small as your percentage is. The guy's got a serious brand. And a highly regarded artistic one at that. A forty-some-thousand-word book, though—that's what we want this to be—it's a bit out of his wheelhouse. This book will fit into some other recent projects he's been doing, though, and, well, for a number of reasons there's a harmony to it all."

At any rate, they talked about details for another few minutes before Merrill (just after, apparently, swallowing a large piece of beef gristle) put down his knife and fork and said, "Okay, Henry, yes or no, in or out?"

Merrill was smiling as he said this, and Henry felt like there was honest warmth coming from him as he advanced the issue to its crisis, so to speak. And Henry was sure that if he asked for more time to think, he'd receive it. But it really was a good proposal, so Henry swiftly replied by saying what he'd already planned to say: "Okay. I'd like to go ahead. I'd like to do it."

Lunch ended quickly after Henry's acceptance, and before long he was in Merrill's offices signing the previously mentioned nondisclosure agreement. "We'll get to the rest of the contract shit in the next few weeks. You can have someone else look it over if you like. But this is just so I can tell you more about who you're working for. But you understand this nondisclosure agreement you're now signing is pretty serious, right?"

"Yes, I think so."

"There's a lot at stake for my client regarding your discretion—reputation and money. Think of this agreement as something like what people sign before they join one of those competition reality shows. So much of the taping happens long before the show is aired, so if someone blows the name of the winners midway through the season, the studio suffers major damage—the whole show is tanked. And that kind of damage can be addressed in all sorts of ugly ways in court. Like getting sued for everything you have."

Henry nodded. It was suddenly a bit frightening, but Henry was a magnificent secret-keeper (ironclad discretion was, in fact, at the core of some of his more mysterious notions of male virtue), so he wasn't particularly reluctant to sign. And when he did, Merrill was able to divulge the more interesting details of the project.

"All right," Merrill said, "here's who you're working for."

The news was fairly interesting—not mind-blowing, as these things go, but interesting. That is, the person he was writing for was not Al Pacino or Queen Elizabeth, but it was certainly an actor who had a solid artistic reputation and someone Henry knew of and had seen perform. His name was Jonathan Kipling. He was in his mid-forties and he'd started his career on the stage in New York—he and Merrill had been great pals in the city when they were younger (even though Merrill was ten years Kipling's senior) and they'd started working together then, although Merrill didn't handle his acting work in later years. Kipling had made the leap to Hollywood via a much-praised independent film about a dying industrial town in New Hampshire, and he'd then gone on to play several important smaller roles in larger movie productions. He was not what anyone would call a true and pure top-shelf star—he was not the lead billing in movies made by studios like Columbia or Paramount (with one exception). But he had high-end name recognition and had even made the various "most beautiful people" lists in the popular magazines.

The one exception to his role as supporting cast member

was the lead in a movie made for young people about a basketball coach who was dying of cancer. It hit all the notes that such a movie tries to hit, and did surprisingly well financially, and this movie was what prompted Kipling to write the picture books for children—his name was now well known among parents looking for nurturing printed culture for their kids. And he was able to pull off the new venture and keep his highbrow status intact because he was also appearing in other more "artistically motivated" movies, playing the roles of an alcoholic, a terrorist sympathizer, and even a failed book editor. More than this, though, and this was something Henry thought with conviction well before he knew who he was working for, Kipling really was an excellent actor—the real thing, as they say. And because of this reputation, Merrill asserted, he could also afford to branch off in more lucrative areas of the entertainment world. For instance, he endorsed a brand of Swiss watches, a sort of environmentally sustainable compact car, and even a line of frozen desserts (which he ate with great pleasure and conviction on daytime television advertisements). He was fairly rich from all this, but he was still looking to continue to leverage his name, and this was why he was hiring Henry.

"Multiplatform is where it's at these days," Merrill said. "There's incredible commercial potential here. A really great book will bolster Kipling's other endeavors, but we're looking for something real, something heartfelt, something artistic, and something I know you can produce for us. Again, I told you this before, Kipling has a strong idea of what this book is going to look like. So you'll be working very closely with him to implement his vision. We think that you can do a great job for us. And if your stab at all this doesn't work out, you're in for twenty grand and you walk away with a great experience and some extra cash to blow on whatever you want."

All of it, Henry had to agree, sounded very appealing.

7

WHAT KIPLING'S VISION was for all this, Henry couldn't say. But the one other important aspect of the meeting, and the one that might answer Henry's question, came at the end when Merrill said that Kipling would very much like for Henry to go (that weekend!) to Kipling's country house in England so they could spend some time "hashing out" what the book would be about.

"I mean, he knows what he wants the book to look like, what he wants it to deal with," Merrill said, "but I think he just wants to lay it all out in person. I don't know too much, so I'll be as interested as you to hear about it. Anyway, I'm assuming you'll want to do this because we'll fly you first class and he's got quite a place over there, so I think it will be a blast."

It was a surprising proposal, and one that truly interested Henry. Now that Henry lived in New York, he did what he could to affect the sort of blasé demeanor of someone who saw great things and rubbed shoulders with great people all the time, but he found that he could not help but be excited at the prospect of meeting someone as famous as Kipling and staying at his country house. After pausing for what he imagined to be a dignified amount of time, he said that he'd be happy to do it. "And I've only been to the UK once," he said, "when I was young."

"Well, time to go as an adult!" Merrill quickly replied. "And Kipling's stuff is big in Britain. I think that's why he's got a place there, but don't tell him I said that. I just think it makes him feel pretty good to be there."

Travel plans were arranged swiftly, and when Henry got off the phone later that day with Merrill's secretary, who Merrill had said would "handle everything," he also decided to figure out his upcoming schedule in general. After several more phone calls, including a very enjoyable one with Whitney (where Whitney said, several times, "Shit, I'd love to go upstate with you!") Henry finally decided on a date—about six weeks away—when they would travel to Pembry Cottage and deal with his parents' unlawfully stored possessions. (He managed to schedule the weekend for just himself and Whitney so he wouldn't run into Aunt Lilly or anyone else who might abuse him for the slaughter of Hannah's Libyan goats.) "And it really is a beautiful house," Henry said to Whitney. "And the lake. Lake Placid is really beautiful. And there's lots to do. We'll have a lot of fun."

"I can't wait," Whitney said. "I can't wait."

At any rate, the meeting with Merrill took place on a Tuesday, and the following Thursday evening Henry was at JFK boarding a flight to London. He was pleased to be flying first class, a thing he'd only done a few times, and he was fairly dazzled by the innovations in luxury travel that had occurred in recent years. The seat that folded into a bed, the television screen on the articulating arm, and a puzzling climate control system that Henry spent most of the flight adjusting and readjusting (with pleasure) according to his mood and activities. He slept for much of the flight, but he was awake to eat his dinner and then his breakfast, and he even drank two glasses of port, served to him in what the menu boasted was "authentic crystal." And when he at last arrived, he felt refreshed and looking forward to the day ahead. Because it was only a weekend trip he also didn't have much luggage—just a single carry-on bag and his backpack, so he was able to pass through the airport with little trouble. On the other side of customs, he found a driver with a sign with his name on it and soon he was in the back of a Mercedes and headed south to Dorset.

And when they arrived, Henry couldn't help but note that Kipling's house was striking in all the ways that a person might expect from a movie actor's estate. It seemed something a person would be justified in calling a large manor, although it was also simple, a white Georgian structure with clean lines and symmetrical windows and elegant but restrained flourishes on the corners and roof joints.

After coming to a stop at the front door (which sat at the edge of a large, flat gravel lot), Henry stepped out. The driver quickly followed—he looked, in fact, as though he would have preferred to be the one to open Henry's door—and soon Henry was ringing the doorbell of the house, the driver dutifully holding Henry's small bag and backpack.

A brief moment passed, then the door opened. Kipling stood on the other side. Henry was a little surprised to see Kipling himself answer the door, although he wasn't sure why—had he expected a butler? But before he could think too much about it, Kipling was extending his hand. "You're Henry!" Kipling said. "I'm so happy you were able to come out for this."

"I'm very happy to be here," Henry replied.

Kipling then nodded at the driver, took Henry's bags, and soon Henry was standing in the entryway and looking up at the curved banister of the house's central stairs.

"This is a beautiful house," Henry said, looking to his left at an ancient mahogany bench that sat in an alcove next to the door.

"I think so too," Kipling replied. "Thanks. I'll show you

around if you like. I'm about to make a late breakfast at the moment, though. Are you hungry? We could eat something and then I'll give you a tour?"

"Okay," Henry said. He wasn't that hungry—he'd been starving at the airport and had bought a large but old-looking ham sandwich and eaten it in the car. Still, Henry was always happy to eat.

Breakfast was good, but straightforward. Scrambled eggs, toast, and coffee. No bacon, which disappointed Henry some-what. He'd imagined that Kipling might have some kind of standing order at a local farm that cured its own meats and that he might have some kind of British artisanal pork belly to start the day. But a newly arrived guest can hardly start demanding that he be fed artisanal bacon, or so Henry deter-mined, and he contented himself with the eggs. They did not talk about the book.

"We'll talk about work on our walk around the grounds," Kipling said before he asked how the flight and the airports had been.

When breakfast was eaten and the tour commenced (beginning outside), the conversation about the book began. As they walked from the house toward a stone folly at the end of a long, almost perfectly flat lawn, Kipling began to praise Henry's work, and to tell Henry how perfect he was for this project. "You know, it's a hard thing, to find someone for a project like this. We're very lucky. I'm very lucky. We wanted a real writer. An artist. Not just some hired person. And Merrill raves about you. I think Merrill was dead right when he said that you've got ample talent and maybe not enough behind you yet to turn us down." Kipling flashed Henry a very warm and, Henry felt, sincere smile at this point. "Of course," he continued, "you've seen the contract, so we'll see how things go. I've worked on enough collaborative projects to know that they don't always work out, even when you've got the very best people. But I feel very hopeful."

"I do too," Henry said, a bit apprehensive now that he had been reminded that his work was to be periodically evaluated. He even wondered if he'd blow the whole thing. But then Kipling began to describe in detail how much he liked one of Henry's stories, and the flattery dampened the anxiety.

Aside from the praise, though, they talked more generally about storytelling and what Kipling was calling "the narrative arts."

"Writing and acting are a lot alike," he said, "and that's why I'm so interested in writing. It's storytelling, like what I do, but from such a different perspective. Sometimes I think fiction writing is similar to an improvisational acting experiment, just inhabiting a character and going where it takes you."

"I've actually thought that as well," Henry said, although he stammered as he got to the end of this statement because he'd never thought anything like this, although it did sound like a good comparison.

"I'd write this myself," Kipling went on, "but I've got so much going on right now. Of course, if this were real, not a book for kids, I'd never let anyone write it for me. I mean, I want this book to be great. Really. I don't see why kids' novels need to be any less artistic than anything else. It's not the real thing, however, is it? And it's just, well, I thought if I had someone to work with . . . I mean, you're the writer. But I have a vision for all this. I'll be working very closely with you."

Again, Henry slipped back into wondering if this was all a terrible idea, but he simply said, "Yes, Merrill said you had some kind of outline. I'd love to look it over."

Kipling shook his head and said, "No, no, I don't have an outline. I don't even know who the characters are, or what happens, or where it's set, for that matter. But those things will come if we think about the thing that's been on my mind for a while, something that's been on my mind for most of my career." He paused for just a moment, then continued, "You see, in this day and age, young people and old people spend so little time together. In our era. Now. In ancient China, it was perfectly normal for eight-year-olds to be cared for by eighty-year-olds, but these days we just pack old people up, and what I'd like to write is a book about a young person, a twelve-year-old, say, who's friends with an old person."

Henry hesitated, not sure Kipling was done, but when nothing more came, he asked, "Who would the old person and the young person be?"

"Well, see, that's why you're such a perfect partner in all this. You've written so beautifully about old people. We thought about trying to get a young adult writer, someone who has experience writing about young people, but I felt that getting a proper artist, someone who can take your perspective, can see things through the eyes of an older person, well, that seemed better. I want this to be the real thing."

Kipling said this last part with deep conviction and Henry nodded with what he hoped was conviction as well, but he was still fairly baffled by the limited nature of the proposal.

"So there's no plotline or anything laid out?" Henry asked again. "It's no problem, it's just that Merrill seemed to think there was some kind of story idea."

"Well, there is," Kipling said, again with sincerity. (They were now walking along a small creek and Kipling was trying to keep track of where he was stepping while at the same time looking Henry in the eye.) "The story is the story of friendship—a friendship between an old man and a young man. That's the heart of it all. It's almost all anyone needs to know."

"Ah," Henry said, after stumbling on a large stone. "I guess that's something to think about," he added, although it struck Henry that if this was what Kipling thought an idea looked like, it would all be hard going. While trying to avoid being too judgmental, it seemed to Henry that Kipling somehow imagined that a story about friendship represented some kind of artistic inspiration (and a well-researched one too, given his thoughts on ancient Chinese culture).

At any rate, the conversation went on like this for the rest of the walk, although Henry also brought up several of Kipling's movies to get him to talk about himself and what kinds of roles he liked most. And the conversation never flagged. At points Henry even found it interesting. (It lasted throughout the walk back to the house, through its multiple reception rooms and bedrooms—including what would be Henry's—and along various hidden servants' sections.) At last, though, Kipling suggested that they take a break from the conversation—the tour was now mostly done—so Henry could do some thinking. "And I've got some scripts I need to get to this afternoon. We'll have drinks at five and an early dinner and we can continue talking then. How does that sound?"

"Good, that sounds good," Henry said.

"And make yourself at home," Kipling added. "You know where your room is. And I have someone in after one today— she'll be cooking for us tonight—but if you get hungry, you can find your way to the kitchen and she'll make you something, and she can get you anything else you might need. I'll be in my study, the room I showed you with all the bookcases, if you need me."

Henry again thanked Kipling, and soon he was (a little confused) standing again near the front door, beneath the large curved staircase, wondering what he'd gotten himself into. It did occur to him, though, as he mounted the stairs toward his room and thought about the conversation he'd just had, that the lack of detail (the lack of any sort of story at all on Kipling's part) wasn't such a bad thing in the end. Henry had been dreading taking orders from someone else in terms of what to write. He'd worried that he might be handed a long and preposterous outline that he'd find impossible to stick to. At least with this situation he wouldn't be burdened with a confusing and ill-conceived plot that he'd be forced to follow. The thing was that friendship between an old person and a young person wasn't much of a start.

However, Henry did spend the rest of the afternoon thinking about it all, and even came up with some interesting ideas, although many of them seemed a bit dark for a children's book—assisted suicide, crippling dementia, obsession-induced murder, etc. The problem with these ideas (aside from simply being too gruesome to give to a twelve-year-old) was that they were so focused on the experiences of the elderly. It did strike Henry that it might be interesting to explore a twelve-year-old's romantic obsession and then the subsequent murder of his love interest, but for obvious reasons he had a hard time thinking that this would fly, especially if the book was mainly supposed to be about friendship.

At any rate, Henry spent the rest of the day wandering the grounds and napping, and by cocktail hour he found himself in the largest of the reception rooms, standing in front of the fire and drinking a glass of whiskey poured over a single large ice cube, once again talking to Kipling.

The matter of the book remained the topic. Henry shared some of his ideas, with the caveat that they were all a bit heavy for a book for children, and Kipling actually seemed surprisingly receptive. "I see what you mean about the ideas being heavy," Kipling said. "But children, Henry, they have an enormous capacity for absorbing and understanding difficult themes, maybe better than any of us." Kipling spoke this last sentence with a somewhat exaggerated spirit of drama and circumspection and Henry once again tried to make an assessment of what might be called his host's turn of mind. Henry loved what he saw of Kipling in the movies, and so did a lot of people. He was definitely a success with the more high-brow critics. And certainly a man who could capture the spirit of a nineteenth century British con man and then, the very next year, have a significant role in a romantic comedy set in Brazil, well, he must have known what he was doing. But Henry still couldn't quite come to any final conclusions about his employer's literary insight, although this would change later that night.

Henry usually dealt with sleep deprivation fairly well, but by eight o'clock, just after a dinner of lamb chops and roasted potatoes, he confessed that the jet lag was catching up with him and that he ought to get some sleep so their discussions the next day would be profitable. As he was standing up, though, Kipling said he had something else for Henry to look at. "I'm a little sheepish about this," Kipling said. "But I've written a few things over the past couple years, and I think you'll enjoy reading them. I think it's important too, so you understand my sensibility."

Henry never had any idea what people meant by the word "sensibility," but he was happy enough to take the stories. And soon he was in his bedroom with a sheaf of Kipling's writings, wondering if he'd be able to get through it all before they reconvened the next morning. Still, the surroundings made him feel relaxed. The room reminded him of his parents' bed-room in Massachusetts—the large bed and the attached bou-doir and bathroom—and as he got in bed beneath what must have been $2,000 worth of Italian linens, he felt very comfort-able and eager to start reading. He didn't make it through the first paragraph of one of Kipling's stories, though, before he realized once again how tired he was. Soon the lights were out and Henry was fast asleep.

And the sleep was deep and very restful, and at four in the morning, when he awoke, he found that he felt very refreshed. It was early, of course, but Henry had the stories to read, and, after going to the kitchen to make himself a cup of instant coffee—there didn't seem to be an accessible coffeemaker— he returned to his room, lay down on the boudoir's purple velvet sofa, and began to work through the stories.

It took about three hours to read Kipling's four stories, although Henry's assessment didn't change much from the start, even if it was the kind of assessment he was never comfortable making and certainly wouldn't share with anyone. The stories were all about gas station attendants and welders and assorted other "real people." They weren't entirely bad. There were some things in the stories Henry found to like. But what struck him (and maybe this was the thing that Henry had been trying to articulate to himself from the first of Kipling's stories) was that they were marred by what Henry could only determine was a stunning lack of labor. It was a common problem, as far as Henry could tell, although he often felt so wretched about people judging his own work that he was very careful not to arrive at this conclusion (even to himself, in his bedroom, with his instant coffee) with too much conviction. The fact was, though, that the stories felt a bit as if they were written during some kind of overnight illegal stimulant bender when the writer believed that the deepest thoughts were the ones written fastest and without afterthought. Of course, Henry had to admit that some people did, indeed, write this way, and although it was not his kind of pleasure, other people often thought a great deal of this sort of thing. Henry had been given these stories in a straightforward exchange, though—Kipling had wanted him to understand his "sensibility"—so it was hard to think of a way to politely say something like, *I hear that other people like this kind of thing a lot.*

At any rate, when Henry finally emerged from his bedroom to greet Kipling that morning—they had agreed to meet for another late breakfast—he felt a deep kind of dread because he wasn't sure how he was going to discuss the stories he had just worked through. He considered telling Kipling that because of the jet lag and the time difference, he'd not had a chance to get to the stories, that he had slept for sixteen straight hours. But he wasn't sure he could pull this off. Henry was simply not a good liar. As he walked down the curved staircase and toward the kitchen, he at last decided that he would use words like "interesting" and "captivating" and even "alarming," all of which were true. And it really was a fact that he found a few things that did appeal to him, including a sort of dishwasher character who evoked a certain amount of empathy (despite his somewhat forced everyman's love of Kerouac and "other writers like him"). But Henry found that any such discussion would, at the very least, be delayed because there was no sign of Kipling, and for the next two hours (Henry left his bedroom at eleven) there was no one anywhere in the house or on the so-called grounds. At last, the person who fed Kipling and took care of his house arrived and told Henry that his host had left for Paris early that morning—on a last-minute trip that couldn't be avoided.

"He emailed me from the airport," she said. "He wanted me to tell you it was a pleasure to meet you and that he's thrilled by the project and that he feels that you're off to a wonderful start. You're also welcome to stay for the rest of the weekend, although Mr. Kipling won't be back for another week."

"Ah," Henry said, not sure how to react to such news. "Well, let me think about what to do. But I don't think I'll be staying, although please thank him for the offer."

8

HENRY SPENT THE next hour or so on the Internet figuring out how to get home, and after an uncomfortable night at a hotel next to Heathrow, he was soon on his way back to the U.S. Clearly it was an odd trip, and Henry wasn't quite sure what to make of it all, but he did find himself upon his return feeling fairly tired and antisocial. Henry found himself, over the next few weeks, refusing several invitations to events and festivities, invitations from Abby, from Whitney, and from various online venues that seemed to invite everyone to everything. (He even got an invitation to a party from the tattooed girlfriend of *Suckerhead*'s fiction editor, although there were also three hundred other recipients.) But instead, Henry was in bed early every night, up early in the morning, and spending his free time reading an enormous amount. He also found himself eating light—not out of discipline but out of lack of dietary interest. Henry had always had a reasonably healthy diet, but he found that he was having lunches and dinners consisting only of leafy vegetables and, perhaps, an avocado or a slice of tofu to spice things up. He drank almost nothing, alcoholic that is, and he lost track of what was going on with the news—he seemed to be accumulating stacks of unread *New York Times*. The reasons for this were puzzling, and Henry was only intermittently aware of this change in mood, but there was one significant thing in his life that was at least in part the cause. Henry had become entirely absorbed in his work, or his job, as it might be more properly put, specifically with a story line he'd started to flesh out and then, because it seemed to be working so well, which he entirely devoted himself to. It was true that he owed an outline to Merrill and Kipling before he started writing, but seeing that Henry never worked from an outline, it seemed that the best way to pursue the story was just to write it rather than perform some kind of duty that wouldn't lead to his best work. Anyway, he always worked swiftly, and he had plenty of time, so if Kipling hated the project, he could simply start over. And he really was in what might be called a trance over this book, and he seemed to do nothing besides write it and think about it.

The one exception to all this, or the one moment when Henry paused to consider his work and explain it to someone, was at a lunch with Merrill, now three weeks after he arrived home from London. Merrill had scheduled the lunch to "keep up with progress," and as they sat down at a fairly austere but expensive Japanese restaurant on Fifty-sixth, Merrill smiled and said, "I can't wait to hear what you've come up with."

And Henry told him, as best he could, although he realized what he was saying seemed slightly disjointed and unformed as he pressed forward. And Merrill slowly began to look more and more quizzical until he finally said, now looking extremely confused, "So, this book, for Kipling, for children, it's a children's book about a catastrophic brain hemorrhage?"

"Well, yes, a stroke," Henry quickly replied. "By its proper definition. But from a different angle. And, actually, two strokes."

"And this was Kipling's idea?"

"No, it's mine. Kipling really didn't have an idea. He wanted a story about a young person and an old person, but nothing more specific than that. This is what I've come up with."

"And the kid, he's the sick one."

"The boy, he's twelve, is injured when he falls from his bike. He has internal bleeding that isn't diagnosed. A clot breaks off and moves to his brain. And then he has a stroke."

"And his eighty-year-old grandfather, who's also had a stroke, but a minor one, has to take care of him."

"The grandfather is all the boy has."

"And it's first person."

"The boy tells the story."

Here Merrill paused and Henry became a little nervous, because it was the only time he'd ever said anything to Merrill when Merrill didn't react with wild and happy enthusiasm. The fact was, though, that Henry was sure it was a good story. He was sure it was working. And before Merrill could say anything Henry continued: "This is really good, what I'm writing. And I'm going to see it through. If it doesn't sit well with you and Jonathan, that's fine, I'll keep it for myself. But what I'm writing is really good. And I think you're going to like it. It's much less dismal than it sounds. It's actually an uplifting thing, two people taking care of each other in the face of terrible hardship."

Again, Merrill was silent, and Henry wondered if he'd made any impression at all with these last points. But finally Merrill cracked a smile and said, "All right, Henry. If you say it's good, I believe it. If you say it's uplifting, I believe it. And I think you're right that you should keep going. If it doesn't work out, it doesn't work out. I do worry about what Kipling will think. It's pretty grim, even if it is in some way uplifting, but you're on a roll and I don't think we should interfere."

"Okay, good," Henry replied, now a little tentative. "But let's not tell Kipling about the story yet. I understand it sounds dismal, so I don't want him to get upset. Anyway, again, if he doesn't like it, he can fire me or I can write something else for him."

"Yeah, it all sounds good to me, so don't worry," Merrill said, nodding, and then added, with real sincerity, "you know, I can tell you love this story you're writing, and it might sound dopey for me to say, but I really think that's always at the heart of anything good. So really, keep going. And I'll keep my mouth shut with Kipling. No worries on that front."

9

FOR THE FOLLOWING three weeks Henry worked with great diligence. He ate sporadically, got plenty of sleep, tried to keep down his coffee intake, and only allowed himself a beer or two if work that day had been particularly good.

It was a remarkable thing—Henry had thought this before—how quickly a person could move through a story if he worked at it steadily. And what he'd been asked for, about forty thousand words, seemed not very much at all, especially since his short stories always seemed to be at least ten thousand words. The bottom line was that at a thousand words a day, which was Henry's typical pace once he became gripped by a story, it added up to nearly a month and two-thirds, allowing ten or so days for various distractions and days when the writing didn't work out. At any rate, by the time he and Whitney were heading north to reclaim his parents' possessions from Pembry Cottage, Henry had something of a draft done. "It's not done-done," Henry told Merrill on the phone the afternoon before leaving for upstate. "But it's close. And it's good. I've reread it a bunch of times. I should have something to give you and Kipling soon."

"Well, that's really great and unexpected news," Merrill said. "So quick! I'll pass this news along. I'm sure Kipling will be excited."

And later that evening, Henry received an email from Kipling telling him this as well. "I'm astonished and excited to hear that you've got a draft done," he said. "I know you want to polish it, but I'm eager to look at it as soon as possible. I can't wait to see what kind of story is unfolding." (This sentence seemed to be good news, since it indicated that Merrill had been true to his word and that he hadn't told Kipling what the story line entailed.)

Kipling continued with other matters, however. "Since you're polishing up the draft now," he wrote, "I thought I'd also send you a few rules of thumb that I live by and that are important for the final product." Kipling then proceeded (in a strangely formatted list with indentations and bullet points) to offer Henry a detailed explanation of what he thought was important to remember about a work of art, "especially a work of literature," although, in the spirit of modesty, he did preface this list with the statement, "I'm sure you know these things, but as a writer in my own right, I never think it hurts to revisit common conclusions about good writing."

Among the points Kipling made (and there were many) were:

- *If you use parentheses and semicolons, it's because you haven't thought through your work properly. Please make sure none are in the final product.*
- *Please be careful with the overuse of prepositions, i.e., use "she awoke" instead of "she woke up."*
- *Take plenty of breaks to sleep and to eat. Hemingway did. So should you.*
- *If you run into trouble, remember that a writer's greatest asset is his imagination. A day of daydreaming is better than a month of research.*

This last point was actually something with which Henry deeply agreed, but its Zenlike phrasing upset him, and, following the rest of the absurd and quite exhaustive list, it dawned on Henry in a surprisingly blunt way that he really did not like Kipling very much at all. Henry's abandonment at Kipling's country home, Kipling's slapdash short stories, and now this helpful-tips manifesto, were all too much, especially since it seemed to go after certain of Henry's own tendencies, specifically in regards to his passion for parenthetical expression.

All the same, the troubling feelings Henry experienced over Kipling's patronizing tone and his incomprehensible aggression toward parentheses was tempered somewhat by the fact that Henry was due to leave for the Adirondacks the next morning. Henry's anger did not dissipate but the prospect of the road trip offered some reason for a more general optimism. He and Whitney hadn't spent very much time together recently, other than a lunch or two, and he thought that a night at Pembry Cottage, and time in the car doing things like chatting and eating junk food, might lead to quite a bit of fun—fun of the sort that he was sure he needed more of in his life.

And by the time Henry was out in front of Whitney's building the next day, he was even more excited. His Volvo was filled with gas—had been serviced, even, just three days earlier—and Henry had loaded the car with various snacks for the trip ahead, including a sort of specialty beef jerky purchased in Chinatown from some kind of famous Chinese maker of this kind of thing—he'd read about him several times on popular Manhattan websites.

Whitney seemed just as excited when he made his appearance, running out of his building in an exaggeratedly happy way (after Henry phoned him from the car) carrying a small weekend bag in one hand and a handle of Jack Daniel's, held high above his head, in the other.

"I'm so excited!" he said as he opened the door.

"I'm so excited too!" Henry replied.

At any rate, it was a happy greeting, and even after Whitney settled in and they found their way to the New York Thruway, they were still just a bit giddy. This happiness continued, through Albany and Saratoga Springs and past Lake George. They talked about books and various appealing women around Williamsburg and also restaurants that had recently opened that they wanted to try. And they talked about more weighty things as well. Whitney gave a somewhat emotional description of his grandmother's death when he was seven, and Henry, who had already spoken several times about his own parents' deaths, once again recounted what it was like to face such tragic events.

They also talked about simpler and more immediate matters, including the prospects for their dinner that night, Henry talking for some time about a local butcher in Lake Placid that sold game meat. "Hunting season is under way, so I'm sure we can get venison if you want," he said with enthusiasm.

This last comment, however, led to an unexpectedly serious conversation about meat-eating and the environmental implications of it all. Both Henry and Whitney were meat eaters, and for Henry's part, it was hard to imagine changing his behavior too much in this regard. But after Whitney eagerly said that he'd been planning on giving up factory-farmed meat (which, incidentally, would not interfere with their venison that night), Henry decided he was quite happy that he had not gotten around to surprising Whitney with his Chinatown beef jerky. He also concluded (because it was on his mind) that perhaps he ought not to suggest they stop at a roadside van he liked just off the New York Thruway that served things like hamburgers and hot dogs. Fortunately for Henry, Whitney was apparently feeling very hungry as they passed the van and insisted they stop. Thus Henry was able to eat a hot dog without feeling too guilty. Whitney ordered a gyro, which struck Henry as the pinnacle of processed meat.

Still, he decided it was probably best not to make this point out loud because Whitney seemed so thrilled by what the person in the van had given him.

And at the butcher's, just ten miles from the camp, Henry felt better. Who could argue with the virtues of buying meat culled from the wilderness? Henry bought two pounds of some sort of venison loin that the butcher recommended, and after stopping at a grocery store for a few other provisions, they were soon passing up the long gravel drive that led to Pembry Cottage.

The house was built on a high promontory that offered an exceptional view of Lake Placid, while keeping it somewhat discreetly nestled within the lakeside foliage. The word "cottage," of course, was used in the Newport way, not in the Beatrix Potter way, and the house was actually a grand late-nineteenth century mansion consisting of seven bedrooms, servants' rooms (now never used other than for kids and guest overflows), large porches and sitting rooms, and a formal dining room with a table that seated sixteen. The dining room had once had at its center a Chippendale table and matching chairs, but the trustees decided that they were in danger of being ruined (by all the children and the drastic yearly changes in upstate weather), and since the house was in need of some unexpected repairs (around 1968) the furniture was sold and replaced with a very nice table that was not, however, a precious antique.

The house was unusual in this part of the world because, rather than an elaborate series of buildings and cabins, as was the custom with most of the great camps in the Adirondacks, it was more like a lodge, a single structure in which all the guests stayed. Henry's ancestors had been criticized by the earlier wealthy settlers for this, but Mr. Pembry had a vision for the area that resembled something closer to Chamonix or Zermatt. In fact, Mr. Pembry was largely credited with bringing the 1932 Olympics to Lake Placid, although he was fairly old at that point.

The house sat on a piece of property composed of about seven acres, including nearly eight hundred feet of shorefront with a magnificent boathouse, built long before zoning laws made such structures illegal. It had four slips, a long dock, and above the slips was an enormous room with a vaulted ceiling, a pool table, a fireplace, and a porch that overlooked the lake. This particular room was generally colonized by the various young people who were there at different points in the summer, and Henry certainly spent many nights playing pool and listening to music there when he was up for weekends with his parents.

At any rate, it was exactly the sort of magnificent second home the rich patriarch of a large family might build for himself, and Henry and Whitney quickly settled in (after each opening a beer). The house was empty for the weekend— it often was this time of year, after the warmer months but before snow and ice brought the winter sports—but Henry had called ahead to the caretaker the family employed, so the heat was on and there was even firewood by the fireplace in the central living room. And starting a fire was one of the first things Henry did, after showing Whitney where to put his belongings, and before long Henry and Whitney were lying across elaborately upholstered couches from the 1920s, drinking more beer and watching the fire.

It was always interesting, Henry thought, seeing friends from one location in a brand-new place, and, as he had expected, the conversation took a deeper turn (that afternoon by the fire, on a walk around the property, during a quick inspection of the items Henry had to bring to the dealer in Massachusetts the next day—all of which were under a white bedsheet with a Post-it note attached labeled "Henry!"—and then into the kitchen, where they prepared the venison and began to eat). They covered quite a bit of narrative ground, but the most startling of the revelations was a detailed discussion of Whitney's father, who had, unbeknownst to Henry, spent two years in prison for some kind of white-collar fraud involving securities—hidden losses of some sort, and three bad years in a row that his father had tried to mask. His father now taught math at a community college—he'd earned a graduate degree in mathematics from MIT before being lured into the world of investment.

"His job he has now," Whitney said as he cut into a potato, "he really loves it. He should have been doing it all along. I guess that's how these things go."

"And you were how old when they arrested him?"

"Twelve. That was something."

"Yeah, I'll bet," Henry said, taking a sip of beer. "I can't really imagine." It was odd, the difference in tragedies that they'd suffered involving their parents. Henry often found it hard to talk about his parents' deaths because everything was so inscrutable. That is, although the pain and the emotion were straightforward, his articulation of it all seemed so confused and often felt very shallow and inexact when expressed. Surely Whitney's sufferings were something close to the intensity of what he had experienced, but there was a measure of disgrace involved, probably making the matter even more difficult to talk about.

"We visited a lot," Whitney finally added. "And they put him in a minimum-security prison, so he wasn't being threatened by murderers. But trust me, it was still a prison, and my dad is a nervous type of man. It seemed like every time we went there he was holding back tears and apologizing to my brothers and me. That didn't make it any easier. It's better, I guess, than some idiotic front involving how other people screwed him or how his crimes were commonplace and that he'd been singled out, although that may be true. Anyway, it's interesting, how a person goes down that road. Not to excuse him at all, but my father was a totally repressed Protestant—not a flamboyant guy who craved money, and not someone you'd expect to get involved with a scheme like this. He made a lot of mistakes in his investments, tried to cover them up, and then tried to cover things up again after another round of mistakes."

"Yeah," Henry said. "I think that's probably not uncommon."

"My dad is a really good guy," Whitney said. "But what do I know? I'm not exactly impartial. And fuck, he lost people's money and lied about it, so maybe he deserved what he got."

It was all a lot to think about, and although Henry said several times that he couldn't imagine having to watch his own father suffer like that, he wasn't sure that he was being much comfort. The fact was that he was also very drunk by the time they had worked through this discussion, and not the good kind of chatty drunk. It was the kind of drunkenness that comes from drinking all afternoon and evening and then eating nearly two pounds of a freshly slaughtered deer covered with sauce made from whipped egg yolks. After a moment of silence, following another remark from Whitney about how happy his dad was now as a math teacher, Henry confessed to the fact that he was nearly at the point of falling off his chair and that it was probably best if they went to bed.

"If I don't go now, I don't think I'll make it," Henry said, standing. "Let's leave the dishes. We'll do them in the morning."

"I'm feeling the same," Whitney said. With that, they found the stairs and made their way to their bedrooms.

10

THE NEXT MORNING, Henry couldn't quite tell if he was still drunk, although after getting his bearings and finally managing to put on his pants, he determined that he was, unfortunately, stone sober but also very hung-over.

He would have liked to have spent that day doing nothing—maybe a Bloody Mary to ease things some and then experiments with Pembry Cottage's waffle iron before a long nap to bring his hangover closer to its conclusion. But they had to leave that day—they needed to get his parents' possessions to the estate dealer, which wasn't open on Sundays—and Henry wanted to get a reasonably early start so he could spend whatever time he needed to with the dealer. After his parents died, Henry had scrupulously assembled his important family artifacts, keeping some with him, others in an expensive storage facility in Boston designed for housing such things, and also in a largish safe-deposit box in the Commonwealth Bank, the Boston bank that also handled his money. When Henry went through the items that morning at Pembry Cottage, he was happy to see that there was nothing particularly meaningful to him, other than an old canvas hat that his father wore on the few occasions he fished from a rowboat on the lake. Henry would keep that—the hat looked quite good on him, as he could hardly help but notice that morning, and this despite the delirium of his hangover. But as for the mahogany writing secretary Uncle Louis had told him about, and an unexpected box of sterling flatware, and numerous other small and forgotten items, Henry was happy to sell it all. There was a pair of pistols that Henry found slightly intriguing—Colt .38s, as Henry determined from the factory engravings. Henry did suddenly remember his father mentioning the guns once, indicating that they were heirlooms of some sort. But very quickly Henry became alarmed that they might be loaded, and after making sure that they weren't (as best he knew how) he decided that these too would be turned over to the estate agent that day. In fact, he concluded with real resolution that he never wanted to hold a gun again.

At any rate, it didn't take long for Henry to gather everything up, and since there was nothing that needed to be carried by two people, he let Whitney continue to sleep and packed the Volvo himself. He wrapped what he could in old woolen blankets that were among his parents' things—it struck Henry that he might actually keep these blankets, since they were quite nice and likely without value—and before long his task was complete.

After that, he roused Whitney from bed. Unfortunately, Whitney was equally hung-over, and the two did what they could to clean, although, by the time they left, Henry felt guilty about the very shoddy job they'd done. But his head was now hurting very much and he had a long drive ahead of him and the guilt soon gave way to the discomfort of once again being on the road.

They took the same route back as they had come, with the exception being that they headed east at Albany and then took the Mass Pike to 495 (where they turned off to buy some hamburgers at a local diner) and then proceeded toward the estate agent's headquarters in Concord on smaller roads while eating their lunch.

And the lunch turned out to be especially good, since they'd grossly overordered, which brought the pleasant sensation of having far more than enough french fries to distract them from their physical distress. Henry even remarked on this, how much he liked having more than enough of this kind of thing. "I suppose it's wasteful, and I don't normally do this, but I really feel relief at avoiding the sadness of getting to the end of an order of french fries when I still want more."

They were then passing through the somewhat scenic village of Kingston, and Henry slowed as he wound through the small town. But the hamburger he was now eating was so good, and he was once again thinking about how pleased he was to have access to so much fried food, that he failed to calculate properly a small turn in the street. And just as he was thinking about how to deal with a bit of mustard that was now on his chin—it stung, actually, which was surprising—he swerved to his left, and then to his right, and then crashed into a parked car.

As collisions go, it was from the very start clearly not catastrophic. He'd been driving slowly, applied the brakes (just not in time), and, in the end, the abrupt stop was at no more than five miles an hour. But the hit was direct—Henry's right fender into the door of a Subaru Outback, and, judging from the sound of the impact, quite a bit of metal and fiberglass had been wrenched from place.

No one was in the car, as Henry quickly gathered, and Whitney immediately said, "I'm fine, I'm fine," when Henry looked over at him. And no one was next to the car, so there were no ancillary injuries. There were a few people on the sidewalk about ten yards away, however, and thus it was with some embarrassment that Henry put his hamburger on his dashboard and got out.

He tried to remain relaxed, but the relief stemming from the lack of real injury gave way to the realization that this was really not good news and certainly would bring him some kind of trouble. He'd surely be reprimanded by someone, and would have to pay for damages, and perhaps this would mean some sort of spike in his insurance premiums. Also, although he well knew that the alcohol was technically long out of his bloodstream, he was definitely still suffering its effects, and when he finally had to explain himself, he wondered how he'd handle it.

As Henry looked at the damages—they were cosmetic but surprisingly substantial—he reached for his phone, deciding it was probably best to call the police, thereby establishing himself as a conscientious and earnest young man, not some kind of hooligan from Brooklyn. But just as he began to wonder if 911 was the appropriate number to dial—it wasn't really an emergency, after all—a police car arrived with New England efficiency and an officer was soon standing beside Henry inspecting the damage with him.

"I'm so sorry," Henry said. "I don't know what to say. I'm not sure how this happened. But obviously it was my fault. I just didn't gauge the curve correctly."

The officer seemed surprisingly relaxed, almost regretful, really. Finally he asked, "Were you on a cell phone?"

"No, no," Henry immediately replied, and then added, with sincerity, "I don't believe in that."

"Were you eating?" the officer asked.

Henry glanced at Whitney in the passenger seat. He was holding a gigantic fountain-soda cup in his hands and had a Styrofoam food container on his lap. "Yes, I was eating a hamburger," Henry said. "But I'll pay for everything. I have insurance."

The cop looked down again at the car, bent his knees, and touched the dent and the broken Subaru fiberglass. Then he stood up, stepped back a little for a broader view, and said at last, "Well, I've seen worse."

And he said it in a very gentle and reassuring tone. It made Henry feel quite grateful, and he was just formulating another apology and another statement of responsibility when he noticed that the police officer was now looking away from the impact and into Henry's car.

Henry wished he'd done something better with his hamburger than put it on the dashboard. He felt like even more of an idiot now. But as the cop moved closer to the car, Henry was surprised to see that the officer didn't look in the front, but in the station wagon's back. Henry began to follow just as the cop turned and asked, "Are those guns?"

"Yes," Henry replied, wondering now if he could stick his hand in and discreetly knock his hamburger to the floor.

"They're yours?"

The two Colt pistols had slid out of the blankets Henry had wrapped them in and were now lying beside the mahogany writing secretary, just below the back window.

"Well, they're my father's. Or they were my father's. He died and they're mine now. I'm actually just taking them to a dealer to have them sold."

"Can I see the registration?"

At this Henry hesitated, then said, "Well I'm not sure I have that."

"You don't have the registration?"

After a pause, Henry said, "I'm not sure what you mean."

"The registration?"

"I've only just picked them up. This is the first time I've really ever even seen them."

"But you own them?"

Henry had already admitted this, so what was there for him to say? "I'm the owner, but I've got nothing to do with them, really. I'm just taking them to be sold. From upstate New York."

Here Henry smiled and, because this police officer seemed

to be a decent sort of man, Henry hoped that his naïveté might cause the cop to be somewhat sympathetic.

And the truth was that it seemed to work. The cop appeared very sympathetic to Henry's answers. He gave Henry a very compassionate glance, even. But this glance was quickly followed by one that seemed very troubled. At last, the policeman said, "Look, I hate to do this—I understand what you're saying to me, and I believe you—but you've got two handguns in there. Thirty-eight Specials, even, it looks like. I'm really sorry, but I've got to call back to the station about what to do about this. The laws are pretty strict, and we're under a lot of pressure nowadays with this type of thing. You need to have your registration with you. They definitely need to be registered in the first place. Especially handguns."

"Maybe they're registered in New York."

The officer again looked a bit disturbed and then said, "To you? Are they registered to you?"

"I never registered them."

"But you're the owner."

"I inherited them."

"How long ago?"

"Um, around two years."

"Yeah," the police officer said, again trying with what seemed like an attempt at warmth, "transporting them across state lines, no registration, handguns, it's just something I've got to call in. I'll try to help you sort this out. I'll do whatever I can for you, but—I'm really sorry—I have to report this."

11

FORTUNATELY, THE REST of the police force and law enforcement officials behaved with the same kind of decorum and sympathy as the officer who arrested them. Whitney was let go within twenty minutes of their arrival, and Henry found himself in a pleasant waiting room that resembled a cheerful and well-run post office rather than a detention center. Henry still expected rapists and pickpockets to be led through, but there was absolutely nothing going on and Henry, as far as he could tell, was the only criminal in the entire building.

And when he was finally questioned by a friendly detective with the last name of Jensen, the mode seemed almost apologetic. Henry did have to explain, with some detail, his "intentions" for the guns. And he was even asked if there was anyone that he was having trouble with, people he "hated" (Henry did not bring up the fairly insulting list of writer's tips he'd recently received from Kipling), and the detective listened thoughtfully to all that Henry had to say and treated his entire situation as a predicament, not a crime. It was, in fact, as though this were all something very unfortunate that had happened to Henry, that he was the victim who needed to be assisted.

It did strike Henry that had he not been a friendly white Harvard grad, he might not be getting so much sympathy. He was sure of this, in fact, and it did make him feel quite guilty. But he was not, it was perfectly true, some sort of gunrunner or violent criminal, although, again, what made this so obvious to the police department? That was the troubling and ugly question.

At any rate, the wheels of justice had to turn as they were expected to, and about three hours later, long after Whitney had been released, Henry was before a judge who was setting his bail for the crime of illegal possession of firearms, "although," the judge added, "there might be additions to this as the investigation continues."

The amount of the bail actually turned out to be fairly light: $15,000, of which Henry had to put up 10 percent. So, $1,500 due, then, paid by Whitney, who'd somehow bought a money order for this amount from a nearby Western Union. And, of course, the guns were confiscated, but the property officer assured Henry that he would take good care of them. "I know it's family stuff," he said.

By this point, however, Henry wanted nothing at all to do with any gun ever again and would have been just as happy if they were lost. The day of jail had, in the end, made him feel very uneasy, despite the kindness of the people who were sending him down the river, as it were, and this feeling continued for some time. Henry had used his one phone call to contact Whitney about bail, so, after hugging Whitney in the front reception room, Henry was quickly on his phone with Lawrence Price, his lawyer—the man who'd so ably defended Henry in the Libyan goat affair. Lawrence was apparently just sitting down to dinner, but he still greeted Henry warmly and said, "I'm glad you called me about this."

Lawrence did what he could to reassure Henry, although Henry, again, was not as panicked as might have been expected. Lawrence admitted that he didn't quite know the scope of everything. "But I'm sure we can work this out," he

MICHAEL DAHLIE

said. "Handguns are trouble, but it's so clearly just a mistake. It would be a terrible miscarriage of justice for them to punish you. It's just that handguns, well, it's not like accidentally walking out of a store with a bag of bananas."

"No," Henry said, now somehow feeling slightly more nervous. "I suppose it's not the same."

"Anyway, I can't do anything this late," Lawrence said. "I can make one or two calls tomorrow, even though it's Sunday. Monday morning I can really get started and figure this out. The thing for you to do now is find some dinner and have a drink. I'll find a way through this for you."

"Okay," Henry said, although he wondered if he detected just a bit of equivocation in Lawrence's voice.

12

HENRY AND WHITNEY drove straight back to New York that evening (the car now full of his nonlethal family possessions) and Henry was still very uneasy by the time they arrived home. Whitney had forced him to eat a plate of some sort of Korean noodles and drink three beers at a restaurant when they got to Williamsburg, though, and this helped, and by Monday afternoon he was having a more specific and useful conversation with Lawrence, who tried to assure Henry that he'd get him through all this.

"There are mandatory sentences with some things," he said, "and we don't know what the charges are, but sentences can be suspended, and after talking to the prosecutors this morning, it seems like no one is going to try to put you away, but the charges, unfortunately, can't be dropped. I've been on the phone to an associate in Albany to see what the law is there, and you really should have registered the guns when you inherited them. Everyone understands that none of this was really your fault, but those were, technically, your obligations. And with guns, these obligations become important. I mean, you're not in any jeopardy as far as New York goes, since you were picked up in Massachusetts, but since they picked you up in Massachusetts, it means that they've got to move forward there."

Henry paused, although only one question was on his mind: "So they could send me to jail?"

Lawrence said, "Almost impossible, but, yes, technically they could. So much comes down to who reviews your case, but you going to jail is in nobody's interest."

Henry was about to rephrase his question when Lawrence continued talking. "Look, you'll be fine. If someone told me about the case, if it wasn't mine, I'd say there's nothing to worry about, but as your lawyer, I have to tell you that there is a tiny risk, although let's not worry about it all until we have more facts, until the prosecutors come up with an idea of what they want."

It was sound advice, but still unsettling. Lawrence was hardly calling to tell Henry that things had been resolved.

And the feelings of uneasiness continued for the next few days—Lawrence had warned Henry it would take some time to hear from the prosecutors. Henry did his best to carry on as normal, although at first he wished he had some kind of full-time employment to provide him with a few mindless tasks that could keep him occupied. Lots of photocopying was what he felt like doing just then. Making one's own days, as the saying goes, is only pleasurable when a person's mind is clear. Still, Henry found that he was able to focus on his writing, and for that week and part of the next, he continued with his children's novel about brain hemorrhages, polishing and cutting the book with devotion until he had what he thought was a draft good enough to pass along. In fact, by Henry's measure, the book was nearly done, and as he prepared to send it off to Merrill he readied himself for the fights that might ensue with Kipling over various details of the story. Kipling, after all, was hardly a reliable reader, and Henry didn't think he could stand another tip sheet on "how to be a writer."

During this time, of course, Henry spoke to Lawrence on

a few occasions. The situation was always the same—they had to wait for the prosecutors to make up their minds about the matter. When Henry sent off his book, now titled *The Best of Youth* (a title inspired by an Italian movie that Henry absolutely adored), his case had not moved forward.

13

HENRY WASN'T SURE what would follow the submission of his novel, but he heard nothing at all for the following few weeks, and he began to worry that they hated it and that they'd been talking about how best to fire him. There was also the matter that it was, once again, the Christmas season—a thing that Henry had mostly avoided thinking about. He passed the holidays as he preferred to, though—alone, drinking lots of coffee, thinking about his parents, and accomplishing minor tasks around his apartment. He also managed not to kill any animals. And Henry followed this routine well through New Year's Day (also spent alone), keeping the anxiety over his novel at bay until finally, on January 3, he got a call from Merrill asking what his plans were for the next few nights.

"Kipling is going to be in town," he said, "and we thought it might be fun for the three of us to go out one night."

"Has he read the book?" Henry quickly asked.

"Well, it's hard to say," Merrill replied. "He has a lot of ideas about the book, but I'm not sure they have much to do with the manuscript. But you know I loved it. I thought it was magnificent, Henry."

Henry was at a loss, but he finally said, "No, I didn't know that."

"I emailed you last week. Something must have happened.

I did it from my BlackBerry. I was in France. I loved the book, Henry. I truly loved it. I have to say, I think you're crazy to think this is a children's novel. I mean, it's simple enough to read, but it's pretty heavy stuff. The hospital scenes with the boy. The recollections of losing his mother and father. I see what you're saying, though, about two people in trouble, on such different sides of life, taking care of each other. I really did find it very affecting, and very uplifting even, given the subject matter, although I think that's what you were trying to tell me before, so I don't think I'm wrong here. Anyway, it's so, so good. So moving."

"Thanks," Henry said, pausing for a moment because he thought he really ought to say more—"thanks" hardly expressed the gratitude he was now feeling—but Merrill quickly continued, "So can you meet up with us this week?"

"Yes," Henry said. "I'd love to."

They agreed to meet that upcoming Thursday, the plan being to have dinner together at a new sort of private club that Kipling belonged to and then to go out from there, probably to a high-toned discotheque or wherever else people like Kipling went. Abby had an important show that night in Williamsburg—probably her biggest so far—and Henry regretted not being able to make that, although in the back of his mind he wondered if he could talk Kipling and Merrill into going.

And in fact the matter of going to see Abby did come up, although Henry actually brought up Abby's gig at a point in the dinner when he was (contrary to the original goals) trying to make an excuse to leave early and alone.

The so-called private club where they ate consisted of an entire brownstone close to the Meatpacking District and, although it was ostensibly a club for artists, it was so lavish and the people there were so expensively dressed that Henry couldn't help but wonder what kind of artists these were. Of course, technically speaking, he himself was both an artist and also unjustly wealthy, so living a rougher-looking life in Brooklyn hardly made him any better than these people. Still, it was a baffling environment.

More baffling, however, was the conversation that unfolded between the three men. After some fairly pleasant chat during the first course, when Merrill told some very interesting stories about his childhood in San Francisco, the conversation drifted. Kipling then became suddenly animated and he began to talk about Henry's novel, which, as became obvious, he hadn't finished and, likely, he hadn't made it past the first twenty pages. This did not, however, prevent him from making some fairly stern pronouncements on its qualities.

"I've given it to my editor and we'll see how she reacts," Kipling said. "She's a genius and she can work magic from anything. But from my own first impressions, I'm not sure you understand what I'm trying to get at. I mean, all the disease stuff. The strokes Merrill was talking about. I want this story to be inspiring, but it's so dismal. This should be about the union of the young and the old, how children and adults need to communicate, to *commune*. It's just so bleak. Your book seems to be about suffering."

"But that's not what it's about at all," Henry quickly said, "and that's definitely not how it ends up." Henry was tentative, though, not quite sure of the tone he ought to be taking.

"Well, to be honest, Henry," Kipling continued, "I'm only just a little of the way into it. But you see, that's the thing. A book needs to pull you through. It's got to be like a freight train. It has to start strong and have so much momentum that a reader simply can't put it down. This is something I believe very deeply, and I haven't seen that in this draft."

At this point, Henry was no longer struggling to understand his feelings. He was indeed offended. Kipling, however, not lacking in psychological perception, added, "I mean, you've given us a lot to work with. I'm hoping you'll stick around for a second draft, but we need this to be good, and good writing comes through careful work. It's not easy. It's hard. Really fucking hard. If you understand that, how hard it is being a real artist, then we can get there."

Oddly, Henry actually felt just a bit of relief with this last statement, since he was now completely convinced that Kipling was a total moron. It was true that Kipling was technically his boss, and if he wanted to continue with the job he'd have to listen to him on some level. But he could also walk away. He didn't need the money, and the contract was not the sort of document that bound him into permanent labor.

Fortunately, Henry was spared from any more rapid calculations on this matter, since the conversation suddenly shifted when, after finally getting to his main course, Kipling began to grow very upset that his steak had been overcooked. He took a bite and said, "This is fucking garbage," in a kind of whisper that was breathy and tight but still loud enough for others to hear. The waiter heard it, at least, and immediately came to the table to ask if there was anything wrong.

At first it looked as though Kipling were going to wave him off, and it even seemed that he was trying to restrain himself. But after a brief pause he said (again, in the same kind of whisper), "This steak is fucking disgusting. It's cooked to a crisp."

"I'm so sorry, but you asked for well done, sir," the waiter replied. It didn't seem like he was trying to pick a fight, but his response also wasn't hesitant, perhaps because it was a legitimate defense: Henry clearly remembered Kipling saying, "I'd like it very well done."

Kipling again looked as though he were restraining himself as he considered the waiter's answer. He didn't lose his temper, if losing one's temper means losing control. But Kipling was clearly very angry—angry in the kind of fastidious, high-achieving way that might be expected (if not forgiven) from an accomplished actor—and he certainly expressed himself efficiently along these lines. "Well, I didn't mean for you to burn the fuck out of it, you little fucking cunt," he said. "Take this fucking thing back and bring me another one."

The waiter quickly took the plate and turned without expression, but the "How about you go fuck yourself" the waiter delivered sotto voce was more than audible to everyone at Henry's table. Kipling stared at his hands for a moment with startling intensity, his mouth tight and his eyes focused. He then unexpectedly smiled, looked over at Henry, and said, "So, I hope you're coming out with us tonight, Henry. After dinner."

The request was delivered with a surprising amount of warmth, so different from what Henry had seen just a second ago. And it seemed sincere. It didn't appear that Kipling was trying to compensate for his earlier anger. But at this point Henry concluded that he absolutely could not go to a nightclub with Kipling and quickly said, "I actually can't go out with you. I have a friend who plays in a band. She plays viola. And they've got a big event tonight at a pretty important venue. In Williamsburg. I have to attend."

"What venue?" Kipling said.

"A bar called Abeline," Henry replied. "I could miss it normally, but it's pretty much the best place to play these days. And to get a Thursday booking, it's a big deal. I'd really love to go out with you. Clubbing. But I can't. It's actually my cousin who's in the band. But not really. She's a forth cousin, which isn't even a relation by most definitions."

Kipling looked at Henry for a moment and Henry couldn't grasp what was coming next—more complaining about his steak, a tearful hug, declarations of artistic inspiration? Kipling's look was just so strange. Finally he said, "Well, that's where Merrill and I are going too, then!"

"But it's all the way in Williamsburg," Henry immediately said. "It's way too far for you both."

"I've got a car waiting. A Maybach, no less. We'll go out, see the show, and then we'll all come back for whatever highjinks are going on in Manhattan."

Henry again began to scramble for a way out, but the best he could come up with was to mention that he was on the list and that it might be hard to get two other guests into the show with him. He wisely refrained from making this argument, however. Given bouncers' familiarity with even the most minor celebrities, there was no conceivable way that Kipling would be turned away at the entrance, especially if they arrived in a high-end limousine. "Okay," Henry finally said. "But I might not make it back to Manhattan. I'm feeling a little tired already."

"Ah, well, I've got something to help with that," Kipling said, grinning and standing up from the table. "Interested?"

Henry and Merrill shook their heads, although it took Henry a second to figure out what he was talking about. Kipling smiled and added, "You're not finding better than what I've got here, my friends. Not anywhere."

Again, Henry and Merrill politely refused.

"All right," Kipling said. "I'll be back." And then he walked off to the bathroom.

At any rate, by the time Kipling returned, his newly cooked steak had arrived, although he barely touched it, and the rest of the dinner was spent talking about an odd kind of project Merrill was working on with a retired athlete who had written a self-help book for single parents. Kipling asked animated questions, and seemed unduly fascinated by this particular father-athlete. But he did also seem somehow to be restraining something else, and just minutes after their plates were cleared by a busser, he became distracted as he saw their waiter walking toward a side door that led to the club's guest rooms.

"Okay," Kipling quickly said, standing up. "Let's meet out

front in a few minutes. This is taken care of. They'll bill me." Kipling then abruptly walked toward the door through which the waiter had passed.

Merrill too stood and excused himself from Henry. "I've got to make a call," he said, not paying much attention to Kipling's sudden departure. "Let's meet on the street."

"All right," Henry replied, a bit confused, but he himself had wanted to leave the table for the past several minutes—he'd gotten a surprising amount of his fish's ginger sauce on his hands and wanted to wash up in the men's room. And three minutes later, hands now freshly washed, he returned to the club's dining room, still wondering if it was possible to elude Kipling and Merrill's company for the rest of the night. This line of inquiry ceased, though, when he saw (as he passed back by their now-empty table) the waiter reenter the dining room, trying to smooth down his now strangely disheveled hair and looking entirely ashen—and ashen was a hard thing to pull off given the dim lighting. More relevant, the right side of his mouth was swelling and bleeding. The waiter put his hand to his mouth as he passed by the kitchen, then walked swiftly toward the men's room. Henry paused for a moment to watch all this, and then saw Kipling appear from behind the door. Kipling spotted Henry and smiled broadly. He walked up to him and said—they were now both close to the landing—"I think that our waiter will be far more polite the next time we come here for dinner." Kipling then swung his arm around Henry's neck and cheerfully guided the younger man down the steps.

14

THE MAYBACH'S INTERIOR was perhaps one of the strangest things Henry had ever seen, and while he had always regarded himself (rightly) as wealthy, New York was showing him once again that there was a world of rich people that he simply knew nothing about, particularly the world of the rich who had some claim to the sort of fame that Hollywood provides. The Maybach felt more like a private jet, with its single-person reclining seats, its buffed-beige leather armrests, and the burled oak panels and brushed steel trim. There were two seats facing forward (the reclining and individual variety) and then a sort of wraparound bench that, Henry imagined, could seat up to five slim socialites. And of course there was a discreet and cleverly disguised bar into which Kipling quickly began to rummage. Fortunately (for Henry's own sense of dignity) Kipling did not pull out a bottle of champagne, but rather a bottle of vodka. He opened it, but then paused and said to Merrill and Henry, "We have beer too, if you'd prefer." Henry and Merrill immediately indicated that they would prefer beer, and soon Henry was sipping a Guinness and finding that he was quite happy to have it.

It was, of course, ridiculous to arrive anywhere in Williamsburg in a limousine, especially of this variety. Even the most uninitiated people of the borough knew enough to arrive at events on foot or on top of secondhand bikes. And Henry suspected that Kipling must have known this too. But he was clearly entirely comfortable with the facts of his financial and celebrity status and Henry was really in no position to try to convince Kipling that their arrival would make for something of an outlandish scene.

What surprised Henry most, however, was how impressed everyone actually seemed to be once they arrived. Rather than haughty looks of disgust as the car pulled up to the entrance, where there was now quite a line, people were generally excited. Certainly no one threw a beer can at them, which Henry had half expected, and, once again, he thought that he really didn't understand the subtleties of his social world at all. More than that, though, Henry couldn't deny that he felt just a bit of pleasure in being part of the show. It was disgraceful, of course. And certainly he'd deny ever feeling such a thing if the matter came up with a peer. But he had to admit that he did, somehow, enjoy it all, and this after he'd grown even more repulsed by Kipling that evening. As they approached the bouncer at the break in the rope where people with special access went, Henry pointed to his name on the clipboard, indicated he had two friends, and they were soon mounting the stairs to the venue.

Once they arrived, Kipling managed to pass easily through the crowd without any fuss. The people were so animated already, and the lights so dim, that Henry and Merrill and Kipling were soon able to find a table near the wall and sit down without too much trouble. That there was a table at all was surprising, but there was still a long line outside and the venue was not yet full.

It took some time for the show to get started. They all ordered drinks and were on to their third when Abby's band took the stage, and *Odd Girl Out* seemed as impressive as always—the viola and the bassoon and the flute seemed both comical and mystifying, especially mixed with Abby's slight voice and her lyrics about being lost in strange cityscapes and dreaming about love.

Abby seemed even more beautiful than usual. She was wearing a kind of sheer dress, and the way it hugged and lighted the shape of her breasts and her legs made it seem that she was wearing nothing at all. It was hard for Henry to believe (as always) that this was the same person who often bullied him into eating more vegetables, made fun of his introversion, and dragged him to parties full of twenty-somethings with whom Henry never quite got along. Onstage, Abby seemed to be a very different sort of person—different from the inhabitants of what Henry imagined was their social world, from any social world he could imagine, and certainly different from Henry himself.

Throughout the concert, Henry had similar such reflections, working hard to suppress any sort of romantic longings, although it was hard to deny Abby's appeal, as was perfectly obvious from the way the audience seemed so lost in the performance. And when the music finally ended, and the lights had been turned up, and Abby at last made her way to Henry's table, it was clear from the glances around the room (although many people had already left) that her charm didn't diminish any.

Henry was quite proud to introduce her to Kipling, which he did after he and Merrill both hugged her warmly. "This is Jonathan Kipling," Henry said, and then, remembering that he was expected to keep the true nature of his relationship with Kipling secret, added, "he's friends with Merrill. He's Merrill's friend. We just found ourselves together tonight."

"It's great to meet you," she said.

"And you too," Kipling said. "I'm stunned. You were wonderful." And then, "We're heading back into Manhattan. The three of us. If you want to come. I've got a car waiting outside."

Henry wasn't sure he liked the sound of that offer, but Abby quickly declined.

"Thanks. Really," she said. "But I'm so exhausted. I didn't get much sleep last night, and shows kind of take it out of me."

"You were truly great," Merrill said, smiling.

"Yes, you really were," Kipling added.

"You were really great," Henry said as well, not wanting to be forgotten.

At any rate, in the next instant Abby was walking back to the dressing rooms, and Henry was once again alone with Kipling and Merrill. They all looked at each other for a moment, still taken with Abby, but at last Kipling said, "All right, then, men, back to Manhattan?"

Here Henry thought that he could take his leave. He said he'd had a wonderful time but that he needed to get home, and despite some more prodding as they descended the steps and found their way to the street, Henry managed to keep up his resistance.

"Really, I should go home," Henry said. "I'm very tired." And after reiterating this several more times, and even refusing a ride to his building—it was only about eight blocks away—Henry said farewell and was soon walking home alone.

15

IT HAD BEEN QUITE an evening and Henry was almost grateful for the hangover the next day, since it allowed him to focus on physical troubles and keep his mind off Kipling's absurd ideas about "literature" and the difficulties that lay ahead of him in the world of criminal gun trafficking. Unfortunately, worries about this latter issue crept back as the hangover diminished, and over the next several days he did what he could to do research on possible outcomes of his case. He learned nothing that Lawrence hadn't told him, other than some surprising information about a few extremely rare but shocking stories of unexpectedly long imprisonments concerning such things, although the truth was that two of these incidents happened in Turkey and the other concerned a man from Kentucky who had quite probably robbed several banks.

At any rate, nearly a week after the night out with Kipling, the call finally came from the prosecutors in Massachusetts and, as Henry later understood from Lawrence, it was not good, but not terrible, and it was in line with what they had expected. "You plead guilty to one count of the illegal possession of a handgun," Lawrence said, "one count of failure to register firearms, you pay a four-thousand-dollar fine, they recommend that you serve no jail time—you'll get a sentence but it will be suspended—and you do a bunch of community service hours, which you can do in New York, on an exchange system that was set up a few years ago."

"So no jail time?" Henry said.

"No jail time," Lawrence said. "You've still got to go up and stand before a judge and plead guilty and all that, but the deal is done as far as the prosecutors are concerned. If you agree, that is."

Henry paused. "And you think I should agree?"

"I think you should agree," Lawrence said. "I could shave a few hours off the community service and maybe get the fine reduced, but what's the difference for you? I don't think we need to piss these guys off."

"Yes," Henry said. "I agree with that."

"The other thing," Lawrence added, "is that they want to get this off their books. So how does next Wednesday sound for a trip north?"

"Wednesday is fine," Henry said. "I'd kind of like to take care of this soon as well."

It was a relief, Henry decided, to get this handled so quickly, although, as Henry assessed the fact that he'd avoided one great disaster that afternoon, he realized that there was something still quite troubling about what had been concluded. He'd now have a felony on his record, and not one that was easily overlooked—weapons charges, of all things. Of course, anyone who heard the story would understand his situation, but if he ever wanted to get a proper job or go to law school, he'd have to write (probably without much of an opportunity to explain) that he'd been convicted of gun crimes. That night, Henry started work on a story about an eighty-year-old woman sentenced to five months in prison for domestic abuse after beating her wheelchair-bound husband with her cane. The story started out as surprisingly funny, and certainly the husband got what he had coming (as details of the story suggested), but the story ended badly for the woman, the conviction leading to a traumatic divorce that left her penniless. At any rate, Henry felt it was a good story, and it was absorbing enough to take him through that troubling week before his court date.

And on the trip north for his court date, in his silver Volvo, Henry found himself thinking more about the story than about his date with the judge, and he determined that he was very pleased with how the story was going. He did wonder if he ought to rewrite the ending, though. Maybe the woman died in prison, just before the jailer brought her her final divorce papers. And walking through the courthouse, and greeting the Massachusetts colleague Lawrence had been working with (he was going to be the one to sit with Henry as he pled), Henry couldn't help but think very deeply about the strangeness of dealing with the American legal system and that he had several other ideas for stories about elderly criminals. And even as he pled guilty, to a judge who struck him as fairly friendly (he smiled and nodded when Henry stood up, at least), Henry thought that the judge might make for a good character in something because he had such a comically bald head. It was of the old sort, waxed to a shine and ringed with a fluffy band of graying auburn hair. Henry didn't imagine that people cut their hair this way anymore and he was thinking with quite a bit of amusement about this matter as he heard the judge's opinions and decisions concerning the legal issue at hand.

"I accept your plea," the judge said, "and I understand the circumstances of this case, and I know that you and the prosecutors have been in touch to bring us to this point. However, I deal with violence and handguns on an almost daily basis, and while the extenuating circumstances of this case are clear, the obligation was yours to take care of these weapons. If more people lived up to their responsibilities, then maybe, even in a small way, we could alleviate some of the problems that face many, many parts of our country. Someone very easily could have stolen those handguns from your family's home and they would have been very valuable for a certain kind of criminal. The crux of all this is the following: I will suspend sentence on illegal possession of handguns, which is the most serious, but I am not going to suspend the sentence on the charge for failing to register firearms, which, while not as dire, will, in this case, mean that you'll serve fourteen days in Essex County Jail. I know this will come as a surprise, but I hope it's the kind of thing that will teach you—and everyone who is a gun owner—that these are not minor issues."

Henry was still absorbed in thinking about this man's strange hair as he began to grasp what was being said. He couldn't help but remember Lawrence's declarations that the matter was a done deal, and that there was no jail time, and this gave him just a bit of irrational security. *There must be some kind of mistake about this*, Henry thought. But as he looked over to the surrogate lawyer Lawrence had hired, the lawyer looked back with what was obviously distress, quickly saying, "It's a safe place. I promise you. Minimum security. It will pass quickly. Quicker than you think. This happens from time to time."

And at this point Henry understood that he would, in fact, be going to jail. It was only two weeks, but two weeks were plenty of time to suffer the worst kinds of prison torments. Henry even began to say something, clearly out of turn, although he only got through "But I . . ." before the judge said, "I know this isn't what you expected, but I don't see any alternative. I will give you five days, however, before you have to report for your sentence. That should give you a little time to arrange your affairs at home, although next Monday, at eight a.m., you need to appear at the Essex County Jail."

And now Henry finally felt the sort of dread a person would anticipate. Physically, that is, in the back of his neck, and he did all he could not to stumble and fall as he walked back through the courtroom and into the large marble hallway beyond.

16

RAPE, OF COURSE, was the only thing on Henry's mind as he drove back to Brooklyn, although Lawrence's colleague assured him that this was a complete impossibility. "It's not that type of place," he said. "You'll watch TV all day. That will be it. The food will be bad. At the very worst you might get shoved around a little by an inmate. But it's all very well run, this jail, and there won't be anyone in there who's particularly violent."

Not particularly violent was not at all reassuring to Henry, nor was the prospect of only being shoved around "a little." And there was no guarantee who would be in there. Perhaps some deranged recidivist criminal waiting around for his next trial would be his roommate, and Henry was quite thin, and mostly without body hair, and, since he took care of himself, he had what could only be considered very nice skin. Womanish, was now suddenly how he felt, and he couldn't shake the thoughts of violent sexual attacks for the four hours it took him to get back to Brooklyn.

It was all very distressing, although a good thing did happen to him just fifteen minutes after he arrived home, even if it was not really good enough to distract him entirely from his impending torture. Merrill called, just after Henry turned his electric kettle on, to say that he'd heard from the editor who had signed up Kipling and that she "absolutely adored!" *The Best of Youth.*

"She thinks it's one of the best things that's ever come across her desk," he said. "She kept saying that she had no idea Kipling had this kind of thing in him. I'm not making this up, Henry. And, believe me, this is sincere, because I've heard a lot of editors trash bigger than Kipling. This woman loved the book. And she's going to speed things forward, which shouldn't be too hard, since the sales team has been planning for a book from Kipling for awhile. She said she wants galleys finished in four months, which is something, and then for the pub date to be nine months from now. It shows that she thinks the thing is done and polished, at least. Anyway, we're very, very happy, Henry, and you should be happy too, because this really is quite an accomplishment. I mean, how it plays out for you will be a little stilted because of the ghostwriting thing, but I don't think you should worry about that. You've got true, true talent, and soon enough I'll be selling a book for you with your name on it."

And for just a little while after that, as Henry poured himself a large bourbon and sat down on his couch to look out at McCarren Park, he thought about what this particular success meant (in its deepest and absurdly romantic sense) and wondered if going to prison might not benefit him somehow in an artistic sort of way. It would teach him a great deal about a world that he really knew little about. And, after all (Henry had this particular idea well into his second very large drink— and bourbon always made him quite drunk), not many young Harvard men had been raped and beaten in prison, although he did then manage to grasp that being raped in prison was hardly a thing to find meaning in, no matter how much you might learn from it.

All these thoughts, though, soon slipped away to something far less speculative and far less philosophical—something very concrete and in the world, in fact. After pouring a third drink (a small one this time), Henry checked his email and discovered a very long note from Kipling. In it he said that he'd finally read the manuscript ("or a good two-thirds of it") and that, while he "liked some of it!" they still had a very long way to go.

The opening of the email was, of course, friendly, and filled with reflective ideas about the nature of art and the difficulties "people like us face when creation is unfolding.

"But I see this manuscript as deeply flawed," he continued, "on a number of levels. I had to skip a section or two because I've got a lot of obligations right now with scripts, but from what I've read, I feel like we're pretty far away from where we want this to be. I'm not saying you can't do it, and I want to keep working with you. I admire you. This manuscript, however, isn't working."

Kipling went on to describe again his feelings about parentheses, which Henry had actually used sparingly, and also offered some ideas about books he ought to read—books by "true writers."

At any rate, it all had a sickening and false angle to it (combined with the unreasonable expansiveness of a man likely using illegal stimulants) and, in the end, it was all simply too much for any thinking person to bear. Henry wondered what his obligations were at this point and planned on calling Merrill for help, but he also wondered whether Kipling's editor— the one who'd been such a fan of Henry's work—might be able to win the debate. Kipling, after all, was so poorly prepared on the manuscript—it was amazing that he had any opinion at all—that Henry thought he might be talked into accepting the book as it was, rather than insisting on things that made absolutely no sense, particularly coming from a person who admitted to having skipped sections of the book.

All this being said, there were other bad things Henry was

facing that were probably more significant than being bullied by celebrity actors. Now that the tedious aspects of his newly-embarked-on professional life had once again interrupted the small bit of peace he'd found in his bourbon, Henry realized once more, very plainly and with all its expected horror, that he would soon be in jail, and that life was short, and that he really needed to avoid worrying about people like Kipling.

17

AND SO THE TIME finally (nearly) came for Henry to head north to face his problems. On the night before, however, Henry planned for himself something of a "last day of freedom" event, although it was only he, Whitney, and Abby who went out. They met in Manhattan at a newly opened restaurant with a famous chef and prices that were far heavier than what the three were used to in Williamsburg. Henry insisted that he pay when he first made the invitation, and he did, in fact, pick up the check, which was surprisingly large after cocktails and wine were figured in (even for this kind of place). By the time Henry was signing the receipt, however, his mind was very far from the expense of the evening or the profound pleasure of the food. He'd imagined this moment before it arrived—when his happy wine-induced mood, accompanied by things like roasted poussin and blood sausage, would begin to give way to feelings of being overfull and far too drunk. He knew that this would be the time when he'd start feeling dread once again, and that, at that point, no subsequent heavy dinner or liquor were going to pull him out of it. Quite surprisingly, though (and it really was shocking), the very intense despair that Henry was now feeling was coming from a brand-new and entirely unexpected source and it took quite a bit of strength not to break into tears through the entire meal.

Abby had been especially happy that night, had chosen her food with some aggression—squab and (without irony) curried goat vol au vents—and after they ordered and as they were sipping their cocktails, she grinned and said, "Something really, really good has happened to me."

It had been quite a bit of time at this point since Henry had made any advances toward Abby, and it was even a substantial amount of time since he'd allowed himself to believe that he still had any feelings for her at all, but he could tell that the next words out of her mouth were going to be about a boy. That said, and as horrible as this prospect was, what followed was much, much worse than anything he could have imagined.

"I've got to tell you guys this, mostly because it'd be weird not to," she said, "but also because it's really on my mind. I know you know him, because you brought him to see me play, but Jonathan Kipling called me the day after the show and asked me out. He got my number from Merrill. Anyway, it's a strange thing to say so soon, just three weeks, but I have to say that I'm in love. I'm really, really, truly in love. And so is he, or that's what he tells me, but we've spent every single night together since he first called, and I don't see that changing anytime soon. I'm going to meet up with him after dinner tonight, in fact."

Abby said other things following this, although by now Henry was lost to a kind of internal dream, half an act of denial and half an act of mental transcendence, trying to avoid what could only be described as crushing sorrow. And he managed to stay focused on this interior moment, this personal mental exercise, for the entire dinner, knowing that if he just let a bit out, if he just made one mild comment along

the lines of, *Are you sure he's the right guy for you?* he'd surely follow with declarations like, *I'm the one you should be in love with!
Me! That guy is the worst fucking person I've ever known.* Apart
from the ironclad legal and contractual obligations that prevented Henry from telling Abby the ways in which Kipling was
an idiot, there was the even more important matter of personal shame that prevented him from speaking in this way.
Weeping at a dinner table was never a good tactic when trying
to prove one's virtue, and at last Henry took refuge in the idea
that surely Abby would soon see through this freak. The sad
fact was, though, that it did seem that she was now clinging to
(enchanted by) whatever illusions Kipling had spun, and that
if they had spent every night together for the past three weeks,
perhaps he too was enchanted, and that this mutual enchant-
ment might last for some time. It was very, very distressing.

Henry managed to survive the dinner (and further discussions about true love) without any kind of outward fit of
despair or anger. As they finally left the restaurant, however,
with Abby off to meet Kipling, Henry finally began to struggle
under the intensity of the pain he felt. He abruptly said he
had errands to run and that he needed to hop in his own cab
and that they'd all be best off finding their own ways home.
"Errands" was a foolish word of prevarication—it was eleven
p.m. at this point, and what errands could he be running?
But he didn't care. And when he got into the cab, he shut off
his phone and before long he was riding the elevator to his
apartment, feeling, he realized, with some amount of dismal
humor (humor entirely shot through with horrible despair)
that he'd found something far worse to keep his mind off
what he was facing for the next two weeks. And as he got into
bed—his own bed, with his own sheets, with a comforter that
his mother had made him in a period of quilt-making enthusiasm when Henry was eleven—he decided that two weeks in

a Massachusetts prison really might be just what he needed to think about how bad things had been over the past month or so. It was hard to tell. Prison was sure to be terrible. But not even the prospect of rape at this point could distract Henry from the pain he was now feeling over Abby. Thinking about Abby and Kipling being together really was the worst thing Henry could imagine, and that night he got no sleep at all.

PART
III

1

ALL THINGS TAKEN together, Henry found McCarren Park to be one of the most calming places in New York City, despite its endless hostile bustle and the tracts of dead grass. Some might argue in favor of Prospect Park or Central Park in the debate over New York's most serene places, but despite their obvious and undeniable beauty, those parks were clearly well-planned artifices, magnificently chiseled pieces of fabricated nature that could not possibly exist in what a person might call the wilderness. McCarren Park, however, actually did encapsulate the chaos of wild frontiers—albeit the chaos of crowded human frontiers—and in that sense it really did represent something close to the natural world. And (and this fact could hardly be argued against) it was absolutely captivating to look at. All that disorder could amuse a man for days, although it should be pointed out that "amusement" and "captivation" are not the same thing, and, in Henry's case, captivation (or mesmerization) was really closer to what he experienced as he frequently looked out from his balcony that fall. It was mysterious, why this was, although the origins of Henry's confused thinking were clear. The mystery was why his view over McCarren Park now provided such an enchanting spectacle at this moment, although by this point in Henry's life there wasn't really much of anything that Henry could rely on to explain his feelings.

That Jonathan Kipling was now a fixture in his life was a fact that Henry simply had to face, and he had done so with more courage than he'd thought himself capable of. And it was also a thing he couldn't permit himself to get angry about, because that kind of anger only led to more distress and the possible (further?) alienation of Abby. And in the past eleven months or so, Henry had only had to face a few interactions with Kipling, mostly at Abby's concerts (which Henry now only attended sporadically), so having to watch Abby with the egomaniac brute was not something he had to put up with very often.

But a new development was unfolding that was leading Henry to the sort of despair that rivaled even a broken heart. It was a thing that certainly made him even more angry—anger he couldn't tamp down—and which seemed even more unfair (if a person believes the words "fair" and "unfair" have any place in describing the course of things like love). Advanced reviews had been coming in for *The Best of Youth* (which Kipling's editor had managed to keep almost exactly as Henry had written it—word for word, really, despite Kipling's earlier criticism), and in just the previous few weeks Kipling was being heralded by the experts in children's literature as something of a modern master. The reviews were in the trade publications—the book was still over a month from official release—so they were mostly the opinions of the librarians and booksellers who spent their days in the pursuit of reading and bookselling and interesting others in books. (English departments in the great universities were still a bit away from assigning Kipling in their graduate seminars.) But trade publications were certainly more important than literature professors in determining the success of a forthcoming novel, especially for the young adult market, and there, in that venue, Kipling was being celebrated with what can only be seen as something close to abandon. As one reviewer wrote, "Truly exceptional writing is not a thing that comes around often, and reviewers have to be circumspect when heaping praise on the latest novels to come along, but here, I believe, we are looking at perhaps one of the best portrayals of a young person's vision of the world since *Catcher in the Rye,* and surely the book rivals the very best coming out now for the adult literary market."

Other reviews were a bit less dramatic, but what was clear from all of them was that the verdict concerning the novel was that it was "a real winner!" and that Kipling ("A man for all seasons!"), already having proven his deep understanding of story via motion pictures, was unquestionably a "magician of the written word" as well.

Celebrity magazines and blogs had also gotten on the bandwagon, declaring his novel to be among the most important cultural events of the year, and these publications in particular led to another aspect of Kipling's rise as a distinguished writer: his Amazon preorder numbers were remarkable. His book moved around the top hundred books on Amazon before anyone (any layperson, that is) had even had a chance to read it. And this only fueled more coverage, again from the blogs and celebrity journals, but also again from the trade publications, which began describing Kipling in longer articles, portraying the beginnings of "a publishing phenomenon," emphasizing that the author's novel could rival the "very best work produced by writers across all genres."

Henry did what he could to take Kipling's success with equanimity, and he even attempted to try to feel a sort of pride concerning what the critics were saying. They loved Henry's work, after all, and that was surely something to be happy about. But when a somewhat highbrow magazine said that the industry was clearly looking at a sort of modern Roald Dahl, here, at this point, Henry finally burst into tears and faced up to the fact that this was all a terrible development. (Henry adored Roald Dahl, even more than Salinger.)

Even through his tears Henry was able to grasp that Kipling's previous fame had, of course, great bearing on the warm acceptance of the book. Kipling was well liked by almost everyone, and he'd already authored several successful picture books (although the reception for those was not what Kipling was now experiencing). The truth was, though, that even the most hardheaded reviewer could not help but be swayed by the fact that the book was written by a Hollywood star. Had the book come out under Henry's name, perhaps the reception would not have been so enthusiastic.

That being said, Henry felt quite strongly that *The Best of Youth* really was an excellent piece of writing and he could hardly avoid facing the fact that a person he truly hated was getting credit for it. Worse, perhaps, there was a good chance that a woman Henry had deep affection for (whatever the slippery nature of this affection) was responding the way everyone else was: with the thought that Kipling was a mysterious and deeply talented man, a great thinker, and capable of who knew what when it came to the creative and narrative arts. It was really all too much to think about, and eventually, after the tears following that most recent review in the highbrow venue, and after two glasses of Pernod (this was Henry's new favorite drink), he turned his gaze from McCarren Park and headed indoors to sit at his computer and try to work on "his own stuff" which, truth be told, he hadn't done much of at all over the past many months.

2

AND IT WAS THIS despair that Henry was now conscious of when he was with Abby. Henry had to remind himself that the bitterness and resentment he felt toward Abby was due to his own problems, not hers. Still, Henry could not help but also feel that Abby had changed in the past months, not in her substance, but in the way the world seemed to wear on her now. It used to be that during their long dinners Abby took a keen and comprehensive interest in reforming various aspects of Henry's life. Now she said things like, "I can't be the one to tell you how to handle a problem like that" and "You have to figure that out for yourself." It was too strange to process, Abby suggesting that she didn't have the exact solution to Henry's problems, since in times past Abby had (as she understood it) the very most precise answer to all of Henry's troubles. *I can't be the one to tell you how to handle a problem like that*—it was extremely unsettling. Henry was sure such words had never passed her lips before she met Kipling. Still, one thing was also true: Henry was getting better at what they call moving on, or, at the very least, somehow letting things rest that were beyond his control.

An excellent place to learn such things, of course, is prison, although his two weeks at the "Essex County Farm," as it was called inside, were surprisingly uneventful. They were almost pleasant, really, in a deep psychological way, since Henry found that he was entirely incapable of altering anything distasteful in his life and simply had to take what came his way. A young man with a bit of money in Williamsburg, for instance, had limitless decisions to make every night concerning dinner. At the Essex County Farm, it really didn't matter if you were in the mood for boiled potatoes or not. That was what was on the tray and that was what you got. And the fact was that if a person liked salty, fatty food, then prison was just the thing. In that sense, the food wasn't too far from what Henry often ate in Brooklyn, with the difference coming in the quality and the freshness of the ingredients. No grass-fed cows were slaughtered to make the Farm's meatballs, and the bread used to make their so-called meatball grinders certainly had nothing like flaxseed or oat bran in it. It was, in fact, the very whitest, fluffiest bread Henry had ever seen.

Henry even found the people to be not too terrible. He was jostled in line a few times, but there seemed to be no culture of rape in Massachusetts minimum-security prisons, and that, after all, was all that mattered. On the other hand, in moments of hope before his incarceration, Henry had also imagined that he'd meet some kind of "old-timer" who would take him under his wing and protect him and tell him stories of life on the other side. Such an inmate, however, never appeared. Of course, Henry's active mental anticipatory life also included fantasies of knowing karate and being able to defend other falsely imprisoned young persons (maybe other young and distraught Harvard men) from gangs of thieves and murderers. This dream too did not materialize. In fact, the only thing that was true, that did match up to his general ideas about prison life, was the boredom. There was simply not much to do in jail.

And one good thing did come from the experience. It was a lesson, as it were, although the lesson came most forcefully early on, as he was being led through the prison on the very first morning when all his horrible expectations and fears were most ripe. The lesson was that there was simply nothing a person could do to anticipate what came next in life and that a very happy trip up north to recover ancient family artifacts could lead to entirely unexpected outcomes and there was absolutely no way to prevent such events. The world was a troubling and uncertain place, it struck Henry on the Monday morning he surrendered himself to the Essex County Jail, and there were forces at work that could very easily alter the course of your life.

This truth about the tenuous nature of life, of course, was something about which Henry did have some previous experience. To get a call one evening in Cambridge, Mass. (after studying several hours for a very important examination about the Hundred Years' War) and hearing a young police officer on Cape Cod (with his own kind of sorrow coming through in his voice) make the announcement that both his parents were dead, well, Henry understood that the world was not a place where planners and schedulers really belonged. Still, jail in Essex County, it was not expected, and even if it only echoed lessons learned long ago, Henry felt he had learned them once again.

3

THE END OF HIS jail term did not conclude Henry's legal obligations, of course, and once he was "back on the street," as it were, Henry set about fulfilling his community service, which turned out not be so terrible and, in fact, eventually led to something quite good in his life.

Henry's lawyer had kept his promise and worked out that the community service be performed in New York (some unlucky Massachusetts resident arrested in New York was doing his work back in Essex County in exchange), and on his first day of community service Henry filled out several questionnaires to assess what skills he had to offer New York City. Henry was surprised by how welcoming the whole process seemed to be. It was as if he'd come to volunteer as a free and concerned citizen. When he met with the official who was assigned to his case, Henry was even complimented on his impressive background and it was suggested that the city was in need of people who could teach some of the things that Henry was good at, "Especially general literacy and writing."

Along these lines, Henry agreed to meet with an HR person at the New York City Department of Corrections, and soon found himself in a strangely secure office near City Hall talking to an astonishingly tall and imposing man who, nevertheless, seemed very friendly. This placement specialist's conclusions were, however, that Henry would not be a good match for New York's prison system. "I don't think you know what you're in for in here," he said, smiling. "I like to hire guys who look like they can take at least one punch if things get dicey."

"But I've been to jail myself," Henry said. "I know what to expect."

"You've been to a rural jail in Massachusetts, which is a little different than what's going on in Rikers Island."

Henry felt a little insulted by this, and he even protested again that he was sure he could handle it. The man smiled again and shrugged and said, "Tell you what: think about it for a few days, but I will say, in the past few years I've had teachers stabbed, beaten half to death, and once, a while back, something even worse happened that you don't want to know about. I can't think this is for you. Especially writing classes. Some of our inmates can get pretty touchy about taking criticism."

Henry left the office assuring the man that he didn't need to think about it at all and that he was positive he could do a good job. But as the rest of the day passed, Henry's bravado diminished, and he decided he might do well to listen to the HR administrator's advice, especially since the menace of rape was once again on his mind.

Another alternative was to work as an after-school tutor for young people—with "at-risk students," as the first placement specialist described them to Henry in a second interview. Henry quickly agreed to this proposal and was given a spot at a school in Bushwick, and soon he was spending three afternoons a week helping several teachers who managed remedial classes.

In this line of work, Henry actually felt fairly competent, and he found that it was easier than he had expected to develop a rapport with the students. Unfortunately, the students (with honest affection) categorically refused to do anything Henry asked them to do. Generally, he worked with groups of four or five students in afternoon study periods to go over homework. But just as Henry would begin to ask if they had any questions about what they'd covered in their classes that day, they'd start asking their own questions concerning things like what kind of music Henry listened to, his various food preferences, and, of course, his romantic life. On this last matter, however, they were impenetrable ciphers, using slang that Henry did not understand at all (but which he was sure described all sorts of astonishing sexual acts) before bursting into wild laughter, often falling off their chairs to extend the theatrical effect. The thing is that they never asked a single question without a broad smile, and on several occasions they told Henry things like, "We like you a lot, Henry. You're a good guy." And it really seemed like they meant it. And while Henry blushed and awkwardly avoided answering questions like, "Do you ever bring your girl a cappuccino?" (followed by wild laughter that would throw everyone to the floor), Henry was willing to talk to them about life and his own experiences, ranging from his parents' deaths to why he didn't like to eat hormone-treated meat. It was all, actually, very pleasurable. It wasn't like community service at all. And this, he gathered, was the reason—his failure to provide any actual useful service, that is—that Henry was finally fired, with one of the most explicit condemnations he'd ever received. "Why does every fucking jackass rich-guy criminal think they're cut out to help young people?" the teacher, a Ms. Ryan, yelled one afternoon. "I have to say, though, Henry, that you, *you* have been the absolute fucking worst we've had. You've wasted everyone's fucking time and as far as I can tell made them even worse readers than when you started. You really think they need a person to sit around and shoot the shit with?"

"Maybe with just a bit more time I could get the knack of

it," Henry replied. He was sincere in this offer, but somewhat certain it would not be well received.

"Listen, any more time with you and they'll all be in jail themselves. Forget it. Sorry for being so harsh about all this, by the way, but you're a total fucking idiot and I have too much to do around here."

Henry left quickly after this, and, despite his hurt feelings, he found himself feeling a certain amount of sympathy for Ms. Ryan. After all, he and his students had, in truth, accomplished absolutely nothing.

At any rate, at his third meeting with the placement specialist, Henry suggested that maybe there was some kind of simple job for him that didn't involve interacting with other people. "I think that dull rather than engaging might be the best thing for me."

The placement man nodded and asked, "Inside or outside?"

After they discussed a range of possibilities, including things like park cleanup and building maintenance, they arrived at what was actually a good match. Henry agreed to reshelve books at libraries around the city. "You'd be moved to wherever they need you," the man said. "Basically, wherever there's a backlog, although that's almost everywhere. And they may ask you to do other things around the libraries, but mostly it will just be reshelving."

"All right," Henry said. "That sounds good to me."

4

AND IT TURNED OUT that Henry liked this job quite a bit. It was easy, his bosses were generally nice, and the work actually seemed to amount to something close to community service: at the end of the day, at one branch or another, a large pile of books was put away and ready for new borrowers. The people Henry worked with were also often quite interesting— the backlogs at libraries occasionally required more than one ex-convict to reshelve them—and Henry interacted with rehabilitated drug addicts, pickpockets, white-collar criminals, etc., although most of the time he and his workmates had headphones on, so there wasn't too much opportunity to chat. There was one exception to this, however, and this exception would end up being very significant in Henry's life.

In the middle of July (now still some months before *The Best of Youth*'s advanced reviews came out) Henry was sent to the Inwood Branch to deal with "a catastrophe." Some sort of crazy person had run through ten aisles of the stacks, pulling off shelf after shelf of books and dumping them on the floor, and by the time the lunatic had been restrained by the security guard, he'd left thousands of books on the floor and in need of being reshelved in their "exact proper order."

Henry was called early on a Sunday morning and asked if he could come in to help "handle this emergency" and was promised double hours against his obligations if he did so. Thus, on a fairly hot Sunday morning at ten o'clock, he arrived at the Inwood Branch, where he met the head librarian (still astounded by her misfortune) and then, to his surprise, found himself being reintroduced to the tattooed and now-former girlfriend (he'd heard they'd broken up) of the fiction editor at *Suckerhead*, the woman who had, apparently, loved the short story he had submitted. It seemed that she was some kind of criminal too, also there to earn double hours toward her own community service debt. It was this elaborately decorated woman (Sasha, again, was her name) who would turn out to be so important.

5

IN GENERAL, HENRY was not easily shocked by other
people's modes of self-expression, and he was certainly not
against what might be called experimental behavior. It was
just that he so rarely engaged in that sort of thing himself.
Henry had never even contemplated any sort of "body art" and
he was normally dressed entirely in bland clothes from popular but reasonably priced stores—lots of solid-colored shirts
and nondescript trousers. But again, this was not because of
disapproval of elaborate dress or physical ornamentation. It
was simply not the sort of thing that he felt suited him. That
being said, Henry could not help but experience a renewed
sense of astonishment when he saw Sasha, because of the
enormous number of tattoos on her arms and legs, and running up her neck. The truth was that he'd never actually seen
her in full light. In fact, he'd never seen her outside of an art-
fully darkened bar, and the harsh fluorescent lighting of the
Inwood Branch actually caused him to avert his eyes as they
shook hands, just after the head librarian reintroduced them.
Henry concluded that his averted glance was only meant to
hide the fact that he wanted to conceal his fascination and
not because of any negative feelings he had. Also, she struck
him now as being surprisingly attractive, and this was a thing
that often made Henry redirect his gaze.

For her part, Sasha managed to say, "I know you." But she also seemed suddenly shy as she said this, turning her head away as well. In fact, in the bright light of the Inwood Library, she almost seemed delicate and nervous, especially since the tattoos that crept up to her face were—Henry hadn't recognized this before—tiny roses. Her face, actually, was mostly free of ornamentation, other than a small clear stud of some sort below her lower lip and a tiny silver hoop in each of her ears. Her arms and calves, on the other hand, were, by Henry's estimation (eyes still averted but quickly glancing across her body) almost entirely covered.

At any rate, this inspection lasted only for a matter of seconds because the head librarian was still so flustered by the attack of the insane man that she wanted to get started right away. She put Henry at one end of the ransacked aisles and Sasha at the other, and soon Henry was listening to some kind of avant-garde musical podcast he'd found on a Canadian website, and Sasha too had her earbuds in. It was not until the end of the day, in fact, that they spoke again, when they both arrived at the center shelf. They quickly nodded and smiled, but as Henry went back to his work, he felt a gentle tap on his shoulder. He turned, pulling out his earbuds, and Sasha said, still smiling, still just a bit shy, "So what'd you do, Henry?"

Henry wasn't sure what she meant by this, so he simply repeated the question. "What did I do?"

"What did you do to get assigned here?" she said. "How'd you get your community service? Unless maybe you're a volunteer?"

"No, no," Henry said. "I'm not a volunteer." And then, after a pause, he added, "Weapons violations. Illegal handguns. I got busted near Boston."

Sasha laughed, although she seemed not to be sure if Henry was joking. At last she said, "Pretty sketchy. I'm impressed."

"Well, it was all a mistake," Henry said. "The guns were

antiques. I inherited them from my parents. I was taking them from upstate New York to an antiques dealer in Massachusetts. I didn't register them properly. I wasn't walking around with illegal guns on purpose."

Sasha nodded and smiled. "Yeah, I figured," she said. Henry wasn't sure if this was some kind of slanted insult, but Sasha was smiling so broadly and now struck him as so nice (and so interested in Henry's answer) that he decided there was probably nothing aggressive in what she had said. And after all, she was a fan of his work, although at the moment he wasn't sure if she remembered writing the note on the back of the rejection slip he'd gotten from *Suckerhead*. Henry did, for an instant, consider reminding her of it, but the only formulation he could think of was, *I just wanted to thank you for really appreciating my writing*, and that hardly seemed like something he ought to say. At last Henry just asked, "What did you do?"

"Got busted for an open container for a third time," she replied. "They give you a lot of hours on your third time, if you're not an alcoholic or homeless, but I really don't actually drink that much. I like to drink in parks. That's my problem. And I'm not very discreet, I guess."

Henry nodded and said, "Yeah, I understand. What's better than drinking in parks? But three times. That's a lot."

"Yeah, and I wasn't even close to drunk for any one of them. It's hard to believe you're not allowed to drink a beer when you're sitting under a tree." Here Sasha hesitated for a moment, then added, "So, listen. I hate to say this, but I've got to leave now. I made arrangements earlier with the officer I work with. The librarian knows too. All the same, I feel bad leaving you. We're almost done, though, so maybe it will only take you another hour to finish up. So is that all right? If I leave?"

"No problem," Henry quickly said. "I can get this done on

my own. And it's a double hour, so it's good for me for that reason too."

"Okay." Sasha smiled. "Well, thanks. Good luck on living down those weapons charges. And I really hope I see you in another library! I've still got a lot of time to serve."

"Me too," Henry replied. "Maybe I'll see you around."

Henry finished up his work for the day as quickly as he and Sasha had anticipated he would. Soon he too was leaving the Inwood Branch, and now thinking quite a bit, much to his surprise, about Sasha.

6

AT ANY RATE, for the next stretch of time Henry continued his various duties with the libraries, and he found the work to be reasonably pleasant. In October, though, now about the time that *The Best of Youth* was getting its prepublication reviews, Henry's duties were changed slightly and he was given an assignment in Brooklyn that he was told would last for a few months. He was a little apprehensive about being placed on a single project for so long—who knew what he was being locked into? But when he arrived at the library's warehouse in Red Hook, he was astonished (thrilled?) to discover that his partner in the project would be Sasha.

He'd spent some time over the past many weeks thinking that he ought to contact her somehow, but he never had the courage to enact the various plans he'd devised. Emailing her to propose dinner, for instance, seemed extremely risky, as did using any of the other popular modes of communication for suggesting such a thing. Thus, when he arrived at his assignment and saw that she was his workmate, he felt unusually lucky.

And Sasha, surprisingly, seemed very happy too.

"It's the gun trafficker!" Sasha yelled when she saw Henry. She was standing with a short, well-dressed man who was clearly in charge of whatever it was that Henry would be doing at the warehouse.

"Yes, it's me!" Henry said, trying to contain his grin. "Are you working here as well?"

"Yep!" Sasha replied. "And I think it's just the two of us!"

At this point the well-dressed man interrupted to confirm that it would just be the two of them. "Just you two, for the next few months," he said. And then, after introducing himself to Henry as Nicholas Boyer, he began explaining the task he and Sasha were being given.

Their assignment (which Nicholas described as he led Henry and Sasha through the warehouse and past countless stacks of boxes) would consist of cataloging thousands of books that had been left to the library by a man named Sam Harrington, who, at the time of his death, owned a gigantic apartment on Fifth Avenue, as well as homes in Litchfield and Southampton. In general, this was not an unusual kind of bequest. People often donated their book collections with the idea that they might do some good once they were gone. Unfortunately, most collections contained little or nothing that was useful to the library. This particular collection, however, likely had among it some books that were worth significantly more than the standard price-per-kilo paid by interior decorators, so the New York Public Library's bibliographers needed a full account before they could make decisions about what to auction off and what to keep in their special collections. Mr. Harrington had obviously been extremely wealthy and had a few items—medieval manuscripts, unusual author letters, etc.— that were immediately culled because their whereabouts and existence were well known. But as for the various Hemingway first editions and books signed by the likes of John Dos Passos and Willa Cather, there was no telling where they were in the boxes. And certainly there were lesser-known authors who had also produced books of value, and these especially would need to be scrutinized by the library's experts.

Interestingly, Harrington had assembled his own extensive catalog, but he'd long ago been lost to Alzheimer's and had never gotten around to computerizing it. And this handwritten catalog had, surprisingly, been destroyed in a small fire, caused by a grandson who had left an untended cigarette in his grandfather's study in the Litchfield property. The fire damaged several books as well, but the bulk of the collection had been elsewhere, and the fire department was able to put out the fire before it swept through the house and into the main library. This story was quite interesting to Henry, especially since he was always fascinated by irresponsible grandsons of rich people. But as he listened to Nicholas give them the details of it all (as they walked in a circle around the warehouse looking at the boxes of books), Henry mostly thought about how happy he was that Sasha was there.

7

AND SASHA INDICATED that this was her feeling as well: "I was hoping I'd run into you again," she said after Boyer's tour. "But this seems like extra good fortune, since this gig will be for the next few months. Not just a day of reshelving books where we don't get to talk."

"Yes," Henry said, and, although he wanted to add more, he stopped because he himself was also so excited that he imagined he might embarrass himself.

"I remember reading that story you wrote about that lonely eighty-year-old guy," she said. "I loved it! I wrote that to you."

And now Henry felt even more nervous, but just as he was wondering how badly he was blushing, Sasha suddenly turned her head and looked away from Henry, and he could see that she was blushing too, surprised, it seemed, by her expression of enthusiasm. It was a strange phenomenon, bashfulness, for someone so well tattooed.

In any event, before long Henry and Sasha were opening their first boxes, each with a laptop they'd been given by Nicholas, and beginning their cataloging project using some kind of simple but highly specialized database program that was, apparently, built exclusively for librarians.

The work was fun, that first day, with just the right amount of interesting subject matter—original copies of *The Dial*, first editions of Jack London and Joseph Conrad, several some-what pornographic French novels (so identified by Sasha, who seemed to speak French). But there was also enough straight-forward clerical work to be done that they could chat as they went, not always having to concentrate too hard. It was a very easy kind of pleasure, listening to Sasha talk about the books she liked and what she liked about Brooklyn and even listen-ing to her give short translations from the French erotic litera-ture: "Her nipples pressed against his cheekbones as she said, 'We mustn't be doing this,'" and "twenty strikes against the buttocks is the thing for you, my lady, although I'll give you just ten if you bring your maid back in to watch."

And they had serious conversations as well—Sasha's father had fled her family when she was two and she spent some time talking about how close she was with her mother despite the fact that they were nothing alike. "She was pretty upset when I moved here to go to NYU, and she loves to tell me that New York has had a terrible influence on me, even though we're really tight. She'd do anything for me, but mostly what she'd like to do is fix me up with a nice boy from Grosse Pointe and de-pierce me, despite the fact that that doesn't really work. And no amount of laser therapy is getting rid of my tattoos."

"Yes, I think they're there for life," Henry said, although just as quickly he wondered if this was somehow rude. But she swiftly replied, "Yep, there for life!," seeming to indicate that she had no problem at all with Henry inspecting her and forming opinions about her body.

Thus, the first day of the new job was patently excellent, and Henry walked to his subway (he only shared three short blocks of the journey with Sasha) thinking about all he and Sasha had talked about and just how lucky he was to be work-ing with her. He did think of things he'd wished he'd said, and good ways to bring up again subjects upon which he felt he hadn't quite performed well enough. The next day, though, passed as well as the first (without revisionist reflections from Henry), and they were on to other conversational topics as soon as the day began. And the following day as well, the conversation was just as happy, although this particular day ended with a bit of difficulty, since it meant that their current work week (both were on the hook for three four-hour days per week) was at an end and that it would not be until the next Tuesday that they'd see each other again. Henry did consider asking Sasha out to something like drinks or dinner, but he concluded that this was too emotionally dangerous, especially since it could lead to a few months of intolerable embarrassment if they had to work together after she rejected his advances. On this account, though, Sasha provided just a bit of a solution.

"Why don't you stop by my job—my real job—over the weekend? I work at a gallery in Chelsea. The show we've got on now is great, and if you came at about six or so you could buy me a beer after we close." To this, Henry agreed, and it was quickly determined that he'd be by late Saturday afternoon to see her at her work. And that Saturday he was indeed in Manhattan, very much looking forward to what Henry was barely allowing himself to consider a date.

8

SASHA WORKED FOR A gallery called Christian Conrad. It was on Twenty-second, near Tenth, and, according to what she told Henry, she'd done well there. Her success, however, was entirely fortuitous, she insisted, coming mostly as a result of the gallery's unanticipated triumphs with three consecutive shows of Eastern European painters who were suddenly in vogue. They were excellent painters, to be sure, but why their excellence rose above the excellence of others was a puzzle.

"I also speak Hungarian," she'd told Henry. "And to be honest, Eastern European people seem to like me. I did a year abroad there, in Hungary, which is why my Hungarian is good. Plus my grandmother, on my father's side, is Hungarian, and she spoke it with me growing up, so I guess the sounds don't throw me like they do most people."

This all interested Henry very much, and on his way to Sasha's gallery he thought about how much fun it would be to hear her speak Hungarian, all the while looking for places where he might take her for a beer. Chelsea always seemed very strange to him, almost as if everyone in his McCarren Park building had aged fifteen years and moved to Manhattan. Still, there seemed to be several interesting places to have a drink, and Sasha would probably be good for a recommendation. And they did end up somewhere that Sasha liked—a kind of Swiss restaurant (they'd just spent an hour looking at the latest lithographs by some sort of rebellious Czechoslovakian person)—and after a beer at the bar they decided to eat dinner there. They talked with the same kind of ease they'd found together at work, and Henry was even relaxed enough not to be preoccupied with the implications of the event. And when they parted (at Sasha's subway back to her end of Brooklyn), Henry didn't even consider trying to kiss her. This is not to say that he didn't want to, but he was just so happy and not feeling any sort of pressure to make a move, as it were, and he embraced her warmly as they said farewell without any kind of awkward advance, wistful sigh, or, as was common with him, a lengthy speech about the "confusing feelings" he was having.

Henry even found that he was excited to work on his writing that weekend, feeling no desire to go out or even to eat anything more than a few bowls of noodles. And on Tuesday, back in Red Hook, things continued as they had the previous week, and when Thursday arrived and their work for the week was done, they once again made plans, this time to meet Whitney and his girlfriend for dinner, although it was all arranged in such a straightforward way that Henry again couldn't bring himself to call it a date. By this point, however, he was fully conscious of the fact that he liked Sasha very much.

9

THUS, IT PROMISED TO be a good weekend, but dinner was not until Saturday, and Friday brought with it a fairly ugly scene for Henry. He'd promised Abby he'd attend a show of hers, which he happily did, despite the fact that there was a chance Kipling would be there—the advanced reviews, by this point, were now out and Henry had, by then, completed his earlier reflections about the soothing chaos of McCarren Park (and his love of Pernod).

"I haven't seen you in over a month," Abby had yelled on the phone. This was true, and it made Henry feel bad enough that he agreed to go to her concert. It really did trouble Henry that he and Abby had been so distant recently, but when he finally arrived at the venue for Abby's performance—it was at a sort of fashionable basement bar on the Lower East Side—he remembered why he'd been avoiding her: Kipling was there, and soon Henry was sitting beside him and having exactly the kind of conversation he'd been working to avoid.

It had already been a bad day on that front. That morning Abby had emailed Henry to confirm plans and had attached a link to a popular morning news program that featured an interview with Kipling. Henry hadn't seen the interview yet and he was horrified to spend the next three minutes watching Kipling talk about how "vital" writing was to him, how it was an "essential component" of his "entire outlook on life."

"This book," he said, "has been one of the most liberating artistic experiences of my life. And as challenging and agonizing and painstaking as the process is, not many things have ever filled me with this kind of passion."

At this point, Henry still wasn't sure if Kipling had even read the novel, and certainly his comments were so vague that Henry had to conclude that his artistic front man still had only a flimsy grasp of what the book contained, other than that it included a young person and an old person ("in a relationship that gets at the very heart of the troubles our nation is seeing today"). Thankfully, Kipling did not expand on his theories about the social history of China.

At any rate, it was all completely repulsive, and so that night at Abby's event, when he spotted Kipling (and Kipling spotted him), Henry did what he could to come up with a reason not to sit together—not to speak at all, in fact. But before he could formulate a proper excuse for such behavior, he found himself seated next to the great author, listening to tales of what a "wild ride this book shit" had been. "And the fucking sales!" he said. "They're already through the roof." (The book was just now starting to appear in stores.)

Fortunately, the music started soon after Henry arrived, preventing any type of real conversation, and Henry found that he made it through the next hour without having to do much more than ask and answer mundane questions about Merrill and the house in England and the weather. When the first set ended, Kipling went backstage to see Abby—Henry declined his own invitation—so it looked as if after another loud set of viola and bassoon music Henry could leave without having to interact much more.

But once the music started again Henry decided to use the

men's room—there had been too many people waiting during the break—and he was startled to discover, as he went into one of the several single-occupancy bathrooms, that Kipling was close on his heels and that he followed him through the door and locked it behind them as they stepped in.

"Hey, hey," Kipling said. "How about a line with your colleague?"

"What?" Henry replied with an inquisitive nod of his head, although he knew exactly what he had been asked.

"Cocaine?" Kipling said, his own head-nod working now, and with the slight smile he added it seemed that Kipling believed this was an offer of some kind of camaraderie. A sincere one. Kipling quickly qualified the offer by adding, "I don't do this every night. I really love it, but it's not very good for you. That's what they say, at least."

"Yes, no, thanks," Henry said, surprisingly feeling a little charitable now toward Kipling, again because this did seem like a friendly gesture. "It's been a while and it's not really my thing anymore." Henry had done the drug only once, in college, and he'd enjoyed himself so much that he drank half a bottle of tequila and vomited on the floor of an apartment belonging to a woman he'd felt he was in love with. After that, he couldn't hear the word "cocaine" without feeling incredible remorse. Henry once again thought of that terrible night and how he had tried to clean up his own vomit with the mania that only coke can provide, and by the time Henry had gotten around to focusing on the issue at hand, Kipling was chopping up lines on the face of a small mirror that he had pulled from his jacket pocket. It was not something Henry wanted to be part of, but he didn't know what protocol was in this kind of situation and he was afraid to open the door to leave, in case someone saw what Kipling was doing. But Kipling started talking again, once more shifting Henry's attention.

"So what do you think of our waitress?" Kipling said, smiling. It was the sort of question to which Henry had grown accustomed—the kindness of others, everyone trying to help him with what they seemed to think was his obvious failing in life.

"Well, I don't think she's really right for me," Henry replied. "And there's someone I'm interested in at the moment, so I think I'm all set." These responses usually ended this kind of conversation quickly enough, but Kipling's next comment was not what Henry was used to.

"Well, she's right for me," Kipling said, "and I'm going to fuck her tonight."

"What?" Henry said abruptly, looking up at his employer with honest confusion.

"I love women like her," Kipling continued. "Bohemian, bleach-blond hair, that tongue stud. She's probably got Rilke lines tattooed on her back."

Henry didn't know how to react, but at last, just as Kipling finished a line, he said, "Are you joking?"

"No. I like girls like that. Don't you?"

Henry still wasn't sure he understood the nature of the discussion they were having. "You're really going to sleep with her?" he said at last.

"I'm really going to fuck her."

Henry paused. "Won't Abby be a little put out by that?"

Kipling lowered his head and then replied, smiling, "Well, Henry, since you're nice enough to ask, I'd say we have an understanding."

"You have an understanding?"

"Well, I have an understanding and I assume she understands it. And don't get pissed at me. You can tell her if you want. I've got nothing to hide."

"But she knows you do this kind of thing?"

"She should assume that I do this kind of thing until I tell her otherwise, right?" Kipling was smiling, but his voice had taken an abrasive tone and his coked-up glare was now clearly signaling Henry to back off. Kipling held his gaze for a moment, then looked back at his mirror—it was resting on the translucent blue counter of the bathroom's sink and Henry suddenly wondered if maybe he ought to reconsider his refusal of the cocaine. Maybe what he really needed was some kind of consciousness-altering experience to ease him through his increasingly confusing world. But then, astonishingly, and without the benefit of the coke, he yelled, "You know, you are such a fucking asshole. Abby's in love with you. You want to fuck our waitress? Abby's in love with you. You're such a horrible person. You are such a fucking horrible person."

Kipling didn't look up from the business he'd embarked on until he'd completed another healthy line. After that he turned to Henry and looked at him with the sort of composure Henry had come to expect from his collaborator. In the next instant, though, Kipling suddenly lurched forward, thrusting his face about three inches from Henry's. And Henry became aware, once again, that Kipling was far taller than him and certainly his actor's regime of exercise and healthy diet had rendered him quite a bit more fit than Henry. Still, Kipling didn't throw any punches, as Henry now expected he might. (Henry was suddenly recalling what Kipling had done to their waiter the night his steak was overcooked.) Instead Kipling just glared at Henry, although his lips were pulled into a deliberate and careful smile. Finally Kipling said, "Henry, don't be such a little fucking cunt. I fucking hate little cunts like you. So don't be one." And with that, he turned back to his mirror. Here, Henry took his leave, not concerned what someone might see when he opened the door.

Obviously, it was a confusing exchange, and Henry wasn't sure what he ought to do in terms of alerting Abby. He decided to keep his mouth shut, but he did manage, later on, to broach with her the more general matter of Kipling's repulsive character.

The show was over and Abby had packed up her viola and come to their table, and after Kipling made a few customary remarks about the excellence of her performance he said, "I've got to meet someone in a little while, and you look utterly beat. Why don't you head home to get some rest and we'll reconvene in the morning?"

Abby paused, took a breath, then said, "I am really, really tired, so maybe that's a good idea."

As she stepped forward to give Kipling (still seated) a kiss on the cheek, Henry abruptly stood and put on his jacket. "I need to go too," he said, and a minute later he was walking out the door behind Abby.

As they passed onto the street, Henry looked over at her and could see, despite the comment's origins, that Kipling had been right. Abby looked completely exhausted, although the weariness seemed psychological as much as physical. And once again, it made Henry furious that she was going out with someone who'd send her home under the pretense of "getting some rest" so he could sleep with the waitress. Still, Henry didn't bring up his encounter with Kipling, although, now that they were outside, he couldn't help but abruptly ask, "Why the hell are you going out with such a fucking asshole?"

Abby's exhaustion suddenly disappeared and now she looked very angry. "Don't fucking start in with me, Henry," she yelled, arching her shoulders. "I'm not in the mood for one of your explanations of family lines and irrational sexual taboos. You and me, it's not going to happen."

"I didn't mean it like that," Henry said, now horrified. And maybe for the first time in the past year or so he was being honest about this matter—he was shockingly void of romantic inclinations at that moment.

Still, he must have also looked very hurt, because Abby

quickly said, "Sorry, sorry, sorry. I'm sorry, Henry. Really. I'm sorry. Jonathan was right. I'm exhausted. And on edge. Very on edge. And you're right that I've had better relationships than this. Practically speaking. I've had better situations than this. Jonathan is hard. It's hard."

Here, Abby paused for more than a few seconds, then continued with a renewed desperation in her voice. "But Henry, I'm so totally fucking whipped. I'm really fucking whipped. And we do have a lot of great things going. He really is brilliant, Henry. You've seen his movies. You were the one who told me how much you liked them. And his book. It's so, so good. I mean, I suppose right now I'm just hoping things steady up some, because, Henry, I really am gone with this one, for whatever reason, so you can't give me a hard time. You really, really can't give me a hard time. It's not going to help. I'm gone. It's not going to help."

Henry was silent. His instincts were still to sound the alarm and beg Abby to reconsider. But he also knew that his inclinations in this regard wouldn't lead anywhere. Abby's assessment was correct—he really wasn't going to talk her out of anything. Henry even grasped that if he told Abby that Kipling was back in the bar seducing their waitress she'd probably just tear up and then tell Henry she didn't mind.

Henry said at last (trying to cast his feelings in a different light), "Look, I'm sorry. I guess we don't hang out like we used to and it makes me sad. But I know that will change back. I know we're friends. I don't have any dismal vision of our future. It's just a little rocky right now and I miss you."

Abby really did now seem to be holding back tears. But she didn't break. She just stepped forward, gave Henry a hug, and said, "Thanks." Then she turned and headed toward the subway, although from behind (Henry couldn't entirely tell) it seemed as though she really was now crying.

10

AT ANY RATE, it had been a terrible day, and Henry was barely able to get out of bed the next morning. But the fact was, as he acknowledged with a blanket pulled tight around his neck, he did have dinner that night with Sasha and Whitney to look forward to. Thus, he eventually roused himself and got his coffeemaker going and soon he was even alert enough to turn on his computer and do some work.

And by the time he arrived at Whitney's girlfriend's house (this girlfriend was named Katie) he'd nearly put the previous night's events out of his mind, feeling very excited by what lay ahead. Sasha arrived shortly afterward (she'd rushed over from another friend's house) and they were all soon drinking beer and Henry found himself feeling much better. But, as the conversation progressed, and they had more beer, and then eventually sat down to a dinner of penne made with asparagus and some type of Bulgarian kale, Henry found himself slipping into thoughts about the events of the previous day and again feeling extremely angry. He tried to address these unwanted feelings with wine, but the more he drank, the more sullen and removed from the conversation he became, until, thinking once again about Kipling's treatment of Abby (and so falsely basking in the glory of *The Best of Youth*'s success), he did something that he could only regard the next morning and in the days that followed as extremely reckless.

It started at a break in the conversation, just after Whitney described a lecture he'd recently been to at Cooper Union. Henry was lost to his thoughts about Abby and had just swallowed half a glass of wine, and, just as it looked like Katie was going to begin speaking—she'd been telling stories that night about the production company where she worked—Henry announced that he'd been witness to an incredible, outrageous, and absolutely stunning literary fraud and that, if he were at liberty to talk about it, he could "right here, at dinner right now, completely blow everyone's mind."

Henry quickly halted, pouring himself another glass of wine and saying that he couldn't continue because he was pledged to secrecy, "legally and contractually obliged to remain silent," he added. But then, as the anger began to take hold again, he went on to say that he was directly involved in the fraud, that he was at the heart of the fraud, but that he couldn't say a single other word about it because his entire inherited fortune, "which is significant," would be in jeopardy.

And then, as Henry once more began to think about how distressed Abby seemed after her performance, Henry slowly began to lay out to his dinner-mates the details of the matter at hand, the details of his situation—his contractual obligations to Kipling, the work he had done for this horrible person, the nature and actions of this freak (who was tormenting one of his closest friends), and in just under fifteen minutes he'd put forward the bulk of the facts of his entire story. He'd sworn them all to secrecy, and stopped every few minutes to say, "You can't tell anyone. Not anyone. Not a single person," to which they all of course agreed. And by the time it was over, his companions were staring at him agape and almost entirely unable to say anything. Sasha managed to break the astounded silence, though. "I can't believe it," she said at last.

"I love—*loved*—that guy. I've been thinking I wanted to read his book, even. Have you seen *The Apartment?* It's one of my favorite movies. He's so great in it." (They all agreed—even Henry.) "But that's the end of my love," Sasha quickly continued. "What a bad guy."

This was exactly what Whitney and Katie said as well, and it felt really good for Henry to hear this, to have the scoundrel denounced and find his friends to be on his side. But as the warmth of the catharsis began to ebb, Henry could hardly help but conclude that he'd quite likely made a terrible mistake disclosing what he was not allowed to disclose, and, moreover, disclosing it to people he liked but didn't actually know well at all (aside from Whitney, that is) and who had no real obligation to him in terms of keeping quiet about what they'd just learned. Henry didn't suspect any secret malice, but who knew what they'd say at the next drunken dinner party? It wasn't too much of a stretch to think that they might, in a moment of excitement, say something like, *You'll never believe what I heard the other night*, and, peppering it with Henry's own phrases like *you can't tell anyone*, divulging the entire story, including a description of Henry's ironclad agreement not to expose Kipling's secret.

It was quite alarming since the consequences of this particular story truly could lead to his complete ruin and the dissolution of his family's entire fortune. Kipling would have a crushing legal case against him if the secret got out, and Henry would have only himself to blame.

11

AND THIS FEELING OF having erred in a catastrophic way continued long into the night, despite the fact that the evening ended in a manner that ordinarily would have left Henry feeling quite exalted. As he and Sasha left the building, she (quite unexpectedly but with charming confidence) put her arm under his, and in the next moment turned him sideways, stood on her toes, and kissed him gently on the lips. The kiss lasted for just a moment and then she leaned back and looked at him with great seriousness. "I love prison guys," she said. "The whole gun trafficker thing, it makes me crazy."

Despite Henry's regrets concerning his confession, he was still able to take enormous pleasure in this. "I'm a dangerous man," he said at last. "You don't want to get involved with me."

"Henry, please, you're scaring me."

Sasha kissed him again, and this time she didn't stop and they kissed for some time. At last, though, Sasha stepped back and said, "Okay, I need to get home. Maybe we can have dinner after work on Tuesday?" She paused, then whispered, "And you can tell me more about what happened to you in prison."

"All right," Henry said in what he tried to make a calm tone, despite his happiness. "Some of it. But not all. I can't tell you everything."

"I respect that," Sasha replied. "Tell me whatever you can.

Whatever you're ready to. I can't imagine how damaged you must be."

Sasha looked like she wanted to continue like this, but she suddenly spotted an empty cab heading down Bedford and said, "Holy cow, I've got to get this." (It was an easy walk home for Henry, but Sasha lived in Clinton Hill, so he let her go, but not without a last kiss on the cheek just as she turned toward the street.)

"I'll see you at work!" Sasha said over her shoulder, and in the next instant she was opening the door of the cab and then settling into the back seat.

So, a wonderful time at that point. But the incidents of the evening quickly returned to Henry as he watched Sasha leave, and the fact that he'd confessed such damaging information was once more a crippling burden. As Henry started to walk home, he vowed he would never ever drink anything again, although just after he arrived at his apartment, he found his way to the balcony with a very large glass of Pernod and began looking out at McCarren Park. On this particular night, however, the view wasn't bringing him any feelings of peace.

12

AND THE NEXT DAY was worse, although his dismal outlook was astonishing. After all, he'd been kissed by a woman he truly liked and who really seemed to like him, and it even seemed as if there could be a future between them. Most times, Henry attributed kissing girls to drunkenness. Even the few longer-term relationships he'd had he attributed to drunkenness, or at least a chronic drinking on his girlfriend's part. At any rate, it was baffling to wake up in a state of such anxiety when something so good had happened to him.

The fact of the matter was, though, unlike Henry's normal assortment of anxieties, this one was justified. It was a very real thing to be worried about, given that he'd done the thing he'd promised not to do and that everything that belonged to him was at stake. The worst thing, though, was to whom he'd confessed it all. It was one thing to open up to Whitney, who Henry was sure was totally reliable in the world of secret-keeping. And Sasha too seemed to be completely upstanding, although the truth was that he hadn't known her for that long, and what if things didn't work out between them? Was it good that she knew so much damaging information? It was talking to Whitney's new girlfriend, though (the production company person), that distressed Henry the most. (She'd even mentioned, after the confession, that her company was in the midst of pitching a show to MTV!) Henry didn't know her at all. And, given Whitney's track record, they weren't likely to be together for very long.

It was a fairly deep problem, and it was made worse when Henry received four more links from Abby that morning. "I thought you'd appreciate these because you're trying to be a writer," she'd said. The insult of the word "trying" aside, the links were to various print interviews Kipling had given on "the writing process" and they were as unbearable as his other interviews, especially since the premise of the discussions (as laid out by the question-askers) seemed to be that Kipling was a brilliant man, a brilliant writer, and almost any information he could give to aspiring young artists would be extremely welcome. And Kipling's responses were excruciating. As Henry read through them he kept conjuring up terrible images of young writers embarking on diets of cold lentils and purging their manuscripts of parentheses and semicolons, since these were, once again, the genius's key prescriptions for "true writing." Kipling also talked about various charitable projects he'd embarked on meant to promote reading and literacy. Along with a new role on a congressional "Literacy Task Force," he'd also been recruited by several youth-centered nonprofits and by UNICEF, which planned to send him on "missions" to the developing world to talk about "my novel, *The Best of Youth*," and how important literacy and reading are to the "human spirit."

At any rate, Henry paced around his apartment in distress for some time after reading the interviews, waiting till just after noon to call Whitney, who was generally a late sleeper. And although Henry woke him up, he didn't apologize or even say why he was calling so early and simply announced, "I need to meet. Can we get breakfast? Or lunch at this point?"

"I'm not hungry," Whitney said groggily. "Can we make it tonight? I think I need more sleep."

"I really need to see you," Henry said. "Really. This is really important."

Whitney sighed, but it was the kind of sigh that indicated he was willing to comply. "I'm over at Katie's right now," he said. "How about we meet at my apartment? We can eat there."

"All right," Henry said. "Half an hour?"

Whitney groaned, but in another second said, "All right. I'll see you at my house in half an hour."

Henry paced for a little while after he hung up, then put on a sweater and a jacket and headed out, stopping by a polish butcher for some sausages and then a liquor store for a liter of cheap vodka and some kind of repulsive Bloody Mary mix that Henry suddenly found himself desperately wanting. Thus, in a little over half an hour, Henry was sitting on Whitney's balcony, hovering over a small Weber grill, cooking his sausages and drinking a very appealing (but, in formal and aesthetic terms, horrible) Bloody Mary.

Henry was cagey about bringing up his main concern— the reliability of the people who now knew his story—and he addressed his situation with a general rehearsal of his anger toward Kipling. Whitney again listened attentively, himself standing up every few minutes to pace and nod his head. He too was drinking a Bloody Mary and becoming more and more glum as the story continued. At last, Whitney stopped his pacing, took a long sip of his drink, and said, "What are you going to do? You've got to do something. This man is a total fucking asshole."

Henry agreed to the asshole part, but quickly reminded Whitney of how powerless he was. "That's why this is all so difficult," he said as he eased a sausage off the grill with his thumb. "I can't do anything. I'm totally trapped. You should have seen the contract I signed." Henry handed the sausage (now wrapped in a slice of rye bread) to Whitney. "There's just nothing I can do," Henry repeated, now almost in tears.

Whitney again nodded, and there seemed to be the beginning of an encouraging speech on its way. But before he could say anything, Henry finally got to the heart of what was worrying him the most: "So, Katie, she seems cool. How well do you know her? I mean, she seems great. So great. An MTV pitch? That's really amazing. You guys seem made for each other. It seems serious to me. How well do you know her? I don't think you should break up with her."

Whitney nodded. "She's reliable," he said, after thinking for a bit about Henry's comments. "She won't say anything. She's not a gossip. But I don't think we're right for each other. I was thinking of breaking up with her."

At this Henry jammed his own rye-bread-wrapped sausage into his mouth, imagining that this might hold back the tears that were surely about to flow. Whitney moved the conversation back to Kipling, though, and, after saying once again, "Katie would never say anything," he added, changing directions (in a very surprising way) from what he'd just said, "This has got to be pretty terrible for you, Henry, but you definitely need to stop reading reviews of *The Best of Youth*. There are just a bunch of people in the world who get away with a lot, and Kipling is one of them. You need to find a way to close the book on it. We'll go out drinking a lot this winter, and you should treat yourself to new skis or something and maybe we can take a trip out West. You could go dick around in Colorado for as long as you like, if you wanted to. Or we can eat sausages and drink Bloody Marys on my balcony every day if that's what you want."

Henry was in fact now making himself another drink, although this time around the pint glass he was using was half filled with vodka. He didn't let his drink-making distract him from what was still on his mind, however. "You can't break up with Katie," he said, a little too pleadingly. "She'll tell people what I told you last night and then I'll be dead. You don't know women like I do."

This was a patently absurd statement, as Henry well knew, although he did think that Whitney's trustfulness was the sort of foolishness that comes to a man when he always has his way. Women, for Henry, never seemed to do anything he hoped they'd do (and this was not a sexist, abstract assertion, but an empirical fact developed from years of direct observation of the world). Still, it was obvious that Whitney couldn't go out with Katie for the sake of keeping her quiet. Despite how obvious this was, though, Henry did manage to propose it in even more explicit terms: "I'm sorry, Whitney, but you have to keep going out with her."

Henry smiled as he said this, though. It was funny, after all. And although Henry desperately wanted what he'd just asked for, he knew it was a completely ridiculous demand. And he even laughed a little, just after Whitney himself smiled. But then, at last, both hands wrapped around his Bloody Mary, Henry did finally begin to cry. The worst person he knew was being hailed as a genius for work he didn't do (for Henry's work!), and it was already selling like crazy. And the girl he'd most been in love with in his life was going out with this man (was "whipped," as she said). And the previous night he'd gotten drunk and done a thing that he was now worried would cost him everything he owned. Surely, Henry thought, as the tears started coming more quickly, this was a thing to cry about.

Whitney appeared quite surprised by all this. But he was also moved (as might be expected from a man with sympathies for Romance languages), and soon he was standing at Henry's side, his arm around him, and then, in an extremely uncommon act of physical kindness, he began stroking Henry's hair, saying, "Things will get better for you, Henry. I promise. And Katie won't say anything. And we'll work out whatever comes along. And you and Sasha were great together last night. She really, really likes you, Henry. I can tell. You've got a lot to be happy about."

It was a remarkable moment, and as Henry continued to cry (over Abby, over Kipling, and over his still-unassuaged fears regarding Katie), he found himself unusually comforted by Whitney's affection. It took a few moments to understand the interaction, but he realized that the last time he'd been handled this way—in a nonamorous mode, that is, and specifically with the stroking of his hair—was by his father, who did this often and even when Henry was in college. The realization made Henry cry harder. The truth was that he was able to take comfort in the fact that Whitney really was a great friend—maybe the best he'd ever had—and that if disaster came, he would (this was true) be able to continue grilling sausages and drinking cocktails on Whitney's balcony. And grilling sausages and drinking cocktails with Whitney, in the end, was something to be very grateful for.

13

So, **IT WAS A** therapeutic barbecue, as they say, and Henry made his way home that afternoon about four o'clock, stumbling as he went, feeling quite a bit of relief. And after he woke up from a long nap, at about seven that night, he was able to make his way to the kitchen to boil a pot of buckwheat noodles he'd purchased a few days before from a kind of Asian health food store that had opened nearby. Soon he was watching television and drinking hot chicken broth from his noodle bowl, and feeling even better. He thought about having a glass of Pernod—as a preventative measure—but the noodles were so good and the television program (a kind of reality show about house builders) was so enjoyable, that he figured he could make it through the night without French alcohol or another Bloody Mary.

And the next morning, as Henry made his way to Red Hook, the respite from his earlier anxiety continued, although it was, sadly, short-lived.

"Have you calmed down any?" Sasha said to Henry as they opened the first boxes of the day.

"What do you mean?" Henry said.

"Yeah, that's the gunrunner in you. Always calm. Well, don't worry. I haven't told anyone. So from my end, you won't get sued. But that Katie, I don't know about her."

But then, glancing at Henry, Sasha immediately said, "Oh, god, I'm sorry. I'm sure, positive, she won't tell anyone," letting Henry know that he'd hid nothing at all of his fears.

"What?" Henry said. "I'm fine. I'm sure Katie will be cool."

Sasha looked at him for a moment, then said, with real compassion, "I really am sure it's fine. I'm sure Katie won't say anything. And what if she did? You can always deny everything. It's not like you're running for office—who cares if you lie?"

Henry nodded. He knew he still looked panicked, but he didn't want to talk about it anymore. He pulled a book from his box and said, "Ford Madox Ford!"

Sasha nodded. "It will be fine," she said again.

"Yeah, maybe," Henry said. "This is a first edition!"

"Pretty cool," Sasha said, nodding again.

"Very cool," Henry replied.

14

HENRY AND SASHA went out that night, and the next, and both evenings ended with kissing on street corners and even kissing a few times in bars. This was not a thing that Henry particularly felt comfortable with (the public nature of their affection), but it was hard to avoid since it made him feel so happy. It also seemed that it was a safe way to let things progress, since Henry always felt that bedrooms and sudden nudity with another person were the absolute worst ways to establish intimacy. This is not to say he was a prude—had Sasha suggested that they go home together he would have agreed with customary enthusiasm. But Sasha too didn't seem anxious to start taking off her clothes, which seemed especially charming since she was so entirely covered with tattoos. Physical modesty simply wasn't what Henry would have expected from a person so ornamented, but the fact was that her shyness did match very well with her personality. At any rate, the bottom line was that there were no complaints on Henry's part. As far as he was concerned, they could spend the next year in straightforward physical embraces and he'd be thrilled about it.

By Thursday, though, there was a bit of a break in their interactions. Sasha had to go west, to Michigan, over the coming weekend. She had a sister who was getting married in a few months and the family was assembling to talk about procedure. "So I won't see you till next Tuesday," Sasha said to Henry as they kissed outside a bar famous for its free assortment of artificial cheese snacks. "I hope you'll wait for me," she added.

"I'll try," Henry said. "But no promises." Henry was actually feeling quite good, at this point, in terms of his capacity for ironic remarks, and he thought that Sasha was helping him quite a bit where this was concerned. But they were soon kissing again and Henry's ideas about his expanding conversational repertoire fast receded as more emotional instincts took over.

The next day, Henry worked on his fiction for nearly twelve hours straight—he was writing a story about a ninety-year-old woman who scandalized her family by piercing her nose and tattooing exotic birds (her late husband was an ornithologist) all over herself. The story unfolded well, in Henry's estimation, and included several comic scenes concerning the looseness of a ninety-year-old's skin and the difficulty of inking a smooth picture on it, and by the time the evening rolled around, he was nearly half done. He only stopped because Whitney called. Henry was quick to say that he was probably too busy that night to hang out, but after Whitney said, "Katie and I broke up," he and Henry were soon at dinner— a German restaurant with an extensive beer list—talking of the implications of this, at first concerning Whitney's well-being but then concerning Henry's fears about her talking about Kipling.

"Look Henry, please, please don't worry about that," Whitney said. "She's totally solid. She'd never sell you out like that."

"But the breakup?" Henry said. "It was mutual?"

"Well, no," Whitney replied. "I mean, yes, officially, but no, it was mostly me."

"How did she react?"

"Well, I suppose I'd have to say that she didn't take it well.

I mean, I've seen worse, but I've seen better. Seriously, what's up with all that anger? Sadness I get, but the accusations of betrayal—I don't understand the logic. You can't decide who to love. It happens or it doesn't. There's no betrayal."

Here Henry paused for a moment before saying, "Holy fuck, am I dead."

"Henry, it's not like that. She was mad, but not at you. Why would she say anything? She really likes you, Henry. And who would she even tell?"

The answer to the question, of course, was absolutely everyone she knew she was pitching to at MTV, plus whatever other contacts she had in the industry. Kipling's story was not the embarrassing behavior of some random Brooklyn freak (like Henry, for instance) but of a person many, many people were interested in. And because of that, it likely wouldn't be long before Henry was once again in court, now for the purposes of losing all his money. He suddenly thought of his great-great-grandfather, who had left the family farm in Sturbridge to become a clerk at a textile mill in New Hampshire, and how he'd gone on to establish the kind of industrial wealth that almost didn't seem to exist in New England anymore. Of course, his father's share (now Henry's) was merely a portion, so it was not as if the man's entire legacy were gone. But Henry couldn't help but think about how this august Yankee ancestor would surely lose himself to fury if he knew that one of his distant offspring squandered such an enormous sum of money because he got drunk and angry one night and couldn't keep his mouth shut.

"I think I should call Katie," Henry finally said.

"You should definitely not call Katie," Whitney replied.

"I just think I need to explain to her what's at stake. I think the other night it just sounded like some kind of ordinary secret, but everything I have is on the line here."

"Do not call Katie."

Henry thought about it for a moment, then said, "I think it would be a good idea."

"Henry, she's not even thinking about you. It would not be a good idea. If you call her, she might actually think that this might be a good way to get back at me. But as of right now, she's not thinking about Kipling and his ghostwriter."

Henry wanted to say more, but Whitney did have a point. Still, would a call really set off that kind of scheming? Maybe Henry could even befriend her. Needless to say, he'd always take Whitney's side in anything, but perhaps she could use a friend, and Henry was usually praised for his frankness and his kindness by women who'd had their hearts broken. Again, Henry sighed, and then nodded, and then began eating quickly, because he wanted to go home to think about how to get out of the trouble he now felt he was in.

And the prospect of calling Katie stayed on his mind into that night and then the next morning, when he woke up early and rehearsed what he might say to her if he called—something about his great friendship for Whitney but knowing the suffering caused by a lost love. At eleven that morning, though—it was now Saturday—Henry got a call from Abby that quickly took him very far away from his current dilemma.

15

"**Henry?**" **Abby said** with a voice so strained that Henry could hardly decipher his name.

"Yes," he said, after hesitating. "Abby. What's wrong?"

She was clearly crying, and after a pause she said, "I'm pregnant."

"What?" Henry said.

"I'm pregnant, Henry," she said, still barely intelligible through the tears. "I don't know how. It doesn't seem possible. But I am."

"And with Kipling? From Kipling?"

"I haven't slept with anyone but Jonathan for almost a year," Abby said, the crying increasing.

"Are you sure?"

"It's Jonathan's!"

"I mean, are you sure about being pregnant?"

"I've been through six different tests—three different brands. I'm pregnant, Henry." Here, remarkably, she started crying even harder.

Henry paused for a moment, entirely unsure of what to do. "I don't know what to say," Henry said at last. "I'll do whatever you need."

At this Abby let forth a loud but halting sob before saying, "Can I come over?"

"Of course."

"Right now?"

"Of course."

"I'm coming over now. I'm leaving now."

Abby arrived about fifteen minutes later, and as she walked in, her eyes were so swollen that Henry wondered how she could see.

"He's going to kill me," she said as she walked through the front door.

"He's going to kill you?" Henry repeated.

"He's going to kill me."

"Kill you for what? How is it your fault?"

"I missed a pill. Or two. He can blame me. But I only missed them because I was out all night with him. You think you can just take it the next morning and everything will be fine. I don't know. Maybe the pills just weren't working right. Henry, he's going to kill me."

"Are you going to have it?" This, Henry realized, was a fairly indelicate question, and also none of his business, despite the fact that Abby had come to see him in this state. Still, it was certainly the question that must have been on Abby's mind.

And here Abby hesitated, seeming to have a great deal to say on the matter. But as she opened her mouth to speak, she burst into tears again, and didn't stop crying until several minutes later, her face pressed against Henry's neck the entire time. At last, though, she pulled away, and Henry insisted that she sit down. He'd made coffee right after he got her call and then suggested that she might like hers with a little scotch in it. He certainly wanted scotch. But it instantly occurred to him that such a thing was definitely not a good idea given the nature of the news. Maybe even the coffee might not be good for her. "I have juice too," he said. "Maybe alcohol and caffeine aren't the best thing for you right now. I have orange juice and I have pomegranate juice and I have two cans of pear nectar."

Again, now seated on the couch with her head in her hands, Abby's tears only increased, and Henry at last did nothing other than sit down and put his arm around her. It was baffling. Even despite the obvious gravity of the situation, he'd never thought Abby capable of such a breakdown. She was always so tough, although it was a fact that she'd seemed so scattered in recent months that maybe this was just the new state of things. And the reason for the breakdown, of course, was monumental—impossible, really, to exaggerate.

But Abby finally relaxed for a moment, and after she asked for a glass of orange juice and then Henry returned with it from the kitchen, she calmed down even more. Or, it struck Henry, she'd at last exhausted herself.

"I don't know what to do," she said. "I don't know what to say to him. If I should say anything. Maybe he doesn't need to know."

This, on the face of it, was very disturbing to Henry, not because he believed Kipling had any sort of right to know, but that Abby was so lost to a person to whom she didn't think she could tell this kind of news. "Don't you think it's a little strange that you'd even consider not telling him? I mean, what kind of relationship do you two have?" Then he added, although he knew as he spoke that it was a mistake, "He's just such a fucking scumbag."

Abby sat up straight and Henry could tell that he was about to be yelled at. Henry took the ensuing abuse gracefully, though, and weathered the recriminations for not being able to transcend his attractions. He quietly said things like, "It's really not like that Abby, not anymore," and he didn't scream things about how it was completely clear that she'd lost her mind. (On this point, Henry was once again astonished that someone as singularly strong and independent as Abby could be so obsessed with a man like Kipling.) But the yelling eventually stopped. And as she put her hands on her stomach and she looked down, Henry concluded that the anger had passed. And he was right, although what followed was even more unexpected. "I don't know, Henry," Abby said. "Sometimes I think a guy like you is who I should be with. It's someone like you who I'd always thought I would be with. Maybe that's why I'm yelling at you. But it didn't turn out that way for us and at this point there's nothing I can do about it. That I find Kipling so attractive still shocks me, but my heart does what it wants to do, not what I want it to do."

It was a confusing thing to hear, and Henry wasn't sure how to respond. At last, though, he tilted away from Abby and said, "There will be a way through this. I promise you. And I'll do anything you want or need. You're in the middle of all this, right now, in the middle of the shock, and I promise you'll feel better in a bit. Or you'll be able to think about how to move forward. Just hang out with me here now and things will get better and you'll think of how to go forward."

At this, Abby started crying once again. But she did manage to choke out, "I don't want to move forward. I just want all this to go away." And this time the crying lasted for several minutes and without any attempt to "talk things through," although Henry imagined that the intensity of the crying now might help some.

And Henry's assessment was correct. Once the emotions had settled, though, she was up on her feet and saying she had to go.

"I'm sorry, Henry," she said. "I'm sorry for dumping all this on you. I don't even see you that much anymore."

"You didn't dump anything on me," Henry said. "You can do no wrong as far as I'm concerned and you can stay here for the next month if you want. The next year. I'll make you dinner every night."

Abby smiled. "That's pretty nice and that sounds pretty great," she said as she began gathering her things, "but you've got to learn not to be such a pushover, despite how much I need it right now."

Abby took a deep breath here and Henry really felt a kind of gratitude and affection from Abby, although as she started walking to the front door he wondered if he'd done anything for her at all.

16

THAT AFTERNOON, Henry distracted himself by working on his latest story, and he also sent an email to Sasha (who replied directly, and with real affection), and he even took a brief and nonpurposeful walk around McCarren Park to think about all that Abby had told him. Had he handled it all properly? he wondered.

Henry called Abby that evening to make sure she was doing all right, but she didn't pick up her phone, so he left a message expressing his various worries, and on Monday, when he still hadn't heard back from her, he left the same message again, although once more he heard no response.

By Tuesday, he was quite a bit more apprehensive, but once he was back at work in Red Hook, in the company of Sasha (now back from Michigan), he felt so good, his sense of anxiety tempered with such overwhelming happiness, that he was able to keep hold of his emotions.

And that night they went out to an unusually traditional French restaurant that served standards like coq au vin and blanquette de veau, and the food was so excellent, and so interesting, and they drank so much wine, that Henry couldn't help but grasp in a very tangible way how happy he was with what he imagined might now be called his girlfriend. And after dinner, after (once again) kissing on the street, Sasha whispered in Henry's ear, "Why don't you come home with me tonight?" Henry was surprised at that moment to find that he wasn't crippled with anxiety about how he might best execute his duties, or whether his potential failures would be written up online, or even on the matter of birth control (although Henry did conclude that they should definitely use some, if it came to that).

And it did come to that. Sasha was prepared, however, and afterward Henry felt quite confident that, if he did later appear as some kind of figure on a website, Sasha's comments would be delivered with warmth and contentment. "I really like you, Henry," she said as they lay on their backs in her bed. "I mean, I really like you."

"I really like you too," Henry said. "This is one of the best nights I've had in a long time."

Sasha turned and faced him. "Me too, Henry. I hope you know that. I'm getting very attached to you. That doesn't happen very easily with me."

Henry turned now as well and said, "It doesn't happen easily with me either. Or it's pretty rare that I feel so good around someone else." Henry almost added, *Except for when I'm with Whitney*, but he caught himself in time because, after all, this was really not the sort of thing he ought to be saying. But Henry quickly concluded that he'd probably be forgiven if he'd said it. Sasha would probably forgive him for such a statement. Henry's lack of anxiety astonished him once again, although he was soon resting his face in the crook of Sasha's neck (just where a bloom of three roses was tattooed) and was once more forgetting about anything at all besides how good it felt to be with her.

17

THE NEXT MORNING, Henry stumbled out of bed and found his pants, and as he did so, he pulled his phone from his pocket, turned it on (it had been turned off for logical reasons), and saw he had two voice mails. Both, according to the call log, were from Abby. The first seemed to be a sort of general check-in, including an apology for not getting back to him sooner. The next, though, left at the end of the night, was so tear-filled that Henry could barely understand what Abby was saying.

And when he called her back he was just as hard-pressed to decipher her words beneath the crying, although he managed to calm her down enough to understand that she'd told Kipling about the baby, and then, after a moment of more intense crying, to get her to understand that he was coming over. "I'm leaving right now," he said.

"You don't want to see me now."

"I'll be over in ten minutes," Henry replied, and quickly hung up.

Sasha was still mostly asleep, but she'd been roused somewhat by Henry's phone call and was able to respond with some sense of awareness as Henry apologized and said he had to go to meet a friend. "It sounds really bad," Henry said. "I've got to go. It's my cousin. Kind of. She's not really a cousin, except for in a technical way."

Sasha put a hand up to Henry's face. "So long as she's related, even just technically, I'll let you go. Anyway, I'll see you in Red Hook in a few hours." Sasha's smile seemed to express such genuine happiness that Henry almost got back into bed. But this instinct was momentary because he could hardly help but realize that Abby was truly, truly distressed—even more than she'd been the last time he'd seen her—and soon Henry was on the street and headed to Abby's apartment.

He really was quite panicked by the phone call. He'd never heard Abby like this at all (not even the last time they were together) and he could only imagine that she'd been up all night in a state of despair over how the discussion about the pregnancy had gone. But when he arrived, when he knocked on the door, when Abby let him into an abnormally darkened hallway, her head down, he began to realize that things were far worse than he'd expected. And as they walked into the main room of Abby's apartment, where the blinds could not entirely conceal the daylight that was coming in at the edges of the windows, Henry himself almost burst into tears. Abby's face was covered with bruises—her left eye was nearly swollen shut—and her lips were so scabbed over that Henry wondered how she had been able to talk at all on the phone. Abby quickly grasped that the dark room was hardly enough to diminish the magnitude of what had happened, although she must have anticipated this and she even seemed relieved to be revealed, and soon she was crying harder than she had so far. This time, though, Henry could make out more of what she was saying, most of which concerned her crushing disbelief that she'd ever find herself in a position like this.

"I mean, getting the shit kicked out of me by a totally fucking high boyfriend is the last problem I ever thought I'd deal with," she said. "I went to fucking Oberlin, for Christ's sake.

I minored in women's studies. I thought this was something the sweater-knitting Peruvian women on my semester abroad had to deal with. And Henry"—here Abby started crying even harder—"I kept telling him how sorry I was as he was hitting me. I kept telling him I was sorry."

After that, Abby gave up trying to articulate the state of her distress. Henry guided her to the couch and helped her to sit, and then he sat down as well, and soon they were embracing and Henry was doing his best to comfort her, although his own state of agitation was itself becoming overwhelming.

18

BUT HE MANAGED not to break any furniture. In fact, he remained entirely in control. He sat with Abby for the next hour, his arms around her, telling her stories that he thought she might find distracting—embarrassing moments at Harvard, plotlines of his latest short stories, a rehearsal of his interaction with the vet after he'd killed all her aunt's goats, and even an involved description of another of his cousins who hated him beyond all reason and had lied several times to get him in trouble when they were young. "He eventually went to Dartmouth," Henry said, trying to make Abby relax a bit more. "I hear they appreciate people like that. Not a Harvard man at all."

They did touch on what Abby ought to do about her situation. Henry implied that they should, at that moment, be on the phone with the police. But Abby quickly said no. Or she said she needed to think.

"I have a friend," she said. "A doctor. I went to her clinic last night. She said the baby is fine and she won't report this. She promised. I don't want to go to the police. Or I need to think about everything, because if I do go to the police, I'll be on every fucking magazine cover in America. So far, the tabloids have just treated me as Jonathan's irrelevant girlfriend. Obviously, this will change that. But fuck, I can't believe I'm even saying something like this. *Don't go to the police?* It's so fucking weird. I can't believe anything I'm saying now."

Henry still thought they definitely needed to call the cops, but for the moment he'd do whatever Abby wanted. And Abby did have a point. It was completely astounding that they wouldn't call the police, but the important thing now was finding some kind of refuge, and tabloid reporters were hardly going to help that. Hopefully she'd change her mind later. It was just so crazy that they weren't getting the NYPD to fuck Kipling up. Still, Henry wasn't going to do anything without permission. He just kept telling his distracting stories, and at last Abby's breathing began to slow, and before long she drifted off to sleep.

Henry, however, hadn't relaxed at all, and as he watched Abby sleep, his mind raced. He did manage to lay Abby's head on the couch properly, and he put a blanket over her, but then he whispered in her ear that he had to leave for a little while, making sure she understood that he'd be back soon. "I'll bring lots of food," he said, "so we can hide out as long as we want." And then he left the apartment because, with some sense of urgency (police or no police), he felt he had something to do.

Henry called Sasha first—it was now a couple of hours since he'd left her in her bed. "I'm not coming in to work today," he said as soon as she picked up the phone. "I've got a really bad thing going on with my cousin. I'll tell you all about it later. But it's pretty serious. So if you could cover for me—tell them I'm sick—I'd really appreciate it."

"Yeah, anything you want," Sasha said, and then, as Henry had been secretly hoping for, notwithstanding the seriousness of his call, she added, "It was really something, last night. I can't wait till I get to see you again."

Despite the fact that he was still feeling such agony over Abby, it was really good to hear this. He managed to maintain his composure, however, and said, "I'll call you later." But then he added, "Yeah, I thought last night was so great. I'm kind of afraid to say anything about it in case I sound completely stupid. But it was so great. I had such a great time."

"Yeah, like I said, me too," Sasha replied. "Me too. Go do what you have to do. And call me later."

"All right," Henry said, and then, after another goodbye, they hung up.

Henry quickly began dialing his phone again. After a few rings, he got Merrill's secretary, and after Henry said he absolutely had to be put through immediately—Merrill was in a meeting—he got to Merrill and asked, "Where is Kipling staying?"

"What?" Merrill said.

"Where is Kipling staying? I'm supposed to meet him at his hotel for lunch but he didn't tell me where he's staying and he never picks up his phone."

"Yeah, he's a dick with his phone," Merrill replied. "He's staying at the Montcrieff on Sixty-second. He always stays in Penthouse Two. Go kick him out of bed."

"Thanks," Henry replied. "I'll give you a call later to check in." And with that, Henry headed for the subway to make his way to Kipling's hotel.

19

WHAT HE INTENDED to achieve with the confrontation was a mystery, but as Henry considered it all, first on the subway, and then walking north to Sixty-second, he decided that Abby was simply a very important person in his life and it was terrible how they'd drifted apart in the past year. Above all, though, he felt much worse about the fact that someone he cared about (unconscious reasons aside) was being abused by what had to be the most repulsive person he'd ever known.

It was strange, though, because as thoughts of Abby crowded Henry's mind, he suddenly found himself thinking about his father, and, in particular, a time when he avenged Henry after a series of fairly humiliating events when Henry was in sixth grade.

Before he went to Deerfield, Henry attended a so-called country-day school in Lincoln, Mass, called the Keller Academy, which educated the various well-heeled children of Middlesex County and its surroundings. The Boston area, of course, has a long reputation for its progressive thinking and liberal restraint, but Henry always knew that it was also true that there was a certain kind of thuggishness that Massachusetts males clung to, mostly out of some kind of concern that the rest of the world thought of them as infirm, Harvard-educated, belles lettrists (like Henry, for instance). And this thuggish spirit, in particular, was most evident on the hockey rink. While young men in places like Minnesota and North Dakota devoted themselves to the purity and elegance of what is, in fact, something of a beautiful and exhilarating sport, Boston-area hockey programs focused on athletic techniques like hostility, spitting, and semi-accidental self-mutilation (for the purposes of appearing more terrifying). At any rate, Henry played in the Keller Academy hockey program and, although he was a just-below-average player, he stayed with it, mostly because of his father's encouragement. His father had played hockey as a young person, was even a second-line left-winger for Harvard's team in the 1970s, and Henry could grasp, even at ten, that it was somehow important to his father that he play. But what Henry could also grasp was that his father realized that he wasn't very good, and that the advantages of hockey had something to do with character-building, rather than being about Henry's fun and glory. Of course, the future was still uncertain. Perhaps there was some tremendous growth spurt in the offing, or Henry's motor skills would undergo some kind of miraculous maturation.

The thing was that, as with all organized sports, there was an extremely important social component of everything, and there was one particular person (another young boy on the hockey team and an absolute star) who despised Henry, and, despite the fact that they were teammates, inflicted the Boston type of thuggishness and brutality on Henry as much as he could, even once going so far as starting a fistfight with him on the bench because, as he said, "Henry was such a fucking pussy." And it was not uncommon for him to bump him on the ice, hit him with his stick on the bench, push him in the locker room, and actively harass him ("It's the fucking pussy") in the Keller Academy's halls and lunchroom.

It was the sort of problem that good parents are tortured

by, especially because it was clear that intervention on Henry's behalf would have a real cost. "Pete," the offender, might have to face a dressing-down by the principal, but what would happen when the authorities weren't around?

Things did come to a head, though, on an evening when the Keller Academy was playing Sudbury Prep and Henry was having a particularly dismal game. Henry's performance had elicited groans from the crowd on three separate occasions, but when Henry's father (and Henry) heard the young bully Pete's father (a thoracic surgeon named Dr. James Paulson) yell in an unusual state of parental agitation, "Take that fucking kid out!" (just after Henry avoided the puck because he was afraid of being hit), it was something of a transformative moment.

The rink was large, but there were not that many people in attendance, and it wasn't hard for everyone to hear such comments. Henry didn't feel particularly bad. He really didn't. Acts of physical bravado never excited him, and his failure to perform them (and the ridicule that might follow) always felt irrelevant. For Henry's father, though, the comment was intolerable. He apparently held his temper through the rest of the game, but afterward, as the fathers greeted their sons as they exited the locker room into the ice rink's food court and video game parlor, he grabbed hold of Dr. Paulson's elbow and said, "This is my son, you dumb fucking jerk, and I want you to apologize to him."

Strangely, it didn't seem as though there was meant to be a fight, despite the crude language and the elbow-grabbing. Even Dr. Paulson didn't seem to think that punches would be thrown. But the emotional and verbal anger of Henry's father had a kind of influence on the physical positions and angles of the two men, and, although it was impossible really to say "who started it," as some sort of law enforcement person might put it, what was a fact was that Henry's father, as he stepped back and put up his right arm (Dr. Paulson had raised his own fist in the air), thrust his elbow into Dr. Paulson's face and (as was perfectly clear to anyone who saw the blood spurt and the man's sudden collapse to the floor) broke his nose in such a painful and conclusive way that there was simply no question that Henry's father's enemy had been entirely defeated.

Of course, good New Englander that he was, Henry's father quickly stooped down to help his adversary and even mopped up the blood with his sleeve and called for an ambulance. (None was called because none was really needed.) And Dr. Paulson, now sitting, feebly insisted that he was just fine, after he managed to put a handkerchief up against his nose. His family, he said, had a long history of weak capillary walls. "I get nosebleeds like this all the time," he said.

At any rate, the two men involved, and the people who stopped to watch, seemed to think that the best thing to do was to pretend nothing had happened and head to their cars. And as they walked through the parking lot, Henry and his father were silent, although as they opened their doors and took their seats, Henry's father began to apologize. It was what Henry had expected, and it followed a standard sort of script about "appropriate behavior" and that it was "wrong to let your emotions lead you to violence."

And Henry did what he could to assure his father that no real harm had been done, that it wasn't really a "fight" but a "scuffle" (Henry was an insightful young literary man even then and understood the rhetorical advantages of precise linguistic distinctions), and that in a "scuffle" a person gets hurt by the event and the emotional circumstance, not by a willful decision.

At this, Henry's father nodded and said, "Well, I appreciate your kind interpretation of everything, Henry." Then, after a pause, he added, "But human beings are just not supposed to behave that way to each other. No matter what the justification." There was then another pause, after which (quite to Henry's surprise) his father added, "But, I have to say, as I think about this with some perspective now, I really loved laying that guy out like that. Dropped him like a rock, in case you didn't notice. I know it was just 'a scuffle.' But this isn't the first time your old man threw an elbow to defeat a villain. And Henry, guys like that, and I say this as a man of great emotional equilibrium, really need their asses kicked."

Henry decided that it might not be the best idea to point out the somewhat accidental nature of Dr. Paulson's defeat and instead agreed that his father had done quite well for himself.

And it was good that Henry restrained himself in this way because what came next was surprisingly moving. Henry's father paused and then said, "And no one will ever treat you badly as long as I'm around. I mean, I don't think you should count on me getting into a lot of fistfights on your behalf. But Henry, I will always be around to take care of you. I'll never let anyone do anything to hurt you."

Even at Henry's young age, he realized the importance of what his father had just said, and as a memory it had always sustained him. And despite the fact that his father was now dead, Henry (as secular a man as he was) still felt that what his father had said about protecting him was somehow, in an emotional if not a spiritual way, true.

What all this meant in terms of what was going to follow with Kipling, though, wasn't exactly clear—a thing that struck Henry very hard as he arrived at Sixty-second Street. But Henry did feel somehow that even timid writers from Harvard had moral obligations, and that protecting people you loved was the only route a thinking, reasoning human being could take. What he was going to actually do on the visit to Kipling's hotel, however, really was a mystery. At the very least, Henry did imagine that he'd be telling Kipling that he'd be going to the police whether Abby liked it or not. But then, once more thinking that he couldn't do that to Abby, he began to imagine that he'd rather follow his father's example and find some clever way to kick the shit out of Kipling (as it were), although this also seemed unlikely. But if he did it, if he found some way to physically injure Kipling, even if it was underhanded and not at all virtuous, well, what could Kipling do about it? If Kipling called the police himself, he'd only make his own exposure likely. Henry couldn't help but feel happy that the thing that made Abby so hesitant to involve outsiders would be the same thing that prevented Kipling from taking any retribution, should Henry, in fact, somehow manage to injure him.

And with this reasoning, after making his way through the hotel's lobby and stepping off the elevator on Kipling's floor, and after spotting a bronze statuette of a naked woman about the size of a wine bottle that sat on a table in the hallway, he came up with a small plan. Figuring that if he could just break an arm or a leg it would make him feel much better, Henry grabbed the statuette and concluded that Kipling would just have to suck up the pain without retribution, unless he really wanted to ruin his career.

So Henry slammed his fist on Kipling's door and when Kipling opened it he was indeed surprised and even looked just a little frightened. Henry stepped forward, his hand with the statue just behind his right hip, and quickly said they needed to talk.

"Actually," Henry said, bringing the statuette forward, "I'm here to beat the shit out of you."

These were quite threatening words, Henry felt, and at the very least he imagined that Kipling would assume some kind of defensive stance and try to explain to Henry that whatever bad things he thought about him were certainly not true. Instead, however, Kipling (a naturally muscular man and a person who, again, clearly spent a lot of time with a personal trainer) stepped forward and punched Henry right in the neck, so hard that Henry could do nothing but fall to the floor and roll over, losing his bronze weapon in the process.

"What?" Kipling yelled. "You're fucking here to avenge your fucking dumb bitch cousin?"

He kicked Henry in the face.

"You think you can come over and fuck with me?" He kicked Henry again. "You cannot fuck with me, and your little bitch cousin cannot fuck with me. I've got too much fucking money and too many fucking lawyers for you to fuck with me, and you, you little fucking asshole, I'm a million times tougher than you, so fuck you and your little fucking sculpture." With this, Kipling bent down, picked up the bronze statue, and clubbed Henry several times on his right shoulder. Kipling then picked Henry up by his collar and his arm, stepped forward, and threw him into the hallway, slamming the door behind him without ceremony.

And so that was it. The door was closed and locked. Sixty seconds and Henry's dreams of revenge were lost.

As Henry lay on the floor, his arm strangely numb, and now bleeding from both his nose and his mouth, he suddenly (and against his will) recalled one of Kipling's movies, a film that dealt with Maine fishermen. Kipling played the upstart younger brother of the stoic leader of a small fishing-boat crew that was trying to cover up a murder—a murder that was retributional, and just, and cheered by any decent and freethinking moviegoer. The thing about this movie—this was what Henry thought about as he struggled to attend to his bleeding nose and mouth with an old cocktail napkin he found in his pocket—was that Kipling was magnificent in it, so totally moving in the small moments when he spoke about justice and compassion and human virtue, that as Henry leaned forward and tried to wipe the blood away from his face, it struck him as one of the strangest things he'd ever confronted: that Kipling could so perfectly play a person that he was so different from. It was entirely confusing—too confusing to begin to pick apart at this point, now, as his attempts to arrest the blood flow from his nose failed and his shoulder now began to throb with astounding pain.

It was here that Henry concluded that he had to go to the police. It was impossible to imagine that Kipling could get away with all this. But then Henry again thought about Abby, and how she was so worried about becoming some sort of tabloid freak, and he decided that he'd never do anything to bring that about if she didn't want to face it, even if it meant he got his ass kicked and couldn't retaliate. It was just such an unbearable idea that Kipling should walk away from all this unharmed.

And the fact was that if Henry did go to the police, Kipling still might win the day—Kipling was right about that, aside from all the bluster about how rich he was. How hard was it for a good PR firm to accuse Abby of being some kind of opportunist, lying about being on the pill or desperate to hang on to the movie star who was so successful and so well loved and probably benefiting her musical career? Plus, could she prove that it was Kipling who beat her up? Why hadn't she gone to the police right away? What, the magazines might ask, was she hiding? And it was also the case that Henry did show up at Kipling's apartment with what was surely, technically, a weapon. What was Kipling supposed to do when Henry arrived? Let the intruder club him to death with a piece of hotel art?

The entire calculation was very distressing. But as Henry

now at last got to his feet, he had another idea, although perhaps it had been on his mind for some time. In the end, as
Henry thought about it, he realized that he did, in fact, have
something over Kipling, at least in terms of his artistic reputation, and in the next moment he was on his phone to Whitney, describing what had happened to Abby and to him, and
then announcing that he was on his way over.

20

WHITNEY WAS STUNNED when he saw Henry at his door. Henry had prepared him somewhat, but only in the more formal details—a split lip and a badly bruised shoulder muscle, etc. Still, he apparently had not quite given Whitney a proper sense of the extent of everything, and there was, of course, the psychological toll, which Henry was sure was completely evident as he saw Whitney's reaction to him.

"You're so pale," Whitney said. "I've never seen anyone so pale. And you're already a very pale man."

"I know, I know," Henry said, stepping through the door. "But I'm okay. Really."

Here Henry even managed a smile, but he immediately began talking again as he walked toward Whitney's kitchen.

"I want you to write an essay," Henry continued. Then, as he opened the refrigerator and took out a beer, he added, "For your free leftist newspaper. About how I wrote *The Best of Youth* and about how Kipling has been lying about it."

Henry opened the beer and then looked at Whitney, who seemed to be avoiding having a reaction to this idea. Maybe he was going to let Henry have his moment of fury and then talk him out of it after he'd calmed down.

"You can put it in the literary section if you want," Henry continued, "but I think it might be good on the front page as well. The day it's published, we'll email copies to every media outlet we can think of. No way Kipling can stop it then because it will already be out there and people will just be reporting on your story. Anyway, I can prove everything. Show me one single word that Kipling ever wrote for this book. We'll subpoena Merrill if we have to. He's not going to lie under oath, although he might get pretty pissed. Or maybe not, given what Kipling has done and given the kind of guy Merrill is. Anyway, I've got stacks of notes and edited manuscripts and a hard drive full of drafts that I wrote. What does Kipling own to prove that he wrote anything? The guy barely knows the names of the characters."

Here, at this point, Whitney allowed himself to react, although the distressed look on his face was a little inscrutable. Finally, he just said, "Fuck."

"He deserves this," Henry added.

"Yeah, but fuck, you're going to be fucked if you do this."

"I want to do it."

"What about that *Survivor* analogy Merrill gave you? The nondisclosure thing. No way you're not going to get crushed by this."

"I don't care."

Whitney looked at Henry for another instant and it appeared as if he were going to speak again, but instead he stepped forward, opened the fridge, and grabbed a beer of his own.

21

IT WAS NOT A difficult article to draft except that the blinding light of passion was tempered a few times with more frank warnings from Whitney as they sat in front of Whitney's laptop and wrote.

"Honestly, you're going to get sued for everything you have and you're going to lose. You know that, right? Tell me you understand that." Whitney said this after they'd just finished constructing a sentence that made clear that Kipling had no hand at all in a single sentence of the book.

"Kipling fucking deserves this," Henry said. Then, after a pause, trying to keep his cool, he added, "And I think the government can't take your house if you declare bankruptcy. I'll still have my apartment."

"Yeah, and you'll have to sell it because what are you going to live on?" Whitney replied. "You're totally unemployable."

It was a good point, but Henry quickly changed the subject by noting that he'd really like more parentheses added to the paragraph Whitney had just typed, and after that the conversation stayed entirely on the subject of the standards of the prose.

At any rate, by midnight, after quite a bit of beer and coffee, the article (officially penned by Whitney) was completed. It was simple and not at all vicious in style—more reportage than polemic. But it laid out the facts of the situation, namely that Kipling, the great literary phenomenon, had hired Henry to write his book for him, and that Kipling had had nothing to do with its creation or editing and that Kipling was now posing as a literary master when he knew nothing at all about how to construct a novel, likely hadn't even read the one he was calling his own. It was quite a satisfying thing to see, especially the quotes that they manufactured and attributed to Henry, but as Henry went to sleep on Whitney's couch that night, with a high-quality down comforter wrapped around him, he wondered if he'd regret all this. Probably he would. At this point, though, again, not to go ahead would be like making an active decision to let Kipling off the hook, which was not a thing Henry could consider.

Fortunately, Henry was so exhausted that these internal ruminations only lasted for a few minutes before he finally fell asleep, the comforter twisted tightly around his neck—a mode of sleeping that Henry had employed ever since he was a small boy.

22

HENRY WOKE UP LATE the next morning and decided that he ought to make it to work that day. He called Abby to see how she was. She sounded fine—or better, or calm—and it didn't seem to her that Henry would do much good for her if he visited. "I just want to lie on my couch and watch TV," she said. "I think I'm more tired than I've ever been."

Henry left for Red Hook shortly after hanging up, but by the time he made it to the library warehouse he suddenly became afraid to see Sasha. Cosmetically, his face had actually come through the fight all right, after the blood had been stopped and wiped away. Still, it seemed likely that he looked terrible and he was quite positive that he smelled very bad. And Sasha confirmed at least some of Henry's more superficial fears when he arrived. "Boy, do you stink," she said when she greeted him. She was smiling, and she reached out to touch Henry's hand as she said this, so it wasn't too much of an insult. Still, it made Henry feel self-conscious. And after stepping away for a second, he was soon explaining what had transpired over the past day and what was likely coming in the time ahead.

Sasha looked genuinely distressed by what Henry said, but mostly she was silent and only nodded when it seemed that her input might be appropriate. After about ten minutes, though, during which time they were not doing any of their work, she finally asked, "So, what, you used to try to sleep with your cousin?"

Henry felt the blood drain from his face (what was left, at least), and his only thought was that, yet again, he'd entirely misjudged the nature of his interactions with another person. And he even began to explain once more that in most cultures that kind of thing was totally normal. But Sasha abruptly grabbed hold of Henry, pulled him forward, and kissed him with unmistakable affection. "I'm just joking, Henry," she said. "Jesus. It's amazing you're not institutionalized. I'm just trying to cheer you up. You look like you've been hit by a truck."

This, Henry could only conclude, was entirely true. But he was pretty happy in that instant, so he endured the insult, although he added, "I think I really do smell very bad. I don't think I can hug you for too long."

"Yeah," Sasha said. "It's really gross. But Henry, man, I really like you, so I'm willing to endure." And with this, she held Henry even tighter, and Henry hugged her back with equal happiness, although now, at last, in the midst of what was, unequivocally, a very happy moment, he realized how truly exhausted he was, and how he had spent the past day and night doing a thing that would surely change his life.

23

AND AS FAR AS life-changing events go, Henry was not wrong to anticipate the magnitude of what came next. (Astonishingly, Kipling had found the article in the online version of Whitney's paper a day before the print version was released—clearly he had some system of monitoring his Web presence.) It was now several days after Henry and Whitney had drafted the article, and Henry was at work at the warehouse when the action began.

Kipling, Merrill, and Kipling's lawyers called his mobile phone every three minutes or so all through work, and for many hours after he'd gotten home. With some legal astuteness, however, Henry did not answer. The lawyers' messages were as expected. They said things like, "You're in violation of your contract and we're now working to bring about restitution for our client." Kipling's messages were so hostile that Henry actually found some pleasure in them: "This book was my fucking idea! It was my fucking idea! Anyway, no one's going to believe you, you little fucking cunt. Who are you? I mean, who the fuck are you? How about I come by and teach you another lesson with some more statuary from my fucking hotel?"

For his part, Henry also left a message with Lawrence saying that Lawrence's legal services would probably be needed soon, although Henry didn't go into too much detail. He'd already resigned himself to losing whatever official case was brought against him, so he was not really yet inclined to call in the lawyers, as they say.

The message from Merrill, though, which came late in the day, was a bit tougher to hear. It was delivered with compassion but it felt very serious. "I'm just not sure why you did this," Merrill said on the phone. "We had an agreement, Henry, and I've got to say that you're one of the most honest and aboveboard people I've ever met. I guess I'd like to know why you did this and, Henry, and I know you know this, this is going to end so badly for you."

Henry did feel as though he owed Merrill an answer, and he arranged to meet him for a drink via messages to his secretary, although by the time they were sitting down in the front room of the Gramercy Tavern the die was cast and the news was spreading and any kind of mediation was now an impossibility. Still, Henry felt calm as they talked, because what was controversial about his decision? Kipling had beaten up one of Henry's closest friends—a woman pregnant with Kipling's child.

"What would you have done for Abby?" Henry asked after laying out the entire story for Merrill. (He'd asked for Merrill's discretion, and Henry knew he'd get it because he was sure Merrill would not want to hurt Abby.)

And to Henry's question, Merrill said, "I would have done the same. Or I hope I'd have had the courage that you did. But Henry, you're really fucked with this. You're really, really fucked. Really, really fucked. You're totally right to have done what you've done, but you're really, really fucked with this."

Merrill was about to continue along these lines when Henry finally interrupted: "Why are you even friends with that guy?"

Here Merrill paused, and it struck Henry that he looked as though he were feeling something close to shame. Certainly he looked very uncertain about how to respond. Still, he managed to produce something of an answer: "Well, at this point, I'd say he and I have an association rather than a real friendship, but we were young together and he was a great friend to me in the past, and I don't know if I know a more talented actor, although how that is, is lost to me now. We have a meaningful past together. How's that for an answer? At this stage in everything, however, I don't know if we really are friends anymore. Let's face it, I think it's evident the guy's got a pretty serious drug problem. And obviously the things you've told me make it seem that the problems are even deeper than that."

Merrill looked truly distressed as he finished this statement, and Henry felt bad as well. But it was the truth that Merrill and Kipling had no business being friends, no matter what kind of history they shared. Merrill was such a better man. And Henry felt confident about his own recent decisions. And he was sure (and happy) that Kipling was now probably in a state of desperation trying to figure out how to manage the problems that Henry had unleashed upon him.

24

IN THIS REGARD, shortly after lunch, Henry received a call from the *New York Times*—from someone named Lisa Bremmer—who said she wanted to talk to him about his role in the creation of *The Best of Youth*. Henry agreed, and when she asked if they could meet, he suggested she come to his apartment so they could look through the hard-copy pages (they'd been described in Whitney's article) that he'd so carefully worked and reworked as he wrote the novel. At this point Lisa also made a specific request. "Can I ask you not to talk to anyone else?" she said. "I mean other media. It's good for me, but it's good for you too. Your story will have a bigger impact if you consolidate it with me at first, and once it's out in the *Times* everyone will want to talk to you, so you can give as many interviews as you can handle."

Henry thought this over for a moment, and then said that he could do this.

"How about five o'clock today?" Lisa said.

"Okay," Henry replied. "Five o'clock is good."

Lisa came over that evening as promised and Henry could hardly help but notice that she was extremely attractive, and (most bizarre) somehow fascinated with him. Of course, Lisa made no sexual advances—Henry was afraid of this, given that he was now involved, as they say. But as Lisa looked over

Henry's printed manuscripts and looked through his emails from Merrill and Kipling, she did seem to grow even more excited by her surroundings and, again, by Henry.

"You know," Lisa said at last, standing up from Henry's computer, "I read the book last night. I can't say I know much about kids' books, but I cried when I read it. A couple of times. It was very moving. I'm really impressed. And from my perspective, at this point, I'm believing all of your claims. So congratulations on such a great book."

Here she paused.

"But here's a question, Henry," she said. "What's he going to do to you now that you've let go with this information? You signed a confidentiality agreement—one that's pretty hard-core, from what you say."

"Kipling will sue me," Henry replied.

"Okay," Lisa said, "so why did you come clean? I'm sorry, but as you might have imagined, I did some research, and you're pretty rich. This is really going to screw you. Pretty hard."

Henry paused and then said, "Can I answer off the record?"

"No," she said. "You can't answer off the record. Sorry."

Henry paused again. "Generally, then, I'd say I did it for the sake of fame and glory. Even if I do lose all my money."

Lisa nodded, said, "All right," and walked back across the room to the stack of manuscript pages. "Fifteen million bucks, you're not getting that back. Not as a fiction writer. I know some big-time successes in your end of things—literary dudes, I mean—and they're not getting 15 million dollars for their work, even across their whole careers." She turned as she said this, hoping that Henry might have something to say, but Henry said nothing.

Lisa spent another hour looking over the manuscripts and rereading and copying emails, and then finally left saying that she'd probably be in touch soon with follow-up questions. And she was in touch again, although far sooner than Henry expected.

"Okay," she said, right after Henry answered his phone, now just an hour after her departure. "Off the record, then."

"What?" Henry said.

"Why did you fuck yourself like this?" Lisa said. "Off the record."

Henry hesitated. "What does off the record mean, now?" he said. "You said no before."

"I won't tell anyone. You seemed like you wanted to talk, back at your place, so why would I say off the record right away? But I want to know. So, off the record."

"Look, this is pretty important," Henry said. "Someone else is involved. And you can't use the information to investigate on your own."

"I'd get fired if I did that, if I screwed you over like that. And journalistic ethics shit, Henry, is really important to me. Almost the most important thing in my life. So all I can say is that I'd rather be sent to Guantánamo than report something you told me in confidence. And, from your end, what you need to think about with this is that it will help the story if I know what's really going on. You've convinced me that you're telling the truth, but it will help the story if you can tell me more."

It took Henry a moment to think about this before he finally repeated, "So, off the record? Definitely?"

"Off the record," Lisa replied. "No joke."

Henry paused, then said, "Well, he got one of my closest friends, my fourth cousin, his girlfriend, pregnant. And when he found out—I think he was pretty high—he beat her up. Beat her up unlike anything I've ever seen. She didn't want to go to the police because then her life really would be destroyed—gossip columnists and tabloid reporters—and so

I ratted him out because I fucking hate him and I wanted to hurt him. And I suppose that's it."

There was silence on the other end of the phone. It hadn't been a long and vivid description, but Henry was sure he'd conveyed everything an ordinary person would need to know, and at last Lisa spoke. "Okay, Henry," she said. "No one will know about what you've just told me from my end, but your cousin, it's Abby Cahill, I'm guessing. Obviously I did some research and know she's his girlfriend—hard to miss it, given celebrity coverage these days. Anyway, I promise I'll never tell what you've just told me."

Then she added, after an even longer pause, "And fuck him. I'm going to fuck that guy."

25

A BIT OF IRONY marked the day the article about Kipling's fraud came out in the *New York Times*. The story was, surprisingly, on the cover of the *Sunday Styles* section (surely more damning for Kipling than if it had been on the paper's front page), but in the *Book Review*, *The Best of Youth* had made it further up the children's best-seller list. It had, in fact, climbed to number one. The sales numbers that put it there clearly came from the week before the story broke, so it wasn't the scandal that led to this. It was Kipling's fame and a quality product, apparently, although Henry couldn't help but wonder how much longer that would last, given the breaking story. He hoped the book would drop from the list altogether, but the reading public, of course, was impossible to predict, and scandal clearly has value when pushing product.

And these brief reflections led to another set of thoughts. They made Henry wonder, as he looked over the best-seller list and then began reading the article, what was, in the end, the damage of all this for a guy like Kipling. The question made Henry feel a little sick, since the answer might be very little. So Kipling hired a ghostwriter. Who would care? The movie world hired writers of all sorts, and usually without giving them any credit at all for the work they did. And (as Kipling made clear in one of his almost twenty enraged and hostile phone messages to Henry) the book might not have gotten any attention at all "if it wasn't for me, you little fucking, fucking cum-drinking pussy cunt bitch!" Henry was sure, though, that the quality of the book had something to do with its success. Had the book been badly written, Kipling never would have been on the ride he was now taking. But Kipling did have a point. Had it been a wonderful book by an irrelevant author, who knew where it would have gone?

The thing was that Kipling was furious—with an anger that Henry had never seen before in anyone—and that, at least, was one indication of the damage Henry had done to him. There might be any number of ways to rationalize the exposure in light of its long-term effects on Kipling's career, but given the wild and uncontrollable nature of Kipling's tirades, it was clear that his being outed upset him far more than even Henry had expected. Kipling had presented himself to the world as a great writer and Henry had taken that away, had recast him with devastating effect as a kind of cultural swindler.

Perhaps equally satisfying was that the article Lisa wrote was maybe one of the most aggressive *Times* pieces he'd ever read. There was nothing about Abby—Lisa had kept her promise—but the essay turned into something of a meditation on contemporary fraudulence (referencing everything from Enron to *The Music Man*) and how Kipling was the latest example of what Lisa was describing as a new and ghastly lineup of villains and liars. In reference to Kipling, Lisa's case fit easily with her larger arguments, simply because Kipling had offered so many outrageous interviews about the "trials and triumphs" of being a "true writer" that his quotes spoke for themselves. And Lisa quoted extensively. And what the quotes all added up to was completely damning, Lisa's point being that Kipling was not just leveraging his name to launch a project or make money, but, rather, had assumed an entirely false persona and then embarked (with great vanity) on a grand tour during which he, again and again, spoke at length of things he knew nothing about and had never really experienced. He'd even recently accepted (Lisa pointed out) an invitation to testify before the UN's General Assembly on the importance of encouraging young people to write more, a testimony that was to follow a dinner he'd agreed to attend in New York to benefit and promote a national literacy campaign that the president was launching. Lisa used the invitations to point out that Kipling's fabrications amounted to the worst kinds of lies, lies far beyond and very different from run-of-the-mill Hollywood magic, and she suggested that if these invitations in New York were honored by Kipling, she at least would be reporting on it and Kipling wasn't going to show up for the events without serious consequences.

It was all quite astonishing to Henry, and he took so much pleasure in reading the article he almost felt guilty that someone else's disgrace should bring him so much delight. But then he thought about Abby again and read the article one more time, just to encourage and prolong his pleasure.

And Henry was sure the story (and the gratification) would continue—there would be plenty of other people reporting on it all. Henry had done as he was asked, though, and hadn't granted any other interviews yet. He'd certainly fended them off, following the initial publication in Whitney's paper, and as Henry thought about the fact that he'd now need to start making the rounds with other news sources, he decided that he might start with the more colorful, celebrity-oriented magazines, although he'd also already been contacted by the *Boston Globe* and the *L.A. Times* and he planned to tell them quite a bit as well. Henry did intend to add one last poetic flourish to the story at this point, though, now that he had a little more control of it all and had learned something from his experiences with Lisa. He planned to explain his motives for his confession as completely accidental—the result of drunkenness and the inability to plug the leak once it got started. (It didn't, after all, seem very prudent to go off the record with lots of other reporters, and certainly they'd want to know why he came forward in the first place.) In this vein, though, Henry would also say that the drunken mistake came in the midst of a discussion about Kipling and what a terrible person he was—in general, not in reference to Abby—and Henry concluded that it might be very illuminating if he described things like watching Kipling cut lines of coke in random bathrooms or listening to him talk about his passion for pierced bohemian women with blond hair.

And so, despite the fact that his entire fortune was now in jeopardy, Henry felt surprisingly happy. But the truth was that thoughts of Kipling's suffering and Henry's avenging Abby were not the only source of these feelings. Other than the scandal that Henry was causing, it was, that morning, a generally peaceful and happy Sunday, and to his left, in his bed, was Sasha, fast asleep and entirely naked. Henry had planned an elaborate breakfast for her, including asparagus and eggs from the Williamsburg Greenmarket, and then, if he could find the courage, he might even suggest that they return to bed to continue once again with the various projects they'd embarked on the previous night. And this was what they did, although Henry also took some time later that day to call Abby to check up on her and see how she was doing. Of course (being a graduate of Oberlin), she'd read the *Times* that morning as well, and all she could say was, "I can't fucking believe this."

"Yeah, I really messed up," Henry replied. "Definitely going to get sued. I got drunk. I never meant for it to get out."

Abby paused, and, it seemed to Henry, halted for an uncharacteristic period of time. And he couldn't help but think that she was linking everything together in a way he hoped she wouldn't. At last, though, apparently with some mercy, she said, "You know what a fan of the book I am. I mean, Henry, it's a really, really fucking great book. You should be so proud. This will lead to something good for you—I promise—but from the article, it looks like you're going to get killed in court. Henry, though, holy fuck, your book, it was great! You've come a long way since you killed all my aunt's goats! I'm sure you're going to get something good out of this."

"I hope something good happens," Henry replied, feeling surprisingly happy, despite his bad feelings at the mention of the goats. "And killed is right," he added. "I am about to get killed."

Henry had, in fact, spoken to Lawrence just before talking to Abby. "The book is terrific!" Lawrence said. "I read it last night. You should be really happy with yourself! But from now on, you should think of me as the guy keeping you out of bankruptcy. It will be an honor to represent you. You'll have your own book before long. And if I rescue some of your money, you can dedicate the book to me. But fuck, it's going to be rough for you. Lot of fucking money gone, even if I do a good job. But here's the deal: I promise Kipling will want this to be over as soon as possible, and we can use our ability to draw it out forever to get him to settle. The settlement will cost you, though. But you're not going to walk away totally poor. And if that's what Kipling wants—for you to lose everything—I've got a PR firm that I use and I can make sure the suit will be in the news every day for the rest of his life. And how will that look? The great phony suing the real artist for telling the truth? Still, it won't be cheap. Kipling does hate you. And he's lost a lot and if he's feeling like he's going to be fucked for a while, he's going to want you to be fucked too. So, you might have to lose as much as nine or ten. Nine or ten million. But you'll have some left, if that's the case, and, as far as I can tell, you bohemian types in Williamsburg don't need very much cash. I had a way-too-young girlfriend last year who lived there, and staying over was like sleeping in some kind of carny's trailer."

Here, Lawrence paused, and then added, "But Henry, and I say this as a culturally ignorant man, your book, it was really good. Really, deeply good. Made me think I need to read more novels, and that's something. So I think you'll be all right."

"That's really nice of you to say," Henry replied, genuinely touched.

And this last point of Lawrence's was actually something that Lisa's article had addressed—concluded with, even, tempering some of the aggression against Kipling. Lisa went to some lengths to point out what an excellent book *The Best of Youth* was, suggesting that perhaps this was one positive aspect of everything that had transpired—that the book had done well not just because of Kipling's brand name but also because of its high quality, and that the world could eagerly anticipate more books from Henry.

Of course, Henry would probably have to wait a while to publish a book of his own—until after he fought off the inevitable lawsuit, for example. After all, Henry didn't want Kipling to get hold of any of his future earnings. And the fact was that earnings were exactly what Henry would be looking for in the time ahead, although he also knew that even what might be considered a successful novel (should he write one) was surely not going to bring back the money he'd be losing. Still, for unknowable reasons, and despite the mysterious loyalty he felt to his thrifty Yankee ancestors, he really didn't feel that bad about what might be taken from him. And, as he thought about all this after hanging up with Lawrence, he wondered how much he could put his apartment on the market for, although it didn't seem like it would have to come to that. Just as he was turning the figures over in his head, though—it was now well into the afternoon—Sasha called while running errands and insisted that she was hungry and that she expected dinner from him soon. "Given my recent kindnesses," she said.

"Yeah, I do owe you dinner," Henry said. "That's undeniable. Your recent kindnesses. I hardly know what to say. Can't stop thinking about them. But I'm about to lose a lot of cash. You know this, right? I'm not the man of great means you knew even a few days ago."

"We'll eat cheap!" Sasha replied. "To practice for when you're poor. Anyway, I don't need much money. Just a tattoo allowance, but we can work that out later. But dinner! Whatever you can afford, now that you're getting jacked."

"You're very compassionate," Henry said. "I'll come up with something." And soon Henry was putting on his shoes and thinking that they ought to go that night to a restaurant in Williamsburg that was famous for serving multiple and experimental varieties of lasagna.

And before long he and Sasha were walking along Bedford Avenue and on their way to dinner, feeling quite happy to be together and very much looking forward to examining the lasagna menu and talking very deeply (with real and intense consideration) about what they'd like to eat that night and what they'd like to drink and where they'd like to go afterward and, still astonishing to Henry, just how happy they were to be with each other.

26

AND IN THE NEXT months, that happiness didn't go away. And life worked out in other ways as well.

With the money issue, things were a bit tougher on Henry than he had hoped, but by world standards he was still extraordinarily fortunate. The final out-of-court settlement was nearly $11 million, a staggering amount of money (no question), but the $4 million left over was enormous too, all things considered.

"It's just enough to keep me around," Sasha said. It was now five months after the exposure of Kipling's fraudulence. "Less than four, and I was out of here."

"Lawrence came through for me again," Henry replied. "Now I can afford to get you that new piercing you've been wanting."

In other news, the third issue of *Suckerhead*—the stock, that is, the printed version—was destroyed in a warehouse fire in Canada, and since the editors had declined the insurance clause on the contract, issue three disappeared into the wide unknowable ether. They did have a fund-raiser of sorts in someone's backyard in Greenpoint, but after funds were tallied against expenditures (the food and beer bill was astronomical) they only made $137, which was subsequently spent on another party to mark *Suckerhead*'s farewell to the world of literature. Henry was invited, with a note on his invitation from the editor-in-chief that perhaps they could talk about a potential resurrection and redemption of all their hard work. Henry did not attend, nor did he RSVP, although his lack of a response to the invitation did make him feel just a bit guilty. It wasn't the best kind of behavior, he thought. Still, he didn't tell the editor to go fuck himself, so perhaps he acted with at least some dignity.

Whitney had made progress of his own as well. He published a translation of a novel by an Italian writer named Christian Frascella to surprising acclaim—he'd done it on his own, with no publication deal, and sold it with the author to an independent press. The novel was initially quite baffling to the literary community, but soon developed a real following, and from there, there was much talk in the city about how the only really interesting things going on in contemporary letters were happening in Italy. Subsequently, Whitney became involved with a string of women and discovered, despite his long experience and exquisite finesse in such situations, that Italian women were far beyond his understanding. Still, there was value to be found in his failure. "If you find out that it's not possible to date three different Italian women at the same time, then you've learned something important about life," Whitney told Henry one evening as they grilled sausages on Whitney's balcony. Henry agreed that this was probably something very good to know.

Most important in all this, Abby decided to have the baby, although with a firm agreement with Kipling that he'd have nothing to do with the child. The commitment came with a financial settlement, though—substantial, in fact, with the threat that, in the interest of providing for her child, Abby would tell her entire story, sucking up her own unwanted tabloid scrutiny, if Kipling tried to back out. Although Henry never learned the exact number, he gathered it was a lump settlement in the millions. So that too deferred some of the pain of the $11 million Henry had lost to Kipling. The money was turning around just as quickly and going toward raising Abby's child. Cosmic justice, as far as Henry could determine.

As for his and Sasha's future, he thought so little about it all (took it so much for granted, maybe) that the relationship could hardly be seen as anything other than one of the best things that had ever happened to him. After they both completed their community service (and vowed to each other never to drink in public or illegally transport firearms again) they made plans—and executed them—to spend the summer in the south of France, near Perpignan, on the Mediterranean and right at the Spanish border. Sasha claimed to have friends there, although it turned out she had none. The strange neighbor she had once known in Grosse Pointe was long dead, as they discovered from a talkative but quite confused nephew. And the family friend from Michigan who lived there had been arrested for some kind of financial fraud just a month earlier and was not around (as he had promised) to take them out and show them the "hot spots."

Still, all they wanted was a little place by the water, which was exactly what they got. Despite the highly polished photos sent to them by the rental company, they were given keys to a tiny one-bedroom shack that had windows that wouldn't close and a shower in the kitchen. But it was right on the beach, which was the important thing, and it had a good, working stove that they could cook their dinners on, and they'd rented a car so they could take provincial excursions whenever they liked. And there was a top-quality fish market less than half a mile away. So what was there to complain about? Nothing, Henry concluded over and over. A man who loses $11 million and disgraces himself in more than one aspect of his life usually flees abroad to disappear or to reassess his future. But Henry felt extremely fortunate with how things were going for him, and he'd even begun work on a novel that he felt was going well—it was about an eighty-year-old journalist who decided to go back to law school after losing a defamation suit launched by a failing film actor. (The journalist's ambition with law school was to learn how to help other aged journalists who were being unfairly sued.) The book was ending up to be quite funny, and since this particular journalist was still reasonably wealthy, and (according to the women in the novel) strikingly handsome, he had quite a good time back in the world of academia.

Sasha hated it. She read his new pages every night after they got into their ancient and comically lumpy French bed, and told Henry that it simply wasn't plausible that this old man would be so sexually desirable to so many young and attractive law students. Henry nodded and didn't dispute this argument, although he did often say things like, "I have an artistic vision and I intend to see it to the end," a response with which Sasha could hardly argue. Likely, the novel wouldn't work out, but he had a strange kind of patience with his work at this point, and if the novel was abandoned by the time they returned to the U.S., what would he have lost? He'd be back in his McCarren Park apartment, hopefully with Sasha living with him—they'd talked quite seriously about this matter—and he'd begin another book. And then perhaps his career as a writer really would take off, and his role in life would become more concrete. If he was lucky, that is, and if he didn't kill any more priceless animals, and if he avoided jail, and if he stayed far away from people like Kipling. These things, though, he thought at last, at this point in his life, he might be able to manage.